I0777241

The Knowing Gene

Robert Lange

The Knowing Gene

Copyright © 2026 - Fourth Edition

All Rights Reserved. No part of this book may be reproduced or transmitted in any form or by any means without the express written consent of the author.

ISBN: 979-8-218-48928-1

This work is a book of fiction. Names, characters, places, and incidents are products of the author's imagination and/or used as fiction. Any similarities to actual events or persons, living or dead, are coincidental.

Third Edition

Published by Sea Parrot Press, Tryon, NC

www.seaparrotpress.com

In loving memory of my father

JOHN B. LANGE, MD
1928-2009

ACKNOWLEDGEMENTS

My many thanks to all the people who inspired, encouraged, and assisted me in the writing, validating, editing, and completion of this story.

To the many individuals who provided critical review and feedback, especially Alison, Renee, Connie, Jasper, Butch, and members of the Hackman-Adams Thriller Writers Group. Thank you all very much.

To all those who contributed to the editing and corrected my many grammatical errors, primarily my mother, Sibyl, brother, Mark, and too many dear friends to individually mention. Thank you for your patience and especially your attention to detail.

And perhaps most importantly to maintaining my momentum and confidence, the many who read my drafts and encouraged me with their enthusiastic responses, especially Michelle and my sister Dorothy Moyer. I'm pretty sure that at least half of you were honest with me about your enjoyment of the story.

A special thank you to the diverse cast of characters at the Trade Street Gallery Coffeehouse in Tryon, North Carolina. This endless source of creative energy and encouragement, not to mention sitcom worthy amusement, helped me slowly but surely move this book to completion.

And Carol, I can't thank you enough.

Cover photo by Lynn Don Bendickson

Chapter One

It was cooler than Jasper thought right, at least until his blindfold was removed. Although he remained terrified, the walls, floor, and ceiling of rock explained the damp cool he was feeling and gave him some bearing for where he was. The presence of other children comforted him little; he hadn't the slightest clue who they were, and they weren't looking terribly happy themselves.

≈

A perfect northern Nevada spring morning was almost over, mid-seventies and not a cloud in the sky. Just to the west stands the magnificent Sierra Nevada Mountain range, bordering the states of California and Nevada. In between lay the more rolling landscape of the Tahoe and Washoe Valleys, with their splendorous blend of smaller mountains and crystal blue mountain lakes. One of these elevations, Slide Mountain, sits just south of Reno, anchoring both Lake Tahoe and Washoe Lake. Standing 9,700 feet, Slide Mountain offers breathtaking views of not only the spectacular valleys, but also the Sierra Nevada Mountain range to the west and the vast desert of Nevada to the east. Thanks to a generous eastward air spillage from the Tahoe Basin, a thermal lift regularly provides local hang gliders ample opportunity to enjoy the beauty the peace and serenity from high above.

1

Winding its way up Slide Mountain, the Porsche convertible's tires screeched as it sped around the curve on the mountain road. Parker shifted gears as he straightened the Porsche out and accelerated on his way to the next curve.

"So, you're coming next Saturday night, aren't you?" Parker calmly asked as Christian relaxed his grip on the passenger door.

A confirmed bachelor, Parker Farr had been unable to outgrow the fraternity years' lifestyle he had enjoyed with Christian almost two decades earlier, despite having become one of Reno's most successful attorneys. Regularly on Reno's "Most Eligible Bachelor" list, Parker was one of Reno's most well-known and recognizable individuals.

"You know how I feel about your parties, Parker. They're always a nightmare of attempts to fix me up," Christian objected. "I mean, everyone is really nice, and the girls are always cute – "

"Extremely cute!" Parker interrupted.

"Extremely cute," Christian corrected himself, "but it's hard to enjoy myself with all that pressure."

"But it's going to be a special one this year, buddy. Besides, I'll protect you."

"Parker, you and I have been partying since our rugby days. I know better!" Christian re-gripped the door handle as Parker rapidly approached the next curve. "This is just another 'Most Eligible Bachelor' party, isn't it? You've been having these for what, ten years?" Christian's eyes widened as he realized what he'd just said.

"Exactly!" Parker downshifted into the curve. "Quite the achievement, don't you think? Reno magazine will be doing a cover story on it and most of the Bachelorette winners over the last twenty years will be there."

Christian's disapproving look was overshadowed by his playful smirk.

"Listen, Christian," Parker began as he turned the steering wheel hard to the left, "I miss Stephanie as much as anyone, but you've got to come out of that shell sooner or later."

"It just doesn't feel right yet, Parker."

"It's been over four years, Christian. Even your little girl is anxious for you to move on."

"Tatum and I will be fine. I will be at the Kappa party at your place next month though."

Parker and Christian Faraday went back to their pledge days a Kappa Rho Phi fraternity at the University of Nevada, Reno. There they formed the tightest of friendships, not only as fraternity brothers, but also as co-captains of the rugby team and members of the school's varsity crew.

It was also at UNR that Christian met Stephanie; accidentally colliding with her during the fraternity's spring 'Naked Marauder' dash around the University's Quad one April evening. Christian was quickly forgiven as she immediately fell for his quick humor and charm, not to mention his boyish good looks and athleticism. The two equally athletic and adventuresome co-eds started dating immediately and quickly became inseparable until her death four years ago. Tatum was their fifteen-year-old daughter, their only child. Tatum not only inherited her parents' zest for living, but also her mother's stunning looks and personality.

"It's only a matter of time before I get you back in circulation, you know," Parker replied as he steered his Porsche into the pull-off behind the blue Dodge pick-up with their hang-gliding gear in the back; joining a dozen or so other vehicles using the spot chosen that day to launch their gliders.

As the two exited the convertible, they heard a familiar voice. "Come on, you two. Conditions are supposed to be phenomenal today. The wind aloft forecast is calling for perfect conditions. It's not to be wasted."

Two years Christian and Parker's junior, Will Graham was the super energetic member of this close-knit gang. Will had abandoned his nine-to-five job eight years out of UNR to pursue his love of aerial sports, eventually earning U.S. and World Championship titles in both hang gliding and paragliding. An enthusiastic promoter of the sport, it was Will's concern for the depression he saw Christian falling into after Stephanie's death that prompted him to arrange this monthly outing among the fraternity brothers still in the area.

The strong thermals of the area generated wind currents capable of lifting experienced pilots well over 17,000 feet, providing gliders unparalleled views of scenic northern Nevada and eastern California. The group was becoming quite skilled as a result of the outstanding conditions and their talented instructor.

"Where's the wind going to take us today, Will? Think we'll make it into California?" Parker inquired as he and Christian headed towards their gear. Parker knew Will loved to circle around Tahoe while the rest of them bounced around the Washoe Valley, trying desperately to get above the 8,200-foot level from where they typically launched themselves. Will had taken more of a Border Collie role with the group since Parker accidentally came a tad too close to the Reno International Airport's Control Zone for the FAA's comfort.

"I'm always expecting you to end up in the Pacific, Parker. According to the soaring reports I'm hearing for today, the Coast Guard might just need to be on the lookout for you in a few hours." Will knew that the conditions were a glider's dream; too bad he was stuck with these amateurs, as much as he loved them.

"I'll just be happy if I can get over 11,000 feet in my lifetime," Christian quipped.

"I'm betting today is that day, Christian. I've got your oxygen systems ready; I'm pretty sure you'll be needing them today," Will noted as he finished up the equipment prep.

Parker and Christian grabbed their gear from Will and headed towards the main east launch site to join the rest of this month's crew.

As usual, Will took off first with the others following his lead. Will had a sixth sense for finding the best thermals. Starting just outside the guard rail, he ran about ten steps down the hill over loose rocks before being firmly lifted off the ground. Initially sinking down to 7,600 feet, he quickly found a strong south easterly, six hundred feet per minute thermal, lifting him well above launch altitude. One by one, the remaining five fraternity brothers followed Will to the launch.

Before long, the pilots were all well above 14,000 feet, heading straight for the rough horizon of the Sierra Nevada Mountain range. To observe the splendor of this amazing creation of nature from the silence of a glider provided Christian an incredible sense of serenity which he had not had in a very long time.

"Better get your O2 ready, boys," Will's voice crackled over the earpieces, pulling Christian back to reality. "I just hit a strong south westerly that's gonna give you the rides of your lives!"

This is going to get even better? Christian thought to himself while a few others were heard making various sounds of excitement over the radio.

Christian suddenly felt the thermal grab him and pull him over Washoe Lake. This was followed by another jolt, which clearly was not the feel of a typical thermal, but more like turbulence when riding in a plane. It only seemed to affect him, not the glider, and knocked him harshly to the right, followed by twisting his body. Just as suddenly it ceased, and the flight was calm again; but not calm enough that he didn't feel the need to get on the radio and ask Will if it was going to be this bumpy the entire way.

Just then, Christian felt another jostle, this time to the left, forcing him to grab his grip tighter when suddenly the glider surged ahead faster than Christian knew was right, no matter how strong the thermal.

"Will!" Christian yelled into his microphone, while the mechanisms of the glider were stressing in ways that they clearly weren't meant to.

Although Will was at least two hundred yards ahead and a hundred or two feet higher, Christian could see Will twist around in his glider looking back at him, only to lose sight of him as his own glider then vigorously pulled him hard to the left.

Suddenly, Christian's direction reversed, facing back towards Slide Mountain.

"Hang tight, Christian. Pull to the right," Will was heard urgently through the earpiece. "I'm on my way."

Trying desperately to control the glider, Christian shifted his body around to no avail. "I'm trying, Will. I've got no control, it's like I'm being pulled." Suddenly, the glider quickly shot up several hundred feet, followed by another turn to the right and sharply down towards the mountain. Christian was then heading perilously close to tree level on Slide Mountain before another unexpected thrust, this time taking him back up and to the left.

Heading straight for Lake Tahoe and losing sight of the others, Christian's usually calm and confident demeanor began to turn to panic. "It's breaking up, Will!"

"Use your 'chute, Christian," Will frantically replied, "just like I taught you."

Trying not to let the twisting and turning overwhelm him, Christian began the procedures Will had made them practice at least a dozen times. Christian began repeating to himself, *Look, Grasp, Pull, Look, Throw, Pull. Look, Grasp, Pull, Look, Throw, Pull*, while looking for then grabbing, the rip cord. Continuing the sequence despite the erratic movements he was undergoing, Christian eventually cleared himself from the glider and the parachute began to deploy as he accelerated downwards.

It was not quite as much of a free-fall as he would have expected; the turbulence continuing, albeit not as pronounced. His body continued to be gently tossed about, although the parachute remained unaffected. Slowly, the movements ceased, a sense of warmth enveloping his body, putting him slightly at ease as he floated towards the rocky slope of the mountain.

Chapter Two

Special Agent Waymon stepped up to the microphone on the crowded steps outside the downtown Reno offices of the FBI. While missing children's cases always gathered a great deal of press coverage, this one in particular had attracted an unusual amount of attention. Not only was the local media represented in the mayhem Waymon looked out upon, but the national media as well. The usual local news vans were now accompanied by big trucks from network news services, including CNN and Fox.

As head of the Nevada FBI, Samuel Waymon usually wasn't involved in the day-to-day management of such operations. However, this case had escalated well beyond the norm. Once the third child had mysteriously disappeared, he knew that this was no normal missing children situation.

Earlier that day, twelve-year-old Jasper Thomas had been riding his bicycle to join some friends at their favorite fishing spot on the Truckee River. Never having arrived, the police later found his bike just off the road with his fishing pole leaning against a tree.

In the twenty-five years Waymon had been with the FBI, this was the most frustrating case he could remember. A middle-aged man with a spare tire beginning to show on what appeared to have been a very fit body in its earlier days, Waymon always had a stern look, with a quick temper to back it up. He had nonetheless mastered the highly political system that was the Bureau, rising in rank from a field officer to one of the most respected Bureau state chiefs – a Special Agent in Charge. He had requested the Nevada position three years earlier to bolster his experience in the gambling world to help solidify his next target, Section Chief of Racketeering for the FBI. Cases like this mildly irritated him as they took focus off his real love of more intellectual criminal activities.

An impressive figure behind the microphone, Waymon stood an imposing 6'4" and clearly gave the impression he was in total control of this, and usually any, situation. He read a brief prepared statement to the gathered press.

"The hearts and prayers of all of us working on this case go out to the Thomas family. Jasper is a bright young man and greatly loved by all that know him. The FBI and local agencies are working tirelessly on all leads and information pertaining to his disappearance. We have no clear indication at this point that Jasper's disappearance is in any way related to the five recent missing children's cases. We do suggest, however, that parents take every precaution with their children to minimize any risk."

He was sure the cases were all related but didn't want to startle the community any more than absolutely necessary.

The questions started flying at him immediately.

"Was there any sign of a struggle where his bike was found?"

"Are any of the families having custody issues?"

"Have the parents been contacted by the abductors?"

"Were any personal possessions recovered at the scene?"

Cutting the questions off, Waymon responded in rapid fashion, "No, not sure, no, and yes." He was not a believer in providing the press with any more information than necessary and, in fact, disdained having to deal with them at all. After answering a few more questions, he excused himself and headed back into the office building, ignoring along the way requests of producers from the national talk shows to schedule individual interview time.

≈

Once inside, Waymon made his way to the situation room, joining agents Dawson and Carver, his key Reno field agents. With various personal, state, and federal rewards for the combined case currently totaling over five hundred thousand dollars, and the national scrutiny of the case becoming more intense by the hour, Waymon was in no mood to hear excuses. This case was alarmingly similar to one in Texas two years earlier; a dozen children disappeared over a four-week period, under equally mysterious circumstances. The perpetrators and children were never found, and the State Bureau chief's career came to a screeching halt as he was assigned to a nowhere desk job back in Washington. Waymon was not about to let that happen to him.

"What's the latest, boys?" Waymon bellowed as he entered the 'war room' where Dawson and Carver were hovering over a map on the conference table.

"Nothing new, sir" Dawson responded. "We've cross referenced all information and still have not a modicum of correlation. We've got agents questioning anyone remotely involved with the boy and residents near the scene, but no information of substance from what we have so far."

"State or local agencies have anything to report on vehicles yet?"

"They're coming up dry. No sightings out of the ordinary and all available surveillance tapes from nearby gas stations and convenience stores show nothing revealing either. We have local teams scouring those areas," Dawson pointed to areas on the map on the table. "State police have set up roadblocks," pointing to other areas on the map, "here, here, and here. But whoever has him is probably long gone by now."

The cases had been scattered around the Reno area; two in the northeast, one south, this one and another in the western suburbs; yet another out near Carson City. There was no pattern in any of the locations – not time of day, similarity in ages, gender, or ethnicity. The only thing consistent was the relative seclusion of the areas where the children were abducted.

Several psychics had called the hotline offering their assistance, but through years of wild goose chases and false leads, the Bureau learned long ago that any information they provided was either too vague or just plain wrong. There wasn't sufficient time or resources to waste on these self-promoters in this case.

"Damn it!" Waymon was clearly frustrated, which was not at all an unusual state for him, but certainly more frequent since this case began. "Increase helicopter thermal infrared monitoring of all rural areas, especially the desert and wooded terrains, for potential hideouts."

Turning to Carver, Waymon continued, "Let's set up round the clock surveillance on all known area sex offenders." Thinking for a moment, he then added, "I want more detailed victim correlation, including blood type and any genetic characteristics.   Compare your individual findings to the organ donor requirement directories."

He simply refused to let what happened to Bragg down in Texas happen to him, even if he had to stock up on Adderall and stay up 24/7 to supervise the case. Before the Texas case, Jason Bragg had been one of the Bureau's most respected senior agents. He and Waymon had practically grown up together in the Bureau and had been friends throughout their careers. Waymon always looked him up during his periodic trips back to headquarters. Waymon had watched Bragg's psyche go from a hard charging, 'whatever it takes' approach, to a much more docile and reserved demeanor. It appeared as if he had resigned himself to counting the days to retirement.

The least Waymon could do for his old friend was to request Bragg's assistance and expertise on this case. Possibly if the two of them to-gether solved the case, it would help get his career, and psyche, back on track. Besides, he had to pursue every possible avenue to get this situation resolved.

Bragg had been consulting Waymon by telephone and e-mail over the past couple of weeks and was due to arrive later that day. Waymon was looking forward to greeting his old friend personally at the airport.

Chapter Three

As the afternoon began to wind down, Parker pulled up to the gatehouse of the quiet gated community of Sierra Vista, just southwest of Reno at the foot of Mount Rose. Christian and Stephanie decided to move their young family there when Tatum was a toddler. When building their dream house, they took full advantage of the huge open spaces and spectacular western views of the rugged Sierra Mountains. Within a year they were followed by Parker, who built his ultimate bachelor pad on a nearby lot.

"Afternoon, Mister Farr, Mister Faraday," the elderly man at the gate cheerfully greeted the two men. "Beautiful day, wasn't it?"

Parker slowly accelerated as the gate began to open. Christian opened his eyes and slowly lifted his head. "Afternoon, Charlie," they spoke in unison, Christian a bit groggily.

"Don't mind him, Charlie, he's had a little too much excitement today."

With the gate fully opened, Parker accelerated into the neighborhood, both men waving goodbye to the guard.

"You sure you don't want to go to the hospital, champ? Last chance."

"Really, I'm fine. Nothing a beer and a little relaxation can't handle."

Pulling into Christian's driveway they noticed a blue Volvo convertible, a clear indication Tatum had friends over, at minimum, her best friend, Nicki.

"Looks like you have to get past the girls first."

"They're probably as tired as I am," Christian replied with relief. "They've had lacrosse practice all day. Besides, midterms are coming up and they're probably studying."

"You're so dense. Even I know teenagers better than that," Parker laughed. "Let me help you inside, buddy."

"Really, I'm only a little shaken," Christian protested. "Don't worry about it."

"Sorry, I'm going to tell Tatum to keep an eye on you, since I know you aren't going to."

Parker was right, and deep-down Christian knew it. Academics seemed to be the furthest thing from Tatum's mind, far behind sports and her newly found interest in the opposite sex. But then again, if she wasn't into those things, he'd be even more worried about her; a fact that he reminded himself of whenever he started getting himself too concerned.

The two men entered Christian's foyer to several girls chatting and giggling under the influence of Taylor Swift music in the room just ahead.

"DADDYYYYYY!" Tatum shouted with a big smile on her face. This was immediately followed by a chorus of the other three teenagers in the room with a cheerful "MISTER FARADAY!"

A total of four fifteen- and sixteen-year-old girls, still in their workout clothes from lacrosse practice, were on the sofa gathered around Tatum's laptop, eating popcorn and engrossed in something on the screen.

Christian had always been popular with Tatum's friends. Never stern or judgmental, Christian had often been more of a cool uncle to these girls than just another boring parent. His easy-going demeanor, quick humor, and ability in disarming potentially contentious situations always made Tatum's friends happy to be around him.

"Hey, Uncle Parker! Have you two been out trying to kill yourselves again today?" Tatum asked.

"Mister Faraday, aren't you a little too old to still be playing college jock?" one of her friends chimed in, making fun of his exhausted look.

"Your dad came pretty close to it today, Tatum. Got in an argument with some pretty intense thermals." Heading towards the kitchen, Parker continued, "Promise to keep an eye on him tonight, will ya? He's a bit shaken up I'm afraid."

Christian rolled his eyes as one of the girls piped in, "Mister Faraday, you'll never make it to the 'stud of the nursing home' if you keep up at your pace!"

"Cute, Baliya." Christian stuck his tongue out at the girls as he sat down in his recliner and turned on the massage control. "And I suppose you girls are up to something intellectually challenging and worthwhile?"

"As a matter of fact," Tatum informed her father as she turned the laptop so the screen faced him, "we're just checking out Nicki's modeling portfolio."

"Now there's something that will get you girls into college," he commented as he noticed the little girl he had known since she was a two-foot-tall tomboy now appear as a high fashion model in her online portfolio. "Seriously though, NikNak," he added as the girl got a look of anticipation of a pending compliment on her face, "you've mastered those crayons on your eyes quite well!", referring to the clearly quite professional make-up on her in the photo.

"I'd reconsider the use of those disposable cameras if you're really serious about this though," Parker added as he returned to the room with a frosted mug of beer for Christian.

Both Christian and Parker knew this was definitely professional photography, even if they weren't aware that it was done by, Carri Trout, one of the most respected fashion photographers in Las Vegas.

As Christian quickly produced a 'got ya' smirk, Nicki took a kernel of popcorn she was preparing to put into her mouth and flicked it smack in the center of Christian's forehead. This was quickly followed by at least a dozen more kernels and a few sofa pillows from the other girls. Christian thanked the girls and began tossing the kernels into his mouth one by one as he retrieved them off his body and chair.

Nicki and Tatum were about the same height, somewhere around the 5'8" mark, although he couldn't keep up with exactly how tall Tatum was. Tatum had definitely inherited her mother's looks, an all-American girl next door with a touch of tomboy. Despite the diverse ethnicity of her friend group, they all seemed to have that kind of look.

Placing the beer on the table next to Christian, Parker whispered, "God help us if they ever try to conquer the modeling world together." Turning back to Tatum, "I've got to run, Tatum. Make sure he rests well. If he faints on you or anything, call me right away."

"Will do, Uncle Parker." Tatum waved to him as he headed out the door. "Thanks for being a good nurse for him today."

"And don't forget next Saturday, Christian," Parker added, peeking his head from behind the front door just before closing it.

"Aren't you girls facing midterms?" Christian frowned. "Not sure those fashion shots are going to help much."

"Oh, hush and drink your beer, Daddy, this is important stuff," Tatum scolded him as the girls got back to the laptop to discuss the different outfits and looks in Nicki's portfolio.

Given the day's events, Christian was much more interested in savoring his beer than verbally sparring with teenage girls, although such rhetorical exercise was often one of his favorite sports. Christian was particularly exhausted this evening.

The girls continued their laughing and gossiping as Christian finished up the recliner massage and downed the remainder of his beer.

Gathering himself, Christian stood up and bid the girls farewell. "See you girls later. I think a long warm soak is in order. I'm afraid you're doing dinner tonight, sweetheart. And I'm famished, so make it good."

With their youthful smiles and exuberant voices, each of the girls blew him kisses, which he returned in a sweeping gesture as he sluggishly headed up the stairs; totally unaware of changes going on within his body.

Chapter Four

Samuel Waymon had pulled a lot of strings to get Bragg's assistance on this case. While it clearly made sense, there were several powerful people in the FBI that still felt the sting from the failure of Bragg to close the Texas case; they were not anxious to have him involved in this case in any way. Waymon had finally gotten approval by convincing the right people that they might have another unsolved case on their hands unless he and Bragg were able to collaborate on comparing patterns and other evidence. Waymon had never been as worried about the outcome of a case as he was this one, not only for the Bureau, but for his own career as well.

For his part, Bragg was anxious to get back out in the field, hopefully recovering his name, and possibly career, in the process.

≈

The sun was just setting as the United Airlines flight from Denver landed in Reno. Inside the plane, Jason Bragg could feel his blood beginning to flow as it had in the past, the thrill of fieldwork rejuvenating his mind and spirit. While excited, he was also deeply concerned that if they were unable to close this case, it might be a fatal blow to what was left of his career.

The friendly smile and send off from the flight attendant as he exited the plane helped put him more at ease. "Thank you, Amy, you have a wonderful day as well."

Entering the terminal, Waymon greeted him with his hand outstretched, "Glad to be out of DC?"

"Samuel! Great to see you again," Bragg responded as he reached out his hand. "Thank you so much for getting me involved. It's great to be out in the field again."

"Hey, thank you! I'm not sure we'll be able to close this without your insight." Waymon, trying to keep his friend's confidence and spirit up.

As they made their way to the parking lot, the two discussed the latest facts and the research Bragg had been doing on the case back at HQ.

"To be honest with you, Jason, we're no closer to who is responsible than the day before the first abduction," Waymon explained as they walked. "These guys are clean, not leaving us a thing to go on. The similarities with Texas are striking.

"This certainly is feeling déjà vu from what I've seen," Bragg replied. "I've reviewed all the case files and compared them to what you have been working on here. There is no doubt in my mind that we've either got the same crew, or a very good copycat."

"Let's just be grateful the press hasn't put two and two together and drawn any connection yet. Any new theories beyond what you pursued in Texas?"

"I'm afraid I haven't come up with any yet. When you and I sit down with your team, jointly we might be able to come up with some ideas."

As they began driving towards the nearby FBI Resident Agency office, Waymon received a call from Agent Dawson.

"We have a reliable lead on some unusual activity at an abandoned motel on the east side of town," Dawson informed Waymon. "Infrared imaging has confirmed several people in the building."

"Warrants in place?"

"In process, sir. Expect to receive them momentarily."

"Okay, coordinate with Reno police, get the building surrounded out of sight, and SWAT in place. Send me the location and I should be there in fifteen minutes."

Reno International Airport is located just southeast of town, not too far out of the way Waymon was already driving. Making the necessary changes on the car's navigation system, Waymon updated Jason, "Looks like you get to enjoy some field action right away. Ready?"

"I've been ready for years, Samuel."

Flipping the switch for the car's lights and sirens, Waymon floored the gas pedal towards the scene.

≈

Waymon directed his car into a long-neglected area of Reno which was littered with abandoned vehicles, assorted garbage, and graffiti-decorated buildings, most of which hadn't seen any maintenance in decades. SWAT trucks and a dozen or so police and FBI vehicles were awaiting Bragg and Waymon.

"What do we have here, boys?" Waymon asked Dawson and Carver as he climbed out of his car to review the scene.

Carver directed Waymon and Bragg to the surveillance truck to view the monitors. "There is no one outside so we've just sent in a couple of agents to the door with cameras."

The four of them entered the truck and watched as a scope camera was inserted under the motel room door. They watched as several twenty-something men sat at a table with a pile of money at one end and packages of some sort at the other.

"What's the drone showing?" Waymon inquired.

Agent Dawson directed him to another monitor and pointed to an infrared image of several people in the room they were monitoring and one person in an adjoining room.

"Doesn't look like a child in that room, but they may be elsewhere," Samuel thought out loud. "Is everyone in position?"

"SWAT leader ready?" Carver spoke into his radio.

"All set," a voice responded.

"Confirm you're seeing three hostiles just to the right of the door, and an unknown in an adjoining room at ten o'clock."

"Roger," the voice responded.

Samuel nodded to Carver, who then spoke again over the radio, "You've got a green light."

≈

The SWAT team burst through the door with rifles strategically aimed at their targets. Four of the team headed to the right with the leader shouting "FBI". The men at the table began reaching for their weapons but quickly thought the better of it and lifted their hands above their heads.

With precision timing, two SWAT officers headed to a door of the adjoining room, kicking it open with guns aimed at the figure on the bed. There they found another twenty-something male being startled awake, instinctively reaching for his weapon, but as he stared down the barrel of the agents' guns quickly changed his mind.

Bragg, Waymon, and the team had been watching the action unfold over the monitor. No sign whatsoever of any children, but clearly packages of what appeared to be cocaine. Waymon instantly became irritated. "Damn!" Waymon yelled. "Just a bunch of drug dealers."

"Still," Dawson noted, "not such a bad haul."

Waymon looked at Dawson and snarled. Right now, he could care less about any other arrests, even if they bumped into one of the Bureau's Ten Most Wanted. He was interested in only one case at the moment.

Chapter Five

The yakking and giggling of the girls was replaced by Beyoncé and Taylor Swift by the time Christian returned downstairs after his long bath. Over in the kitchen, the centerpiece of their home, chopping could be heard as Tatum prepared dinner.

Stephanie's primary passion, apart from being married to Christian and raising Tatum, was cooking. Stephanie's father was a chef of his own wildly renowned Chicago restaurant and Stephanie learned the love of food and the art of cooking from him at a very early age.

When they purchased the lot in Sierra Vista, Stephanie claimed all design rights to the kitchen in exchange for allowing Christian free rein with the rest of the house. As a gift to the couple, Stephanie's father not only assisted her with the design of her dream kitchen, but also picked out and provided them with the finest professional appliances and cooking utensils. The floor and walls are Italian marble, the countertop Rocky Mountain granite, and the extensive cabinetry exotic hardwoods. In the center of the kitchen stood an enormous island for cooking and casual dining, complete with top of the line gas cooktop, food preparation, and sink. Above the food prep area was an iron pan rack from which hung the finest gourmet cookware.

Entering the kitchen, Christian admired Tatum as she chopped peppers and onion like a pro. Watching her reminded him so much of Stephanie. Stephanie and Tatum would spend hours together in the kitchen and Tatum learned quickly, now moving around the kitchen and managing the equipment like a seasoned chef. She definitely developed the same love for the art of cooking her mother and grandfather had.

"Something smells wonderful, sweetheart," Christian greeted as he gave her a kiss on the forehead.

"You're lucky I love you and you're aching so bad, Daddy, otherwise you'd be having frozen." Tatum slid the chopped vegetables into a waiting pan.

"You'd never do that to me, and you know it."

"After that anchovy smothered stuff you made for me last week, I wouldn't feel too confident about anything I might put on your plate," Tatum smiled impishly as she handed him some plates to set the table with. "So, you're going to Uncle Parker's party next Saturday, aren't you?"

"You know how I feel about his shindigs, Tatum, they aren't fun without your mother by my side. I'm tired of being cornered with yet another woman who thinks she can hook me."

"Maybe one of them would be right for you. Besides, if you would just find a nice woman, she could help me take care of you."

Tatum had wanted her father to begin dating for some time. As much as she loved her mother, she knew her father needed someone to share his very affectionate spirit with. Besides, Tatum really did miss having an older female around.

"How many times have we had this discussion, Tatum?" Christian replied with a tinge of frustration in his voice. "Have you ever seen any woman who could in any way compare to your mother?"

"Just because someone isn't perfect doesn't mean you can't have a meaningful relationship."

"Besides, we make a pretty good team, the two of us."

"A team of what? Psycho chefs?" she replied. "In a couple of years I'll be off to college, and you'll be in this big house all on your own."

"Oh, I think I'll be able to hold down the fort just fine," Christian replied as he exited to the patio to set the table.

≈

While dinner cooked in the oven, Christian joined Tatum at the kitchen table where she was watching the evening news.

"Anything interesting in the news today, sweetie?" Christian inquired as he sat down next to his daughter.

"Another kid has gone missing. This time it's a twelve-year-old over near the Truckee."

They both watched as the video from Samuel Waymon's press conference aired.

"I don't think they have any idea what's going on," Tatum added. "They've apparently come up clueless in all these cases recently."

"I just don't understand this kind of stuff. What the hell is the matter with people that they need to do this to children?" Christian was never one to get angry, but any harm to innocent children, or animals, really bothered him. "I want you to be extra careful, Tatum. Who knows what's going on out there? Please stick with your friends while you are out. Don't go anywhere alone. Okay?"

"I wouldn't worry, Daddy. If anyone got a hold of me they would end up paying you to take me back,' Tatum joked as she went over and gave him a kiss on his nose. That was her special place; not even Stephanie had been allowed to kiss Christian on his nose. "Besides, we travel in packs and usually have lacrosse sticks. Who would want to mess with us?"

That put Christian a little at ease, but this whole situation really disturbed him nonetheless. He couldn't remember anything like this in his many years living in the area. Tatum was his only child, and he wasn't expecting to have any more.

"The FBI has not been able to link any of the families, but the few clues police have released regarding the abductors certainly makes it appear as if they are related," the news anchor reported. "With so few clues and the continued serial nature of these disappearances, it is highly recommended that you and your children take extra precautions until the abductors have been apprehended."

≈

The adjoining patio was one of Christian's favorite spots. The tile from the kitchen continued out onto the patio, which had a 240° view of the mountains. It was here that Christian had frequently enjoyed Stephanie's incomparable meals and company as they savored the amazing northern Nevada skyline, including sunrises and sunsets.

The sun was just setting over the rugged crest of the Sierra Nevada Mountain range as Tatum joined her father, carrying her latest culinary masterpiece. "Voilà!" Tatum proclaimed as she placed the plate on the table in front of Christian. "Bon appétit."

≈

After finishing dinner, they cleaned the dishes and the kitchen together before Tatum headed upstairs to study for her upcoming midterms. "Remember now, if I'm going to be able to retire at fifty, you need to get a scholarship," he reminded her for the three hundred and seventy-second time.

"I think it would be good for you to wait till you're sixty-five, Daddy," Tatum suggested. "All you're going to do every day is go out and try to kill yourself anyway," she added, followed by a playful sticking out of her tongue.

As Tatum disappeared up the stairs, Christian went into the family room for some serious relaxation prior to getting ready for another week in his architecture practice. Just as the kitchen was Stephanie's design playground, Christian had paid particular attention to the design of this room. He felt strongly that this was where the family would spend most of their time together. He wanted a warm relaxed atmosphere which would encourage conversation and quality family time.

The large two-level octagonal room featured expansive floor to ceiling custom windows on the western walls, French doors leading out to a large patio, with more magnificent Sierra Nevada views. Inside, the room had extensive wood moldings and ample bookshelves to encourage reading, Christian's favorite indoor pastime; he deliberately did not include a TV in this room. A large two-sided fireplace was shared with the kitchen and framed on this side by river rock, floor to ceiling. A balcony from the upstairs hallway on the east wall incorporated the room into the living level.

Hung about the room were personal pictures going back to when Christian and Stephanie played intramural sports together in college. There were all sorts of sports and recreational pictures; some of Stephanie's modeling photos, including her Maybelline and Clairol campaigns, as well as a few movie posters from films she had been featured in. Also scattered about the room were Tatum's baby pictures and many photos of Tatum and friends as she was growing up. Christian was a perfectionist when it came to making the room a gallery of their lives. It was definitely the most inviting room in the house; the three of them enjoying many memorable moments here.

Christian relaxed back in his massage chair and pressed the control, starting the vibrator and massager, a well-deserved treatment after the long, and very unusual, day of hang gliding.

The chair was one of his favorite pieces of furniture. It was a gift from Tatum two years earlier. After seeing him stretched out in pain after a long weekend of whitewater rafting with his friends, Tatum snuck one of his credit cards from his wallet and purchased this top-of-the-line massage chair, which she presented to him for his birthday the following week.

One of the many things Stephanie taught Tatum was how to deal with her father. "It's often easier to seek forgiveness than to get permission," she would tell her daughter. "This is particularly true with your father, especially if the intentions are good." Stephanie taught her that a tilted head, a pair of raised eyebrows, and a slight frown would go a long way towards turning her father into Jell-O. She also warned her, "I wouldn't recommend you trying that on me though!" Whenever the 'charm' approach didn't work, Tatum would quickly regroup with her formidable debating skills, which usually left her father speechless. *She's gonna make one damn good attorney*, he often found himself thinking as she quickly outmaneuvered him. If there was ever a man that was wrapped around his little girl's little finger, it was Christian. Once he got over the sticker shock of her 'gift', he realized she was thinking only of his best interests and was quickly forgiven; as usual.

Christian had strategically placed the chair so it could easily swivel for maximum sight of either the fireplace or the panoramic view through the massive windows. He kept his stereo remote stored in the chair's side pocket and his current reads a short reach away. Emotionally, it was the safest place in a house full of memories of his beloved Stephanie. That it may have put him another month away from retirement was just no longer important.

This was definitely an evening for some mellow jazz. Christian was a prolific lover of music, all kinds of music. One could just as likely find him tuned to opera as country, rock, or Broadway musicals. He loved to drift off to sleep with classical however, preferably Mozart or Chopin. But a quiet evening after a day like today called for a little soothing jazz; John Pizzarelli Trio or Harry Connick, Jr. Nothing could make him float into relaxation more than a light massage and gentle jazz.

As Christian eased back in his chair and began to lose himself in the music, he reminisced fondly on the day, recalling the stunning images from the magnificent flight. He smiled as his thoughts turned to Tatum's excellent dinner and how well her mother had trained her in the kitchen. Eventually his thoughts turned to the missing children's report and a sadness temporarily overwhelmed him, but he eventually began floating off into the music; the children remaining in the back of his mind.

After several minutes of total relaxation, Christian's head suddenly became flooded with information. He suddenly sat upright, quite startled. These were not the kind of thoughts that come from one's imagination, they were as clear to him as anything he knew unquestionably as fact.

It was the missing children. He knew everything about them; their names, what they looked like, where they lived, their height, weight, and their favorite colors. He knew their parents' names and addresses. He knew exactly how they were abducted, as if he had seen each abduction himself. But most importantly, he knew where they were and who had them!

None of this seemed possible to Christian as he stood up and walked around the room to contemplate this information that appeared in his head out of nowhere. There was absolutely no question in his mind as to its validity. "Tatum!" he anxiously called into the intercom. "Come down here! Quick!"

Pausing from her geometry, Tatum wondered what in the world was so urgent. *Am I in trouble?*

"Is it good or bad?" returned her voice over the intercom. She always asked him that, trying to figure out if she needed to brace herself for something she might have done wrong.

"It's weird! Just get down here right away," he replied as he sat down on the sofa, his mind spinning.

"Sit down," Christian quickly instructed Tatum as she entered the room. "I need some help."

"Sure, Daddy. What's up?"

"That story on the missing children on TV, how many did they say there were?"

"Six. Four boys and two girls."

Yep, he knew that.

"And their names?"

"They only mentioned two names. The one abducted today, Jasper Thomas, and a girl from last week, Natasha something. I don't know the others. Why?"

Christian had only peripherally followed the story. Handing Tatum his iPad, "Here, pull up the latest news on the case."

Tatum could clearly see a certain anxiousness in her father as she had never before witnessed. Perplexed, Tatum searched for the story. "What's this all about?"

"I'm not sure yet."

"Here it is," she pointed to the screen.

Not looking at the screen, Christian inquired, "The names of the other kids, are they John Patterson, Kerrie Phillips, Mark Delford, and Austin Blake?"

"Hmmmmm," she pondered as she scanned the story. "Here they are. Mark Delford, Kerrie Phillips, Austin Blake, and John Patterson. Those are their names."

Tatum looked up with a puzzled expression on her face, "How in the world did you know that?"

Ignoring her question, he continued, "John disappeared last month on the twenty-eighth on his way home from school; Kerrie on the thirtieth walking to the mall; Austin, on the second of this month, after little league practice; and Mark on the eighth on his way to school. Right?"

Tatum scanned the story, replying "Hmmmmm. Right, right, right, right. How do you know all that?"

"I have no idea, honey, I just know it. I know it as clearly as I know my name or your name or that Reno is in Nevada. What's really scary is that I know just as clearly where they are and who is holding them!"

Tatum sat in disbelief as Christian instructed her to find the hotline number. "Daddy, there is no way you can know all that. You could get in real trouble making a false report, you know."

"I'll remember that if I am ever tempted to make a false report. In this case, however, I do in fact know where they are."

Despite her reservations and objections, she provided the phone number.

Christian dialed the number on his phone and the voice answered, "Missing children's hotline."

"Yes, I know where the six missing children are and who is holding them," Christian quickly informed the operator, an officer with the Nevada State Police.

The hotline had been receiving dozens of tips per day, and it was this officer's job to sort the real from the unlikely, and the urgent from the back burner. "Let me understand this, sir, you know that the children are alive and where they're being held?" the officer responded with a bit of skepticism in his voice. He'd received a lot of calls, but not one claiming to have such detailed information, and he was not yet convinced that this caller really had any information that was of value. Since the total local, state, and private reward level exceeded the half-million-dollar mark, plenty of people were trying to cash in on it.

"Yes. They are all together, being held by two men and a woman. They are locked up, but all safe and reasonably well taken care of. They are being held at an abandoned mine just southwest of Virginia City. The old Willet Silver Mine," Christian stated with high levels of confidence and urgency in his voice.

His interest peaked, but still not convinced, the officer continued, "Okay, sir, and how are you aware of this information? Have you seen them?"

"No, I have not, and I can't explain how I know, but I assure you that you will find the children, as well as their captors, exactly where I said."

"Did someone give you this information, sir?"

A tinge of frustration beginning to show in his voice, Christian's speech picked up cadence, "I'm not quite sure, but I can guarantee you will find them there. But be careful, one of the abductors plays lookout in a shack outside the mine. You'll need to approach from the rear and cut off his communication with his two accomplices inside the mine holding the children. Otherwise, you'll jeopardize the kids."

The officer was beginning to think he may be for real. "Thank you, sir, we'll check into this right away. Could I get your name and best number in case we need to get back with you?"

"Christian Faraday. 775-555-6413. Listen, if you doubt me, let me add that Austin had a wallet with five dollars, a library card, and a Best Buy gift certificate. Karie had an iPod, and Jasper, of all things for a twelve-year-old, a Kindle in his backpack."

Christian was totally perplexed, but at the same time he was absolutely one-hundred percent certain he was correct.

Chapter Six

While Waymon and Bragg were reviewing the complexities of the case in the 'war room', Agent Dawson entered with a sense of urgency.

"We've got what looks like it might be a legit lead. Caller claims he is absolutely positive that all the children are alive and being held in an abandoned mine near Virginia City."

Waymon looked at him skeptically. "What's your take on the credibility?" They received so many tips that it was a tough call on what to follow-up on. They already had one false raid today and he wasn't looking forward to another, especially this late in the day.

"I listened to the recording and believe it's solid." He provided some personal information on the kids which hasn't been made public. He wouldn't say how he knew where they are, but he was very specific and insistent."

"I'm listening."

"This is what we've got." Dawson pressed the 'Play' button on the tablet. Waymon and Bragg both raised their eyebrows in interest as they listened to Christian's voice.

Once the recording concluded, Dawson continued while pulling up a satellite image on his tablet, "Infrared gives us what appears to be two warm automobiles in two different shacks, and a body in one of those as well."

"Smart, hide in a mine where we can't pick up anything on imaging. That would also explain this ever so faint warmth at the opening of the cave. Let's get everyone in here and evaluate potential actions," Waymon told Dawson. "If this lead is for real, we need to approach this scene carefully. Get the roads in and out of the area blocked off, making damn sure everyone remains well out of sight. Put some drones up there for more real-time imaging."

Bragg added, "And check property ownership and assess the need for any warrants."

≈

Within ten minutes the conference room was crowded with leading representatives from the local and state police, FBI, and the head of the SWAT team. In front of them on the conference table was a detailed topographical map of the area around the mine.

After introducing Jason to the team, Waymon played the recording for all those gathered. He then showed the real-time infrared images on the large screen on the wall."

"As you can see, the call appears legit. We've got slight heat here, which looks like the mine entrance. The two separate shacks here," pointing to another spot on the image, "clearly have warm vehicles inside them, with one body obvious in this one."

Waymon then directed attention to the topographic map on the table. "There is one road leading to the mine, which is otherwise surrounded by rough terrain. This leaves them, and us, only one path for vehicles." Turning to the head of the SWAT team, he continued, "Any thoughts on how to approach this, Jeff?"

Jeff Perry, a lean man in his mid-thirties, was an ex-Navy SEAL. Jeff had been heading up the Nevada SWAT operations for the last three years and had yet to have a failed operation. None of his men had been injured, much less killed, and all suspects apprehended without fatality; although a few had wished they hadn't put up a resistance. Jeff was an extremely serious man and had rarely been seen to crack a smile.

"My team can handle this terrain easily," Jeff responded. "I'll send several men in on foot over this minor pass, right here," as he pointed to a spot on the map. "There's access from the river just east from where they can reach it. Once there, we can neutralize the suspect in the shack from the rear while simultaneously securing the mine entrance. Even the slightest sound will echo in an area like this so some flyby sound cover would help, but not so close as to be suspicious. Is there any information on the shacks, or the mine itself?"

Agent Carver opened a file on the mine which contained some old black and white photos, displaying them on the table. "These are the two large storage sheds, both wooden construction and probably quite rundown, meaning anyone inside has lots of missing sideboards to look out of on all sides. As you can see, the one infrared picked up the body in on the right has two levels. This tells me that individual is the lookout," he explained while using a pointer to identify the buildings as he spoke. "If you look at the entrance of the mine, it appears about fifteen feet wide and about ten feet high. According to the mine maps it goes straight back, but records indicate there was a cave-in and it's now pretty much closed up about 100 feet back, leaving no exit other than the main entrance."

"Taking both the lookout and the cave shouldn't be a problem," Jeff noted. "The problem is that we don't know how the kids are being held within the cave. We'll have to deal with that in real-time. This shouldn't be a problem if we are able to quickly disable the two suspects inside."

Waymon pondered the situation while Bragg inquired, "Given the terrain, how close can we get backup vehicles in without danger of being heard?"

"I'd give it a quarter mile minimum, but I'd probably keep it at least a mile or two until we've cleared the lookout," Jeff responded. "We'll have feeds to all monitors. Once we're ready to enter the mine, pull your vehicles to this point," he said while pointing to a spot on the map just outside the visibility of the mine entrance. "All lights out."

"Okay, let's get our teams coordinated and get moving," Waymon instructed. "Jeff, give us your time parameters and we'll have the back-up ready to go. Dawson, coordinate all state and local. Carver, get the flyby arranged based on Jeff's signal. Arrange for nine ambulances and have the closest hospital on standby. Have cars at all residences ready to deliver the parents to the hospital with psychologists on hand for each of the six kids in the event we're successful. Have a dark van with assorted press but don't give them any information and no communication allowed until we give the go ahead. This is the highest security."

Waymon did not want another public raid which didn't yield results.

The men in the room then dispersed to their tasks.

≈

Their way lit by the reflective light of the almost full moon six well-armed SWAT team members dressed in desert camouflage made their way over the crest where two hills met behind the mine. Silently they continued to the base of the hill within twenty yards of the smaller shack. At the same time, two SWAT snipers stealthily positioned themselves one hundred yards in front of the mine, ensuring a clear view of both the shacks and the mine entrance. One of the members set up a thermal infrared camera aimed at the two-story shack to monitor the individual in there.

Jeff Perry assessed the situation. The night was calm and the air still. The only sounds to be heard were the occasional muffled child's cough coming from inside the mine and music playing at a very low volume from the second-floor shack. That would help with the sound cover, but only slightly. The site was virtually unchanged from the black and white photos he saw in the FBI conference room, although a few additional abandoned vehicles now littered the area.

Jeff reached into his backpack and pulled out a wireless monitor which controlled and displayed the image from the camera set up by the other team. He could see the image of the individual in the shack, seated and relaxed. The man was positioned in front of a window and could easily be picked off by one of the snipers. However, until it was firmly established that these were criminals, there would be no fatal shootings.

Using the controls, Jeff zoomed to the mine opening on the left, a wood structure with a door covering the entrance. He was able to make out the thermal images of two people lying on either side of the entrance and several grouped together further back in the cave. Repositioning the camera to the smaller shack he confirmed that it was uninhabited.

Back in the surveillance van, Waymon, Bragg, and the other key personnel watched the same images with a sense of great anticipation.

"You've got a go from here," Jeff heard Waymon from his earpiece.

Jeff whispered in return, "Order the first pass."

Dawson spoke into a separate microphone and gave instructions to commence the first flyover pass. An F-16 based out of nearby Nellis AFB had been circling just south of the area awaiting the command.

As they waited for the flyover, Jeff silently signaled instructions to his men. Two of them were to flank the cave opening, two others to the other side of the larger shack, and the last one to a trailer fifteen yards this side of the shack. While they were well aware that they had no more than a seven second window for noise cover, they had been trained to move almost silently over most terrains. The intense desert silence, even with the low radio volume, was of concern enough that they might nonetheless attract interest from the lookout.

After several minutes the sound of the jet came within earshot and Jeff gave the signal for all teams to move in. The teams dispersed in their assigned directions, with Jeff and his partner going to the trailer; his partner carrying a large rifle-type weapon. As the sound faded, all teams were positioned. Jeff took another look at the monitor and observed that the individual in the shack appeared undisturbed, clearly unaware of their presence.

Jeff's partner prepared the weapon, using the thermal infrared scope to aim in at the person on the top floor of the shack. This 'thermal gun', a new development from Oak Ridge National Laboratories, could be aimed through a wall and had a range of 50 yards. Using radio frequency exposure, the thermal gun quickly raises an individual's body temperature to 107°. Given that even a slight fever can impair a person's physical ability, at this temperature the victim is nearly 100 percent incapacitated.

Reno law enforcement activities, even those coordinated by the FBI, did not normally have access to such advanced technology, but this case was of such importance to the Bureau that they had been supplied with all the latest gadgets along with personnel trained in their use.

Jeff whispered into his microphone, "All systems go," to which he heard Waymon respond, "You've got a green light."

"Go for it," Jeff whispered to his partner.

The two agents stationed at the mine entrance braced themselves in the event something went wrong and they would have to rush the mine sooner than planned. Two agents on the opposite side prepared to round the corner to enter the shack.

Inside the surveillance van, the team watched as the yellow, orange, and only slightly red figure first became entirely red and stiffened up, then fell limply into the chair.

"Team two, go," Jeff ordered.

Instantly, the two SWAT officers rushed into the building and up the steps where they found a man in his late forties slouched in an aluminum beach chair, completely immobilized. At his side was a table with a radio, a coffee thermos, pistol, and a walkie-talkie. Quickly, one officer removed the walkie-talkie and aimed his rifle directly at the man's forehead. The only muscles he was capable of controlling were his eyes; moving them to see the muzzle of the rifle pointed directly at him.

The second officer secured the man's wrists and ankles with zip ties and taped his mouth to keep him quiet. "Team two secure," he whispered into his microphone as he headed back down the stairs.

Jeff and his partner, who by now had laid the thermal weapon on the ground and removed rifles from slings on their backs, quietly hurried over to the cave opening. Already there was an officer kneeling down, carefully inserting a thin flexible scope into a crack in the old wood planks that covered the entrance. They were joined by one of the officers coming out of the shack. Jeff leaned down and adjusted the frequency on his monitor, watching as the scope slowly entered the cave.

In the surveillance van the agents watched the same images on their monitor. With their lights out, along with the caravan of police vehicles behind them, the van slowly made their way to a spot just out of sight of the mine entrance. Meanwhile, the two sharpshooters grabbed their bags and ran from their post to join the rest of the SWAT team.

As he watched the interior of the mine become clear on the monitor, Jeff indicated to the officer controlling the scope to point it to the left. On a cot, he could see an adult sleeping soundly, with a gun on the floor next to him. Jeff pointed to the right and the scope turned to the opposite wall where another adult, apparently female, also asleep, and also with a gun on the floor next to her. Jeff instructed the officer to point the scope straight ahead. The monitor displayed what appeared to be a wire mesh wall beyond the cots. Past that were several children, all lying on the dirt floor. There did not appear to be any indication of booby traps.

"Check the door," Jeff whispered to the scope operator. The scope cable created a U-turn, and the monitor displayed the inside of the door where no internal barricades or extra locks were evident. Jeff indicated to the officer to exit the scope.

Stepping back, Jeff pulled the other officer with him. "We're going with a flash-bang, get your goggles ready," he whispered to them, referring to a device which sets off a bright blinding light lasting a fraction of a second while setting off a loud sound. It is very effective in temporarily blinding and completely disorienting a suspect, allowing law enforcement to enter a room and secure a situation.

"Place the explosives on the doorknob. If it's locked, we'll have to blow it. As soon as the door is open," he pointed to one of the officers, "toss in the flash-bang no more than two or three feet. I'll go in first and cover the suspect on the left, the rest of you follow in order. Mark, you secure my guy. Tom, you and Bill take the right cot. The rest of you head to the back and check out the kids."

The team returned to the mine entrance, putting on their goggles and preparing their weapons. Once the explosive had been placed next to the door handle, Jeff whispered into his microphone, "We're ready to go in."

"Proceed at will," Waymon responded. Waymon had grown to trust Jeff's judgment, without question, after the many missions they had participated in together over the last few years.

Jeff stepped up to the door which, as expected, was unlocked. The suspects obviously felt they had things well covered, and it wasn't worth the hassle to keep locking and unlocking every time they went in and out, even at night.

With the team all in place, Jeff nodded his head to go ahead. The door was thrown open, and the flash-bang was tossed in between the cots. Just as the two suspects on the cots looked up from the sudden sound of the door opening, the flash-bang went off, completely stunning, blinding, and disorienting them.

By the time the suspects on the cots began to orient themselves and were able to see again, Jeff and Tom had kicked the guns out of reach and had their rifle barrels pointed straight at the suspects' heads. They encountered no resistance. As they were zip tied, the rest of the team was back at the wire wall, an officer in the rear of the pack with a lantern.

"It's okay, kids, we're here to take you home," one of the SWAT officers told the children as another pulled out a pair of bolt cutters, breaking the lock on the wood frame wire door.

Fortunately, none of the children had awakened when the door burst open due to the distance to their cage. They were not aroused until the noise of the flash-bang, thereby missing the bright light. At first terrified, they quickly realized that the police were there to save them, and they rushed to the cage door; it had been a long time in the cave for most of them and they were anxious to get out.

Outside, the area was bright as daylight with most of the vehicle headlights pointing straight towards the mine entrance and shacks. The ambulances had backed into an area between the shacks, ready to load their charges and head off to the hospital.

Inside the FBI van, Waymon and the rest of the team had been watching the scene inside the mine unfold from the officers' body cams. As a camera panned the children's faces, Dawson matched their faces against those of the missing children.

"They're our kids," Dawson confirmed, "all of them."

"Great!" responded a clearly relieved Waymon. "Get the psychologists to the cave entrance to prepare for their assigned kids. Open up the press van and get the word out to the rest of the media."

Waymon had arranged for several of the local press to be present under the condition that if there was something to report, they would be the first on the scene; otherwise they would just have a long midnight ride in a windowless van. There were several print reporters and photographers, as well as reporters and cameramen from a couple of the local TV stations.

"Go ahead and pick up the parents and get them over to the hospital."

≈

As the kids were released from their cage, they passed by their abductors secured on their cots. Some glared at them angrily straight in their eyes as they rushed out of the cave to the awaiting group of psychologists and paramedics, who each greeted the child assigned to them, escorting them individually to their ambulances. Nearby, photographers and cameramen were capturing the scene on video while Agents Dawson and Carver briefed the reporters on the operation.

Waymon and Bragg made their way through the scene and into the cave to assess the situation.

"What do we have here, Jeff?"

Looking through the wallets on the table, Jeff replied, "Looks like Jerry Schmitt and his wife, Amanda. I found another license for a John Ferris; I assume he's the one out in the shack."

"Bag up any evidence and get their phones analyzed for accomplices," Waymon instructed. "And once the kids are clear, take these two out and in for questioning. I suspect there's much to learn and Agent Bragg will definitely want to assess any relationship with the Texas case. You've got cameras waiting out there, so give the press a good look. I assume they don't need an ambulance?"

"No. They're just a little pissed off, that's all. I've got an EMT checking out the guy in the shack just to be safe though."

"Good work, Jeff. Another flawless mission."

"Thank you, sir."

"Find anything back there?" Waymon asked as he turned to one of the officers looking around the caged area.

"A bit of filth, but nothing notable. It doesn't look like they were well taken care of, but not abused either," the officer responded.

"Okay. Once the evidence is bagged let the press have a peek, but just from the entrance, I don't want them disturbing anything. They can get a few quick shots then out they go."

≈

The three suspects were escorted to FBI vehicles; photographers given an ample opportunity to record the event. Waymon, flanked by Bragg, called the reporters over to give them a statement.

"I'm pleased to say that, thanks to the tremendous coordination of the FBI with local and state agencies, as well as the assistance of a concerned citizen, we have recovered all six missing children who appear to be in good health and physically unharmed. They are currently on their way for full medical evaluation and to be reunited with their families. I'd also like to thank Special Agent Bragg from Washington, who has been critical in helping us close this case. I'll have a further statement later. For now, feel free to look about the scene and direct any questions to either Agent Dawson or Agent Carver here. And remember, you are dark until we give you the go-ahead to make this public, which should be within a few hours."

Waymon hated answering questions, so he and Bragg hastily exited, leaving Dawson and Carver to handle the reporters.

"Get this wrapped up in half an hour then go by and pick up the guy that called in the tip for questioning," Waymon whispered to Dawson as he passed him on his way to the cave.

Chapter Seven

The digital display on Christian's bedside clock read 1:47 a.m. as he was aroused from a deep sleep by the sound of his doorbell. Despite the excitement of the evening, he had had no problem falling asleep earlier. Not only was he not one to have trouble falling asleep at night, but this had been a particularly exhausting day; the exhaustion he was felt down to his cellular level. A middle of the night wake-up call was the last thing he needed after the unusual day he had just experienced.

Christian lay in his bed in a semi-conscious state until Tatum barged into his room.

"Daddy! Can't you hear the doorbell?"

"Wasn't that a dream, sweetheart?"

"No, it wasn't. Now will you go down and answer it so I can get back to sleep?"

Christian stumbled out of bed in his boxers and T-shirt and retrieved his bathrobe from the back of the bathroom door. He was so groggy that Tatum had to make sure he didn't fall back in bed. "Who in the world are you expecting at this time of night?" she asked.

"Don't blame this on me—it's probably one of your boyfriends," Christian quipped back. "Oh, I forgot—you just sneak down to the basement window to meet them!"

"Yeah? Like when?" While she actually did that from time to time, she was hoping her father was just joking. Christian gave her a knowing smirk, even though he was indeed just joking.

As Christian descended the stairs, Tatum sat on the top step, being far too curious to ignore such an event.

Rubbing his eyes, Christian turned off the security system and opened the door to find two men standing outside.

"Good morning, Mister Faraday," Agent Dawson greeted him while holding up his FBI badge. "I'm Agent Dawson. This is Agent Carver."

Christian looked at their badges and was satisfied that they were indeed Federal agents. "FBI? It's nearly two in the morning!"

"We'd like to talk to you about your call earlier this evening—the one about the children at the old Willet mine."

This snapped Christian to his senses. The peaceful sleep he had been in made him forget this earlier call to the tip line, almost thinking it must have all been a dream.

"Uh, sure. Come on in," Christian widened the door and gestured for them to come inside. Through his yawns, he somehow managed to ask, "Did you find the children?"

"Yes, Mister Faraday, that's why we are interested in speaking with you. Your information allowed us to successfully raid the cave and rescue the children; all six of them." Then, in a more serious tone, Agent Dawson continued, "We're keenly interested in how you were aware of their location and the other details you gave us."

"So, they're safe?" Christian pointed them to the chairs in the family room. "Please, have a seat."

"Yes, Mister Faraday, they are all at Washoe Medical Center with their parents. They have you to thank for that. We all greatly appreciate your assistance in the case," Carver reassured him.

"I really don't know anything more, I gave the operator everything I knew; including all I knew about how I knew. If you had simply called, I could have told you that and saved you a trip out here."

"Mister Faraday, we would really like to explore that last part in a little more detail. Are you acquainted with any of the individuals involved?"

"No, this time yesterday I didn't know anything at all other than there were a bunch of missing children. For some reason, as I was resting yesterday evening, it just came to me. I really know nothing more than that."

"You do understand that we find that a bit far-fetched, don't you?"

"Absolutely," Christian was beginning to get a little agitated. "I find it a bit far-fetched too, but that's the way it is. You did want me to pass along the information, didn't you?"

"Yes, Mister Faraday, you –"

Christian cut him off, "Please. It's Christian."

"Okay, Christian. The FBI must pursue that explanation. We really need a better understanding than, 'I just suddenly knew it.'"

"I wouldn't mind a better understanding either, but that's all I have. So, if you'll excuse me, I've got a meeting with an important client first thing in the morning. And I'm sure your wives would love to see you at home instead of out here in the middle of the night."

"I'm afraid it's not that simple, Mister Faraday. We're going to need you to join us down at the office to explore this further."

"Fine, I'll come by tomorrow after work. I'm afraid it's a bit of a busy day."

"Actually, we'd like you to accompany us now."

"As I mentioned, I need to get back to sleep for a busy day ahead."

"That won't be possible. Would you like a moment to get dressed, or come with us as you are?"

Christian stared at Dawson, understanding he really didn't have a choice in the matter. They were the FBI, messing with them clearly wasn't going to do any good.

"Whoooooooooooa," came a voice from the stairway as Tatum ran down the steps. "You aren't taking him anywhere. Didn't you hear him? He helped you out all he can and needs to get some sleep. Can't you appreciate that at least he was responsible for rescuing the kids?"

"This is my daughter, Tatum." Christian explained. "She's a bit protective of me." Turning back to Tatum, "It's okay, honey," Christian assured her. "I've got to go but should be back shortly."

"We're not sure how long this will take, Christian. Do you need to make any arrangements for your daughter?"

"No, Tatum will be just fine. And this will NOT take very long." Christian gave Dawson a stern look.

Christian and Tatum went upstairs. "Don't worry, sweetheart, everything will be fine. You get some sleep and I'll be back before you're off to school."

He went to his room and slipped into a pair of slacks and a shirt. "Turn on the security system and go back to bed. I'll see you at breakfast."

Gently giving her a kiss on her forehead, Christian then headed to the door with Dawson and Carver.

Once the men were out the door, Tatum turned on the security system. Leaning back against the door, her eyes widened, an idea hatching in her excited head.

≈

Christian sat on one side of the nondescript table in a nondescript interrogation room at the FBI offices with Agent Dawson across from him while Agent Carver paced the room. Christian was well aware that he was being observed by others on the opposite side of the large mirror on the wall.

"Listen, yesterday was a normal day. I woke up and I knew very little about this case. I spent the day hang gliding with friends, came home, had dinner with my daughter; before which we watched a news story on the kids. As I was resting after dinner, I suddenly became aware of everything I passed along to you. I called you immediately. That honestly is all I know. I don't know the abductors, never met them, never heard of them, and don't know anything else about them. You now know everything I know."

"So, what you're telling us is that out of thin air, all this very detailed information just popped right into your head?" Agent Carver clarified with quite a skeptical tone in his voice. "Exactly where they were, who was with them, the best approach to the mine. Doesn't that seem awfully unusual to you, Mister Faraday?"

"Duh, of course it does. It would to any rational person," Christian sarcastically retorted.

"Are you a psychic or something, Mister Faraday?" Dawson interjected.

"Well, my daughter often calls me a psycho."

As the men sat stoically, clearly absent a sense of humor, Christian became uncharacteristically serious with a stern look on his face. "No, I am not a psychic. I'm just a normal guy who thought he was doing people a favor by passing along important information that I, for whatever reason, came across. I have no idea how I came across it. I have no idea where it came from. If this is how you treat people that are trying to help, no wonder you have so much difficulty solving cases!"

≈

The interrogation had clearly reached an impasse as Waymon and Bragg watched from behind the two-way mirror.

"I think it's time for you to play 'good cop', Samuel," Jason suggested.

"Yup. Those two aren't getting anywhere," Waymon responded as he arose from the table he was leaning on. "Let's go."

The door to the room opened and Christian looked over to see Waymon and Bragg enter the room.

"Hello, Mister Faraday. I'm Special Agent Samuel Waymon and this is Special Agent Jason Bragg from Washington," Samuel smiled as he extended his hand.

As Christian shook their hands, Waymon continued, "I first want to thank you for assistance on this case. We had been working several angles, but your information was invaluable in bringing the pieces together. I know I speak for every parent in the Reno area when I say, thank you very much."

Christian began to relax as it appeared someone actually appreciated his call. "I'm glad I could help, but I'm afraid I don't understand the reason I was dragged out of my slumber in the middle of the night."

"We're terribly sorry about that, Mister Faraday. You have to understand this is highly unusual and brings up many issues that we really need to understand very quickly."

"What kind of issues couldn't wait until I got a full night's sleep and through my morning meetings?"

"To begin with, there is a lot more to this case than just the six children abducted over the last few weeks."

"I really don't know anything else about it."

"And we must understand how this information just appeared to you."

"I told you –"

Waymon raised his hand, "Yes, I understand. But you have to understand that such an explanation suggests that you are a psychic, although you yourself don't believe that. So where does that leave us?"

"No further than when your men woke me up back at my house, and all we have to show for it is a lot of lost sleeping time."

"One thing I've learned over the years, Mister Faraday, is that there is always an explanation. It's not always obvious, but there is an explanation to be found." Waymon calmly attempting to put the situation in perspective, "Nothing ever happens out of thin air. There must be something else involved, and together we need to figure it out."

Christian rolled his eyes and laughed. He shook his head as he put it down into his hands. The room sat in silence, the FBI men looking at one another awaiting Christian's response.

Exasperated with the FBI Officers and their questioning, Christian began to think about the children. *Why were the children kidnapped? Who were those people? What more could the FBI want from me?*

After a few moments, and exactly as the night before, knowledge about it all began flooding into his head. Once again, not things he was daydreaming about, but things he innately knew to be fact.

Suddenly, Christian popped his head up and blurted out, "Operation Python!"

Waymon and Bragg immediately sat up, clearly startled, and looked immediately at one another.

"How in the hell do you know about Python?" Waymon demanded, knowing that the name of Bragg's fatal career case in Texas was still highly classified.

"Twelve kids. Texas. Four weeks. Five years ago. Your case," Christian blurted out as he pointed to Bragg. "They are now in Montana, on a farm forty-five miles northeast of Shelby."

The agents looked at each other in total disbelief.

"And the racketeering case in Vegas you're working on," Christian added, looking straight at Waymon, "you're on the wrong guy. Williamson is being set up by Malone's mob organization. At this address," he began writing an address on a piece of paper, "you will find all the evidence you need to close the case, plus a lot more."

Again, the agents were speechless, not quite sure how to react. They realized they were on to something but didn't quite know what. Christian himself had a look of astonishment mixed with self-satisfaction.

"Operation Wicker is a sham. Your St. Louis office has framed three guys to the tune of fifty years each to cover up their own incompetence. Waymon, your son is ranked second in the state in pole vault. Agent Carver, today is your daughter's thirteenth birthday; boy do I feel sorry for you! And," Christian added with a smile on his face as he looked at Agent Dawson, "your daughter has a cat named 'Pinkerbell'!"

Just as Christian sat back, took a deep breath, crossed his arms and smiled broadly, the enormity of what just happened hit him. Jumping slightly forward in his chair he blurted out, "How did I know all that?" Slowly sitting back again he grinned, "Hey, this is pretty cool!"

Although all were taken aback, Jason Bragg was too invested in the first response to care about the rest. "The kids in Montana? Are they alright? Where exactly are they?"

Concern for the kids quickly overtook Christian's curiosity over his unexplained knowledge and he got serious again. "A ranch called the TriangleT. Off Route 200. Get me a map and I'll be able to show you exactly."

Bragg signaled to Carver who rushed out of the room.

"They are living in a converted barn. A small religious cult is indoctrinating them while making them work the ranch. There are three adults there, Including the wife of one of the men you apprehended earlier tonight. At 7:00 AM they will be expecting their morning update call from the group you just picked up. The kids here were to be the latest addition to their flock."

With the sense of urgency and fascination clearly building in the agents, Christian continued, "The adults live in separate houses. The compound is about a mile down a dirt road off Rout 200. The kids are generally healthy, although not exceptionally well taken care of. Some serious brainwashing going on, however."

"Are there any others, or just the twelve from Texas?"

"A few others. One from Wyoming, and two from Iowa. Additionally, there are two kids that are children of the adults there."

Carver returned with a state map of Montana and Bragg spread it out in front of Christian, who picked up a pencil and marked a specific spot on the map, "This is where you will find them, and I'd get there before 7:00 AM, local time."

Bragg turned to Waymon, "You don't mind if I borrow these two for a bit, do you?" Pointing to Agents Dawson and Carver.

"They're all yours. They will make sure you get any resources you need. Dawson, get the jet on standby in case you guys need to get up there."

As the three agents left the room, Waymon's mobile phone rang. "Waymon," he snapped as he answered the phone.

"Mister Faraday's daughter and attorney are out here demanding to see him," responded the voice from the front desk.

Damn, Waymon thought, *I don't have time to deal with this.* "Tell them Mister Faraday will be busy for a while."

"I don't think you understand," shouted Parker Farr's voice over the phone, apparently having grabbed the phone from the security guard. "If I don't see my client immediately, I'll have the press down here in twenty minutes and you'll be spending all day trying to explain why you're holding the actual hero of this case."

"Just a moment, I'll be right out." Samuel turned to Christian, "I'll be right back, Mister Faraday."

Unaware that it was his friend who was on the phone, Christian responded, "This has all been quite exciting, Agent Waymon, but I'd really like to get home and get some sleep tonight."

"We still have quite a bit to discuss. I'll have some coffee brought in."

Christian started to object, but Waymon was out the door before he could get more than a couple of words out.

≈

The silence in the meticulous penthouse condo overlooking the lights of the San Francisco skyline was pierced by the shrill ring of the mobile phone on Marcus West's nightstand.

Despite the clock reading just after 3 AM and being awakened from a deep slumber, his life-long training enabled Marcus to be fully alert within seconds and answer the phone with all his senses intact.

After listening to the caller for about thirty seconds, Marcus responded, "Thanks. You'll be seeing us shortly. Cover us the best you can. Good work."

A brief moment was all he needed to decide which number to send an urgent text to. "Airfield. 4AM. Urgent." After pressing 'Send', he pressed another contact, which quickly answered. "Need a jet ready immediately. Destination, Reno." Hanging up, he hustled quickly to his exercise room for a quick workout before heading to the shower.

≈

In the lobby of the FBI offices, Tatum was pacing the floor, ready to pounce on the first agent that showed their face. Parker attempted to assure her that everything would be okay.

Waymon opened the secure door and introduced himself, stretching his hand to Parker. Tatum, not concerned with formalities given that her father was being held somewhere behind those doors, rushed towards Waymon only to be stopped by Parker's outstretched arms grabbing her at her waist, preventing certain collision with the agent.

"Where is my father?" she screamed as Waymon stepped back, quite startled.

"It's okay, Tatum. I'll handle this," Parker assured her. "I'm Parker Farr, Mister Faraday's attorney. We'd like to see him immediately."

"Mister Farr, Miss Faraday," Waymon shook Parker's hand and nodded to Tatum. "Mister Faraday is fine. We're having a very productive discussion, he is being immensely helpful in several ongoing investigations. We really appreciate all his assistance."

"Be that as it may, he has every right to have his attorney present."

"He hasn't been charged with anything, Mister Farr."

"Then you have no basis on which to continue to hold him, Agent Waymon."

"All his assistance has been voluntary. In fact, we've got a team getting ready to nab some bad guys up in Montana, thanks to your father," Waymon smiled as he looked at Tatum.

Parker had little patience with such condescending attitudes. "Let me be quite clear. If I don't see Mister Faraday within sixty seconds, I'll make sure there are as many lights and cameras on your front steps in twenty minutes as you had out at the mine this evening," Parker giving Waymon a very stern look, "Do you really want such a public display as to who is doing all your work for you?"

Waymon knew he had little choice. Given all the information Christian had already provided, Waymon had less time than ever to deal with the press. Additionally, there was potential for Christian's ability to become public. That would not only discount any credit the FBI could take for this success, but also take the media focus off of this case and on to the unusual ability of Christian Faraday.

Waymon was also acutely aware of Parker's legal reputation. He would have to yield and let Christian go home and sleep for a few hours. Somehow, he would find a way to grab Christian in the morning.

"Okay, Mister Farr, Miss Faraday, please follow me," Waymon conceded as he headed to the secure door leading into the inner offices.

Tatum gave Parker a high five and the two followed Waymon through the secure door, down the hallway, and into the interrogation room.

"Daddy!" Tatum yelled as she ran to give her father a hug.

Christian was relieved to see his daughter and good friend as he returned her hug. "Thanks for coming, Parker."

"No problem, you know that," Parker reassured him. "What exactly is going on here, Christian?"

"It's really weird, I just close my eyes and think about something and all kinds of information about it just pops into my head. I don't know what's going on. But I do know that I'm exhausted and really need to get some sleep."

"So am I, and I think Tatum has school in a few hours." Parker turned to Waymon, handed him one of his business cards, and firmly stated, "I think Mister Faraday has given you enough food for thought for tonight. Call me if you need any further assistance from him."

"Thank you, Mister Farr, and thank you very much for your tremendous assistance, Mister Faraday. We're very grateful and I look forward to meeting with you again. Soon." Waymon knew that he had to be much more diplomatic in order not to alienate Christian—or Parker either for that matter. This was definitely the most significant find he had encountered in his long career and could possibly propel him well beyond his current ambitions if he played it right. On the other hand, things could spiral out of control if he screwed it up.

After showing the three of them out, Waymon tracked down Bragg to see how he and his men were doing.

"Looks like I'll need your jet, Samuel," Bragg exclaimed as Waymon entered the room.

"Not a problem. You certainly deserve to be there." Waymon was not too concerned about the Montana situation as he had much bigger things on his mind. "Have my boys made all the arrangements you need?"

"They've been great. Surveillance, SWAT teams, state and local all lined up. Our boys in Montana are coordinating things from here on out. I just need to get in the air. Where's Faraday?"

"His bratty kid brought his attorney down here and I had to let him go home."

"You released him?"

"It's clear from the range of information he had that he wasn't involved with the kidnappers. I can't really hold him for having psychic ability."

"You are aware of the implications of the ability we witnessed?"

"Painfully so. Don't worry, I'll have him back in a few hours." The intense look of concern was clear on his face. "I'm not sure what he's got going, but being able to summon up any desired information on demand makes him a very valuable asset."

"I don't understand it either. We've never had any notable success with psychics, and he doesn't even claim to be one."

"Can you imagine the cases we can get closed if this guy is for real?" Agent Dawson naively interjected.

Waymon had been around the Bureau for a long time. So had Bragg. They were both well aware that much of their confidential information as well as internal 'dirt' could be jeopardized, not only to the public, but within the intelligence communities as well. "No doubt. But it's not quite that simple. Do you have any idea how much damage he can do to the Bureau?" Samuel snapped. "Get some men on him; I want a team on him around the clock and a full briefing on the guy at zero seven hundred."

Chapter Eight

Mornings, even Monday mornings, had never been a challenge for Christian. He was an early riser by nature and loved to start the day off with a good workout to prepare his creative juices for his architecture projects—usually well into his morning routine by 5:15 a.m. His daughter, on the other hand, never liked seeing daylight before 11:00 a.m., unless it involved a special event with her friends. School simply didn't rate as a special event.

Arising on this Monday morning, however, was proving to be quite the challenge. Despite his exhaustion from the events of the last twenty-four hours, he nevertheless mustered enough energy to drag himself out of bed, be it an hour and a half later than his usual 5:00 a.m. He was just in time to make sure Tatum was up in time to get ready for school. Tatum was a freshman at not-so-nearby Laurel Ridge Academy, and her friend Nicki was due to pick her up at seven.

Struggling out of bed, Christian stumbled into Tatum's room. "Morning sweetheart." Christian was always cheerful, especially with Tatum, no matter how tired he was.

Tatum, while usually just as pleasant, was not quite as agreeable in the morning. "Go away, Daddy," came her voice, muffled by a pillow.

"Monday morning! Let's boogie!"

"I was up half the night. Monday can wait."

"Come on kiddo, let's get moving. If this old man can do it, you can too."

"Okay, okay. I'll be right down."

Christian stood in the door whistling until Tatum pulled herself out of bed and headed into her bathroom, "See you downstairs, sweetie."

"Whatever."

Christian headed down the steps and into the kitchen and, by habit, straight to the coffee pot, where the coffee maker automatically had his coffee hot and ready. As Christian started to pour coffee, he realized how quickly since he arose that both his mind and body had become remarkably refreshed, actually feeling as if he had already exercised. Setting down his coffee, the sudden energy surge compelled him to squeeze an orange instead.

Usually, Christian just quickly prepared a muffin and fruit for Tatum. This morning, he was feeling particularly imaginative and decided to whip her up an omelet for a change.

"Wow, what smells so good down there?" Tatum's voice sounded from the stairwell, only slightly more awake than when she went into the shower.

"Have a seat and get ready to enjoy this morning's gastronomic specialty."

"Oh please," Tatum rolled her eyes as she plopped down at the table. "You're awfully chipper this morning for someone that only got a half a night's sleep."

"Just another beautiful day, sweetheart." Christian placed a beautifully prepared breakfast plate and glass of fresh squeezed orange juice in front of her.

"So, Daddy, are you still super smart this morning?"

"I don't know, let me see," Christian sat down with her and closed his eyes for a moment. "Today you'll be getting back a science test you took Friday; ninety-four. You messed up questions two and seven. Your locker combination is ninety, two, twenty-eight. Your Latin teacher has a pop quiz waiting for you. And oh, you forgot to put your calculator in your backpack for school today."

"Wow, that's really cool! What questions are on the quiz?"

Christian laughed, "Sorry, kiddo. You have to earn your own grades, you know that."

"But it will help with my scholarship," Tatum tilted her head down and looked up at her dad, remembering her mother's guidance, "and you'll be able to get to that retirement sooner."

Damn, she's going to be a great lawyer someday, Christian smiled. "Save it for the debate club, sweetheart. Let's see what's going on with the news this morning."

Christian picked up the remote control and flipped on the TV.

The now solved missing children mystery dominates the local, and even national, news this morning. After showing footage of the mine area and several reunions of children with their families, the news accounts moved to the morning's raid on a Montana ranch where fifteen other missing children had been recovered in a related case. Christian observed Special Agent Bragg as he touted the successful conclusion of this over five-year-old case.

"Is that the same thing you told them about last night?"

"Yup, that's the one. They seem quite proud of themselves, don't they?"

What are you going to do with this new ability, Pops? Isn't this going to change things a little bit?"

Christian smiled, "Hopefully I'll be able to finagle some good business out of it."

Tatum dropped her fork, and her jaw, pointing at the TV. "That's our house!"

Sure enough, the Faraday house was front and center on the TV screen with a news reporter in the foreground. "This is the home of Christian Faraday, the caller that tipped off authorities to the location of the abandoned mine containing the missing children and their abductors. It is unknown how Mister Faraday knew of the location, or if he is anyway associated with the abductors."

"Daddy, what are they doing? Are we going to start getting harassed because of this?"

"I'm sure it will be fine, honey. I'll go see what's going on," Christian got up, urgently heading to the front door. "You finish getting ready, I'm sure NikNak will be here any minute."

Tatum started to take the last bite of her breakfast when she looked up to see her father at the door. "Daddy!" Tatum exclaimed as she started to run after him. "You only have –"

Too late, the door closed behind him.

"– your boxers and a T-shirt on," she finished in a more resigned voice as she leaned up against the wall, raising her hand to her mouth, giggling.

Outside, Christian stood in his Hawaiian boxers and T-shirt, surveying the scene of several news trucks on the street. *KOLO-ABC, KTVN-CBS, KRNV-NBC, even CNN. What's going on here?* Christian thought as he watched the reporters and cameramen rush across the lawn towards him. Just as they were about to reach the entrance, Tatum's had reached out of the front door and pulled her father back inside.

"Go get dressed, Daddy. I'll take care of this until you're decent."

Christian looked down at his attire and snickered, "I must have looked pretty silly out there." He leaned down to kiss Tatum on the forehead, "Thanks, sweetie. I'll be right down."

"You're such a dufus," Tatum told him as she rolled her eyes. Grabbing her backpack and lacrosse stick, Tatum took a deep breath before opening the door to face the crowd of reporters. Fortunately, Tatum had inherited her mother's natural acting ability, nurturing that skill in drama clubs and debate teams. As Tatum composed herself in front of the door, the reporters and their cameras organized themselves in front of her.

As several reporters began to speak, Tatum pointed to one of them. "Was that Christian Faraday just out here?" the reporter, a young Asian woman asked, sticking her microphone towards Tatum.

"Yes. That was my father. He'll be back out in a moment. Is there anything I can help you all with?"

"What is your name, young lady?" another reporter asked.

"Tatum Faraday."

"Is it true that your father placed the call that identified the location of the missing children?"

"Yes, and I hear that they are all fine and reunited with their families. Isn't that great?"

"How did he know about the mine, Miss Faraday? Did he know the people involved?"

"Beats me how he knew, but I do know for sure he doesn't know any of the people involved. I'm just thrilled about those kids, though. I cried when I saw those reunions on TV this morning. Did you guys see that?"

"That was amazing. How did your father feel about it all?"

"Of course he's thrilled; he loves helping people. He's the most caring person I know. I'm sure no one is happier than my dad for those families. Is there any new news regarding the kids? Are they all back home now?"

Tatum also inherited her father's ability to disarm people and get them to relax; it appeared to work on these reporters quite nicely as the questioning turned into a dialog.

"Two are still in the hospital, but the rest are back home," replied one of the reporters.

"I hope those bad guys get it good!" Tatum said as she held up her lacrosse stick and put on a mean look on her face.

The reporters laughed, one of them adding, "I'm sure they will have a lot to answer for, Miss Faraday."

The door opened behind her just as Nicki's Volvo convertible pulled up the driveway. Christian, now dressed, walked out of the house and gave Tatum a kiss on her forehead. "Well, guys, I'm off to school now. Take it easy on my dad, please; he didn't have much sleep last night." She then whispered in his ear, "Go get 'em, Daddy. And don't make a fool of yourself. There are probably going to be lots of cute women out there watching." Tatum turned and winked to the cameras before running off to get in Nicki's car.

While no stranger to press conferences due to his years of introducing his architectural accomplishments, Christian was not quite the show person his daughter was. Due to his own modesty, he certainly was not comfortable being the center of such an exciting story, especially having to talk about himself.

"Good morning, everyone." He said to the reporters while nervously waving to them.

The reporters started at once, all aggressively calling out, "Mister Faraday," followed by a flurry of questions so quickly that he couldn't distinguish one from another.

Christian gasped and held up both hands, "Whoa guys, I can't understand any of you. Let me try. I guess you are all here because of my call about the missing kids."

As a round of affirmative responses, along with follow-up questions were thrown at him, Christian held up his hands again for them to settle down. He then continued, "There really isn't much to tell here. I came upon information relevant to the case and passed it along to the FBI. Kids home safe. Bad guys caught. Everyone happy!"

The reporters resumed asking questions, which Christian still could not make out, resigning himself to ignore their garbled words and deciding to just point out reporters one at a time. Not much for the stereotypical slick reporters, he picked out a young man that seemed more down to earth than the others, indicating for him to go ahead with his question and signaling for quiet from the others.

"Exactly what information did you provide the FBI and how did you come about it?" he asked.

"Well, the FBI had a pretty strong investigation going. I simply stumbled upon a few details that helped them connect a few dots. I'm sure they would have had it resolved in a few days anyway."

As a follow-up, the reporter continued, "It's being said that you gave them the exact location of the mine."

"Well, I guess I helped them narrow down the location and what to expect, but they're the ones that pulled it off and saved the kids."

Christian then pointed to the CNN reporter.

"How are you involved that you knew about the mine, Mister Faraday?"

"I'm not involved at all, I just happened across some information."

"What was your source?" the reporter pressed.

"I had no source. I just *knew* it."

The reporters became unusually silent for a moment, not quite sure how to react to that statement. Finally, one of them spoke up, "You just knew it? Are you a psychic, Mister Faraday?"

"Do I look like a psychic? Is there a neon hand in my window?" he joked as he gestured back to one of the house windows behind him. Unfortunately, he began to get carried away. "I don't know how I knew it, the same way I don't know how I know that your nephew was just awarded a soccer scholarship to UNLV, and your sister," he pointed to another reporter, "is about to move with her family from Portland to Boulder. And that van down there," pointing to one of the news trucks, "has forty-seven thousand two hundred and thirty-six miles on it."

As the reporters stood stunned and speechless, Christian realized what he had just done, although not quite sure where the information he just blurted out even came from.

"Oops!"

Gathering himself, he smiled and added, "I guess that about covers it. I'm afraid I've got to get ready for work now. You guys have a good day." As he turned to the front door, he noticed a dark blue sedan parked across the street with two mysterious characters in it. He paused just long enough for reporters to begin barraging him with more questions before quickly heading into the quiet security of his house.

With the door locked behind him, Christian went back to the kitchen to clean the dishes. As he watched the TV footage of the event that just took place, including his initial appearance in boxers, Christian grabbed one last bite of his English muffin and gathered the plates off the table. While loading the dishwasher, he suddenly stopped. *Holy shit, not them too!*

Chapter Nine

In the FBI conference room, Samuel Waymon and Agent Dawson watched the television news accounts from the previous evening and earlier that morning, paying particular attention to the scenes from Christian's house.

"This is quickly getting out of control. I shouldn't have let him go last night."

"I'm not sure pissing him off by keeping him in custody would have been such a wise move in the long run. You need to play the long game with this guy," Dawson replied.

"And the damn leaks. Can't these local agencies keep their mouths shut? We don't even know where this guy is getting it all from. Is his report ready yet?"

"Right here, sir," Agent Carver was just walking in and dropped off copies of a file marked 'Christian Faraday – Top Secret", on the table in front of Samuel. "Squeaky clean. A little wild in college here in Reno, but pretty much your typical jock and fraternity stuff. Master's in Architecture from University of Virginia with his own very successful practice here in Reno. Married to his college sweetheart, Stephanie Pulitzer, formally of Chicago. Mrs. Faraday was an actress and model until she died of cancer four years ago. Hasn't been on a date since. One child, you met her."

Waymon rolled his eyes.

"Spends most of his spare time on outdoor recreational activities. No known vices. Financial and tax records appear clean. No unusual travel or communication activity. Parents both deceased, no siblings. No known investigative or paranormal associations. His best friend you also met, one of the top attorneys in Nevada."

"A regular all-American guy, huh?" The frustration was clear in Samuel's voice. "Is there nothing in here I can legitimately haul him in for?"

"Not a thing," Carver replied. "Not even a parking ticket. Whatever this guy has going on, it's not through any traceable means."

"Let's assume he's telling the truth, maybe he tapped into some long hidden sixth sense and we've got a legit psychic on our hands," Waymon stopped and took a deep breath, "which is going to be hell selling to Washington. But let's assume that's the case. We've got to get the situation under control and him in our camp, immediately."

"The guy doesn't seem to have any ulterior motives and appears to be genuinely interested in helping people in bad situations. We can clean up a lot of our cases in short order if he is willing to be as helpful as he was last night. If we appeal to his apparent concern for injustice while respecting his personal space, he –" Agent Dawson started.

"Damn his personal space," Waymon interrupted him. "This guy's life as he knows it is over. Now that his ability is becoming public, everybody and their brother will want a piece of him. We've got to get him in our house and contain him. Besides ensuring primary access, damage control is a priority."

"Damage control?" Carver asked.

"If Faraday can summon up helpful information, he can no doubt undermine the Bureau with knowledge of our sensitive information as well. You heard what he said about the St. Louis office last night. Hell, the entire United States could be in jeopardy if he fell into the wrong hands."

"What about his daughter?"

"We'll have to bring her in as well, I suppose," Waymon responded as he rolled his eyes. Tatum was just a little too spunky for his liking. "Get a few boys to bring him in. Never mind. On second thought, you two get over there yourselves. This has got to be handled carefully, I want you two to personally bring him in without raising any red flags. Give him the civic duty line. Tell him we have a couple more critical cases with innocents in imminent danger that urgently requires his insight. Whatever it takes, even if you have to end up violating a few of his civil liberties."

As Dawson and Carver headed out of the room, Waymon picked up the phone on the table, "Get me the Director."

≈

In front of the Faraday house, KOLO-ABC was the last of the news crews to wrap up. As they drove away, the sedan pulled into the Faraday driveway. Its driver, a polished man in his early fifties, and the passenger, an attractive African American woman who appeared around thirty, exited the car. Both looked slightly menacing, wearing their black sunglasses. They both appeared trim in their perfectly tailored dark suits; hers with a skirt hemmed just above the knees.

Christian stepped out of the shower just as the doorbell rang. Wrapping a towel around his waist and another to dry his hair, he pressed a button on the intercom. "Yo."

"Mister Faraday?" a man's voice responded.

"That would be me. Just getting out of the shower at the moment. I'll be down shortly."

"Mister Faraday, this is urgent government business. We need to speak with you immediately."

"I'm sorry, Agent West, you'll just have to wait until I get some clothes on. This is Agent West with the CIA, is it not?"

The words Christian spoke into the intercom were merely confirmation of their earlier briefing regarding Christian's reported ability. Nonetheless, they were both surprised. "Thank you, Mister Faraday, we appreciate your help. We'll be right here when you're ready," the man responded.

"And good morning to you as well, Agent Johnson." Christian added.

Momentarily flustered, the woman blushed, then smiled as she replied, "Thank you, Mister Faraday. Good morning."

Marcus West had been in the CIA for over thirty years, joining the Agency right after a stint as a Naval Intelligence Officer. A third generation Naval Academy graduate and son of an Admiral, Marcus was brought up old school in a very disciplined and structured environment, developing a mix of personal integrity, character and patriotism.

This background, combined with his outstanding academic performance at Annapolis and exceptional service record, caught the attention of the CIA. He was actively recruited as his service requirement neared completion. The opportunity to take advantage of the resources of the CIA as he honed his investigative talents was too much for Marcus to resist.

Emotionally detached by nature, Marcus loved exhilarating field missions, managing to avoid lengthy Langley assignments with their mindlessly boring social and political interactions. The challenge of real-time analysis in intense, sometimes life-or-death, situations continued to excite him. However, he was also quite content planning strategic missions, patiently watching and waiting as the pieces invariably fell into place exactly as he had carefully planned.

A bachelor, Marcus spent his spare time in the pursuit of fitness, often accompanying Navy SEAL friends on exotic, high-risk 'vacations'. Marcus felt as though he had indeed lived a charmed life, the perfect upbringing and the perfect career. Retirement, if it ever did occur, would no doubt be just as charmed, perhaps becoming the next Ian Fleming, making an exciting life ever more intriguing through some sort of fictionalized version of himself.

Heather Johnson, on the other hand, could not run harder or far enough from her past. Her upbringing was far from the privileged life of an Admiral's son, but her personality was immeasurably more advanced than Marcus', albeit haunted by the events of her youth. Yet it was this childhood that shaped her into the driven, overachieving woman she had become.

Her father was but a fleeting memory, seen on rare occasions between his stints in prisons for crimes which spanned the entire spectrum of illegal activity. Her mother tried to hide her from him as much as possible during those times he wasn't incarcerated. The last Heather had heard of her father, he was involved with some organized crime figures, and that was back when she was a teenager. For all she knew, or cared for that matter, he was wearing concrete boots at the bottom of Lake Michigan. Her mother had tried desperately to provide some sort of stability for her, working in a variety of servant roles, usually live-in, to some of New England's wealthiest families.

It was in these upper-class homes that Heather learned to appreciate the value of education and culture, especially since the first six years of her life were spent in the horrid conditions as the daughter of a junkie drug dealer who paid little attention to the responsibility of either a wife or a child. Without question, the arrest of her father was the best thing that ever happened to Heather and her mother, who got her act together and scraped by, barely making a living until her death as a result of brain cancer during Heather's first year in college.

Thanks in large part to the influence of these wealthy environments, but in no small measure due to her own brilliance and buoyant personality, Heather was determined from an early age to escape the lower economic and sociological spectrum of society and make something of her life. Her grades were almost always flawless and her drive and passion in extracurricular activities, which were in large part an escape for her, was boundless. In addition to the almost parental admiration of her mother's last, and exceedingly wealthy, employer and several academic and athletic scholarships, Heather was able to attend Amherst.

At university she played women's tennis and studied psychology and sociology, graduating summa cum laude. Although she had plans to attend law school after graduating, the intrigue and lifestyle offered by aggressive CIA recruiters changed her planned course. Although financially rewarding, Heather determined that the life of an attorney would be too confining for her; perhaps due to her independent personality, or perhaps the internal demons from having such a derelict father which continued to haunt her.

Her current life suited her fine. She lived alone in San Francisco and traveled extensively on assignment, thriving on the never mundane experiences and soaking up foreign cultures and languages. Her difficult life experiences and CIA training had tamed her innate exuberant personality to a powerful charm she could turn on and off at will. Despite her strong personal characteristics, Heather had a deep-rooted fear of relationships stemming from her childhood, allowing only a few very special people into her life as friends. Heather's personal life primarily consisted of belonging to a rock-climbing club, an outlet she used to escape into a solitude which both comforted her and kept people from getting too close on a personal level.

Neither Heather nor Agent West were in a terribly patient mood as they awaited Christian's arrival at the front door. In addition to having to wait for the reporters to depart, the 3 AM wakeup call was beginning to catch up with them. They were also keenly aware that the FBI was watching Christian; it was only a matter of time before a confrontation would take place if they didn't get Christian into their control immediately.

Christian opened the front door. "Hi, guys. I guess I might as well invite you in. Something tells me you aren't here to deliver flowers."

Both maintained their stoic look as they thanked Christian and stepped into his house.

"If I may get straight to the point, Mister Faraday," Agent West began as he and Heather sat on the sofa Christian had directed them towards. "We are fully aware of your powerful, for lack of a better term, psychic ability."

"Rule number one, Agent West. I don't have conversations with people wearing sunglasses inside."

West and Johnson uniformly turned their heads towards each other momentarily before reluctantly removing their sunglasses. "We'd very much like for you to accompany us to our offices to discuss several situations."

"Everyone wants me to 'accompany' them," Christian mimed quotation marks. "Do you know I spent two hours in the middle of the night last time someone wanted me to 'accompany' them? Which, by the way, was just a mere few hours ago." Christian was getting irritated. "I don't mind helping, but I have demanding clients and a very expensive teenager to support."

As usual when working with many of the more superior agents she was often assigned to, Agent Johnson had to smooth the all too direct edges of her partner. "Mister Faraday," she began in a compassionate and friendly voice as she looked directly into his eyes, "We do understand you have an active life and many commitments which require your attention. We really don't want to disrupt your routine any more than absolutely necessary." After a brief pause while maintaining direct eye contact, she continued, "But I'm sure you can appreciate that, were you to spend a brief period of time on a few very important and time-sensitive issues, you could probably save several lives and resolve a few severe injustices."

Christian was completely disarmed by her intense blue-eyed gaze, a rarity among African-Americans, surrounded by her stunning good looks. "I – um –," stumbling through his words as he gathered himself, "I see what you mean, Agent Johnson. Is there anything in particular I can help you with right now?" Christian, never one to be flustered by members of the opposite sex, was a little startled by his behavior.

"Mister Faraday, we'd really like you –" Agent West began before Agent Johnson put her hand on his shoulder, interrupting him and continuing in his place, "to be absolutely comfortable helping us. Possibly we could be a little more flexible and go over a few things here. That way, we can see how it goes before we ask for any more of your time. Would you have a few minutes for that now?" Heather subtly added a slightly sympathetic facial expression. "I think you'll find that it would be time well spent, not just for you, but for your country."

Agent West was trying hard to contain his impatience, but he had worked with Agent Johnson enough to trust her diplomatic skills. Her psychology education, combined with her polished demeanor, had managed to keep several interrogations from getting out of control, and had even kept him out of trouble from time to time. West was never the romantic type, but he had often thought of pursuing Agent Johnson romantically. An outstanding agent, smart and beautiful to boot.

Christian thought for a moment. "Sure. Let me call my office and let them know I'll be arriving a bit late and to postpone my early meetings." He was not happy about this, and he knew this morning's client would not be either. There was a final review of an office building design before submitting for final permits. "Excuse me for a moment," Christian stood up, retrieved his mobile phone, and stepped into the kitchen.

"Heather, we've got to get him out of here before those Bureau boneheads get their act together," West whispered as Christian disappeared from the room.

"I am fully aware of that, but we need to deal with the fact that this guy is fiercely independent and clearly not intimidated by much. If we don't spend a few minutes getting him to realize the importance of his contributions to get him on our side, we'll lose him completely. If we force him out of here, not only won't he be very cooperative, but he'll probably get that attorney involved, causing us no end of grief," she whispered back.

Marcus knew she was right; she always was in these types of matters.

"Okay, guys. My secretary is putting out the fires for me, but I'm likely to be interrupted by a phone call or two," Christian announced as he reentered the room.

"That's perfectly understandable, Mister Faraday. We do appreciate your priorities," Heather reassured him.

Agent West pulled a recorder out of his jacket pocket and placed it on the table in front of them. "Do you mind?" he inquired as he pressed the 'Record' button.

"First, it's Christian, not Mister Faraday."

"Alright, Christian," Agent West continued, "just what is the extent of this psychic ability of yours?"

"I hadn't really thought of it as a psychic ability. I don't see images or visions. Information seems to just be available to me if I give a moment or two of thought to a particular subject. Trivial information, such as your names when I was on the intercom, doesn't even appear to require any conscious thought at all."

"That's fascinating, Christian," Agent Johnson commented, continuing her subtle charm offensive on him, focusing her eyes on his. "How long has this been happening?"

"Just since last night. I was relaxing after dinner and suddenly became aware of all the information about those missing children. I thought it was some sort of fluke, but later when I 'accompanied'," Christian put up his hands, once again imitating quotation marks, "the FBI, they asked me several other questions on related subjects I would have no way of knowing anything about. After few minutes of focus, I knew all about them, including much more than they wished I had."

"Any idea what prompted this, Christian?" Agent Johnson continued.

"I really don't know. It just started yesterday, no funny mushrooms or anything."

"Mister Faraday," Agent West started as Christian visually corrected him, "I mean, Christian. People don't suddenly start having paranormal capabilities out of the blue. There must be an explanation."

Christian stopped to think for a moment, his facial expression slowly changing to that of astonishment. *Hang gliding. The erratic thermal was actually a cosmic cloud of some sort!* He suddenly realized what had happened to him.

Catching himself, he remained silent, not wanting to let on the excitement of his realization. Christian changed the subject and decided to put the CIA agents on the spot. "Agent Carver. He's your guy. You planted him in the FBI! That's how you knew about me and what is going on. If you can't play nice with your sister agency, how do you expect me to be able to trust you?"

Ignoring his accusation, yet nonetheless taken aback by it, Agent West showed his frustration with how the discussion was proceeding. "Christian, we really must get to the bottom of how you acquired this power."

"What is it you want, Agent West, to save lives or figure out my personal life?"

Once again, Agent Johnson saw the need to keep the discussion focused and not risk alienating Christian. "It's alright, Christian, we can deal with that at a later time if you wish." Her interjection caused Christian to lower his head while raising his eyebrows at her. "If at all," she corrected herself, resetting her voice to a more conciliatory tone at the same time. "Let's get back to the saving lives issue."

Christian relaxed after seeing Agent Johnson give Agent West a subtle look, as if telling him to back off.

"Fine idea. How can I help you?"

"What can you tell us about Operation Plastic Pan?"

Christian sat back and closed his eyes. They sat in silence as two CIA agents looked at Christian, then at one another, while Christian contemplated the question.

Christian opened his eyes and sat forward in his chair, shooting them both a serious look. "Please, you two, I thought we were going to try to make this quick. Why are we wasting our time with closed cases?"

The agents looked at each other. Obviously, this man knew things he shouldn't.

"I'm sorry, Christian, we are just trying to start by calibrating the validity of your information," she calmly replied.

"I can accept that." Christian relaxed again. Agent Johnson seemed to keep putting him at ease, he noticed. "Okay. To begin with, the guys you have naming these operations are costing the taxpayers way too much. Other than that, Plastic Pan is an operation both of you worked on, along with three other agents out of San Fran and a handful from your Hong Kong station. You had an employee of a Silicon Valley government contractor passing encryption technologies to a front export holding company in the city. The holding company then delivered the technical specifications to an import company in Hong Kong, where it was then passed to a Chinese agent."

The agents glanced at each other before West replied, "Very good, Christian. I think we're in sync now."

"Not quite, Agent West. You got everyone involved in that operation and expelled all the right 'diplomats', but that is just the tip of the iceberg of a much larger operation. You didn't even get close to the puppeteer. He's a narcissistic ex-military guy operating out of Houston that's been setting up these kinds of deals for over ten years now, leveraging contacts initially established while stationed at various embassies around the world. His name is Ron Higgins, and he's got active deals transferring weapons technologies to two eastern European countries, financial technology to France, and pharmaceutical manufacturing technologies to Nigeria. That doesn't take into consideration his recently completed deals. You should probably rename the thing to Plastic Kitchen and call him the Plastic Chef."

Even two seasoned CIA agents like West and Johnson couldn't hide their shock at this information, all of which was completely new to them. They had personally closed the case.

"Did I pass the test?"

Agent Johnson recomposed herself, "Very nicely, Christian."

"Great, can we get some real work done so I can get on with my day?"

"That was a pretty substantial start in and of itself, Christian. We had a few things in particular we wanted to discuss, but perhaps it would be best if we allow you to simply share what comes to mind." Christian was clearly impressed with himself, and Agent Johnson wanted to let him feel he were in control. Hopefully he would be comfortable enough to let loose and begin spilling information. "Please continue, Christian."

Agent West stiffened up and started to object as he had his own agenda. Agent Johnson glanced his direction and he stopped himself.

Christian leaned back in his chair and closed his eyes. On this occasion, the pause was several minutes, leaving the two agents anxiously awaiting Christian's next treasure trove of information. Even with all of Agent West's experience in the Intelligence Community, he had never experienced anything remotely as exciting. While the senior agent began jotting notes, Johnson focused her attention on observing Christian. She noticed what appeared to be an ever so slight glow in Christian's skin, assuming the early morning daylight streaming through the large wall of windows behind him was playing tricks on her eyes.

After several minutes, Christian slowly opened his eyes and smiled. "You guys ready?"

Christian began rambling off an extensive list of national security compromises, ranging from international drug smuggling to terrorist cells around the world. He gave them information on a few internal CIA leaks and double agents. West and Johnson listened in amazement during fifteen minutes of details down to names and addresses, bank account numbers, complex personal and organizational relationships, and location of critical evidence in important cases. He wrapped up by throwing in a few scandalous accounts of CIA's behavior and telling them that grassy knoll shooter had passed away. However, he did pass along who hired the shooter and exactly where they could find his rifle.

"Hoffa's location will cost you extra."

Christian took a deep breath and asked if anyone would like some orange juice. "I just squeezed it myself this morning," he added with a smile and look of great self-satisfaction on his face.

"It might not be a bad time for a quick break, don't you think, Marcus?" Agent Johnson suggested. "I'd love some of that OJ myself. Marcus?"

"You two go ahead. I think I'll call some of this into Langley."

Christian invited Johnson to accompany him into the kitchen and she stood up and followed him. "You've got a lovely home, Christian. Have you and your family been here long?"

"Actually, it's just my daughter and myself." He paused and pointed to one of the many pictures of Tatum in the room. "This is Tatum. Her mother," he stopped and picked up a picture of Stephanie with her arm outstretched as he kissed her hand, taken while they were hiking in the Grand Canyon, "passed away four years ago. Breast cancer."

Agent Johnson could sense the pain Christian felt as he gazed longingly at the picture of his deceased wife. "They are both very beautiful. I'm sorry to hear about your wife," she added as she observed many pictures of them around the room, most in the middle of various outdoor adventures. "I gather the two of you led an active outdoor life."

"Very," Christian whispered before snapping back into reality. Resuming their way into the kitchen, he continued, "Tatum nags me regularly about getting too old for all this, but I could never give it up."

"I know how you feel, I spend most of my spare time outdoors as well. I'm partial to glacier skiing and rock climbing. Fortunately, being with the Agency affords me lots of opportunities to take advantage of my passion."

"Such as the time you had to rappel down that glacial crevice wall to retrieve the flash drive from that North Korean agent you sent to the bottom with your left foot across his chin?"

Agent Johnson again managed to contain her surprise. "That would be one example, yes. For some reason, sitting at a desk all day never appealed to me."

"Nor being in a courtroom either, I should imagine," he nonchalantly added, referring to her close brush with law school. Christian reached into the refrigerator and pulled out the pitcher of orange juice.

"I can see you're not one a girl can keep too many secrets from," she laughed, blushing as Christian poured orange juice into a glass.

"Something tells me life is going to be a little different for me from now on," Christian noted, staring blankly at nothing in particular. Up until that point, Christian had really taken this ability very lightly. He hadn't spent time dwelling on it, preferring to think that it would be useful for not much more than basic information for everyday use. He had now come to the realization that there was much more to this ability than he'd originally thought. His life, as well as Tatum's, would be suddenly taking a drastic turn. Sensing the concern in his voice, Heather put her hand on his arm and looked him straight in the eyes, making sure he paid attention to what she was about to say.

"Christian, for whatever reason, you've been given this gift. It's a gift that in all likelihood can help all humanity, not just the CIA or the American people. There will most likely be some hardships for you and your daughter, but the rewards will no doubt far outweigh any challenges that you're presented along the way. Besides, since when were you someone that shied away from a little challenge?"

Christian was touched by her sensitivity to his situation, as well as her insight to his character. "Agent Johnson –"

"Please," she held up a hand to stop him, while giving him a charming smile, "Call me Heather."

The combination of her eyes and lovely smile stopped his thoughts in their tracks. *She's done it again!* No one but Stephanie had ever been able to slow his brain while simultaneously causing his heart to quicken. He smiled and corrected himself, "Heather."

Heather returned the smile as he continued, "I assure you, any motives I may have would be completely unselfish. But what makes you think that your Agency or the Bureau gives a rat's ass about what's in anyone else's best interest when they've got such critical agendas of their own? How much energy does the CIA put into solving Africa's famine problem or unemployment in Iowa? Besides, I know lots of things that, I assure you, your superiors don't want anyone else privy to."

Heather hadn't really thought about it in those terms. "I completely appreciate your skepticism, Christian. I hope you'll look at me as your advocate within the CIA. I promise you that I will ensure your efforts are only focused on positive activities and that politics stay out of your work with us."

Her powers of comfort and persuasion were not working as well as usual this time. "I'm sure," Christian smiled, "and I know this for a fact by the way, that your concern and intention are as pure as you've said. Unfortunately, there are bigger forces at play here than either you or I have any control over. This is already way above your pay grade."

Agent West entered the kitchen with his usual 'all business' approach. Christian looked at Heather, raised an eyebrow while tilting his head in West's direction then tapped his orange juice glass against hers. Downing his juice, he gave her a wink.

"I just spoke to Langley. They're very interested in continuing this discussion with a broader audience immediately. I'm afraid I'm going to have to insist you accompany us to our office, Christian."

Expecting to have to play interference again, Heather started to speak up, only to be cut off by Christian, "I guess I can understand that now. I'll need to be back in time for dinner though. I need to help my daughter study for the midterm she has tomorrow."

Heather was stunned but pleased by his unexpected cooperation. "Thank you, Christian. I knew we could count on you."

Christian turned off the kitchen lights and followed them to the front door. Picking up his cell phone, Christian called his secretary. "Things have taken an unexpected turn this morning. Have Gary review the design with the client and cancel all my appointments for the remainder of the day." Pausing for a moment, he continued, "Tell Gary I'm sorry, and if he needs to speak to me today, he'll apparently have to go through the CIA. I'm suddenly some sort of a national treasure."

"So I understand from the news," his secretary responded. "You also might be interested that your boxers are the talk of the office."

"I don't guess I will be living that down anytime soon, will I?"

"That, and the cute legs."

"Great. Just what I need." Turning more serious, "Tell Tom to get to the ER right now and tell them he needs a brain scan immediately. No questions, just have him do it."

Christian disconnected the call and closed the door behind him. Reaching into his pocket he then turned to his escorts, "Hang on a second, will you? I need to get my keys and my wallet."

West nodded at the door for him to indicate they would wait.

"It will only take a minute." Christian went back inside, leaned his back against the door for a moment, then quietly ran down the basement steps, out the back door, and across his yard into the woods.

≈

As agents West and Johnson waited patiently at the front door for Christian to return, Marcus briefed her on his call. "Instructions are to return straight to the plane and get him to Langley directly. We're not to let the FBI in on it at all. The Directors will probably end up duking it out, but we want him in our possession before that happens."

"What's the problem here, Marcus?" Heather looked concerned. "Shouldn't this be a centrally coordinated cross agency approach?"

"Everybody has their skeletons. We're going to want everybody else's before they get ours."

"I can tell you from my conversation with Christian that he's not going to play the usual political game. Not only that, but he is clearly as concerned about humanitarian issues as he is national security."

"He'll play ball no matter how we tell him to. He really doesn't have a choice. The bottom line is that he must be immediately contained. There's too much potential for damage to the Agency."

"Don't underestimate this man, Marcus. He's likely to be a step ahead of us if he senses anything is off."

Having been on several missions with Heather over the years, Marcus had a profound respect for her in so many ways—intellectually, physically, and emotionally. She was strong-minded, fearless, beautiful, and smart. *The perfect agent. The perfect woman. If she just wasn't so soft on issues of this sort.*

Chapter Ten

The morning sun of the cloudless spring day was just too much for Parker to resist. As demanding and dedicated as he was to his law practice, Parker nonetheless had a great appreciation for the beauty of the Reno area. He relished every moment of the outdoors he had the opportunity to take. Given his interrupted sleep the night before, Parker decided to work at home this morning, taking his meeting via conference call by the comfort of his pool.

"Thank you, Sunye," Parker said, smiling at his attractive Chinese housekeeper and cook as she delivered his tray. Parker enjoyed starting his day with breakfast on his expansive patio overlooking the perfectly groomed property. He often enjoyed watching the early morning sun burn the dew off the grass while listening to birds chirping as they hustled about their morning business. There was no more civilized way for a man to start the day, at least not by Parker's standards.

"Yes, sir, Mister Parker, sir," Sunye bowed before turning around and going back into the house.

Despite his daredevil approach to most things in life, Parker was a very neat and orderly person, almost OCD. Everything in his life was always perfectly laid out, not that he liked having to do anything to make it that way other than initially setting up whatever arrangements necessary to have everything in pristine condition. When he came downstairs in the morning, he was already showered and perfectly dressed for whatever occasion the day's plans might call for. His breakfast was always awaiting him, perfectly timed and perfectly prepared. Sunye always laid his folded newspaper on the table with his morning vitamins on a small plate next to the freshly squeezed orange juice and hot coffee.

Parker made sure he took the time to savor this perfect beginning to his day. This daily ritual reinforced the 'master of my universe' mindset he approached each day with. It worked so well, in fact, that anyone associated with him simply accepted his total control. Fortunately, his exceedingly positive nature and friendly demeanor endeared everyone to him, to the point that even rivals couldn't help but respect and like him.

Sunye had been Parker's full-time, live-in maid for many years prior to his move to Sierra Vista. They had the perfect system. His cleaning needs were minor, but he was very particular about his house always being immaculate and each item where he needed it, when he needed it. Sunye fixed his breakfast, cleaned the house, did his laundry, ran his errands, prepared his dinner if he was expected home, and generally kept his domestic life organized so he could concentrate on being the carefree bachelor he so loved being.

Sunye was intensely loyal and dedicated to ensuring Parker's domestic life was seamless for him. Parker rewarded her service with double the market value for someone in her position, full benefits, a car, as well as several luxury VIP Vegas vacations for her and her husband. Parker received way too many of these trips as courtesy of his various gaming industry clients.

Living with her in a guest house on the property, her husband took care of the groundskeeping as well as bartender duties as needed from time to time.

No one was going to be able to steal this five-foot gem away from him and mess up his perfect universe.

As Parker read his newspaper and enjoyed breakfast, soaking in the universe he was master of, he looked up to see Christian in the distance, running out of the woods that adjoined their properties. The properties were large enough that, when combined with the rolling terrain and vegetation, the houses were totally out of view from one another, although Christian could occasionally hear the music that played during Parker's parties.

Given what was in the paper and what he earlier observed on TV, it really wasn't too much of a shock to see Christian show up at his house for help. He was, however, just a little surprised to see his friend emerge from the tree line, run around the tennis court, and jump over the diving board in such a hurry.

Casually returning to his paper, Parker awaited Christian's arrival. The news accounts of the children's recovery and the mysterious caller, who by now had been identified in the television news reports, fascinated him. He so enjoyed comparing press accounts to reality, which was something he was often very involved in as a high-profile attorney. Parker often knew the behind-the-scenes truth of the hyped-up media reports. They were just another source of amusement for him in his perfect universe.

"Damn, I'm glad you're home," an almost out of breath Christian exclaimed as he climbed the final steps to join Parker on the patio.

"Damn, I'm glad to see you in something besides those boxers you had on earlier. You probably have half the entire female population of Reno all aflutter. Sorry to say, but it really didn't do anything for me."

"I know how you prefer me in Speedos. I'll try to remember that next time I decide to publicly humiliate myself," Christian quipped back as he plopped himself down in a chair across from Parker.

"I'd appreciate that," Parker replied, looking up from his paper and jokingly forming his lips into a kiss. "So, what's up? Haven't I gotten you out of enough jams in the last twenty-four hours?" Parker casually sipped his coffee as he awaited Christian's urgent issue.

Sunye returned with a tray holding a cup of coffee and juice for Christian. "Good morning, Mister Christian," she smiled with a bow.

"Oh, hi, Sunye. Thanks, I'd love some," Christian smiled.

Sunye smiled as she placed the coffee and juice on the table in front of him, "Nice boxers this morning, Mister Christian."

"Thanks, Sunye. Remind me to pick up a pair just like them for your husband," Christian replied with a smile.

"Oh, no, Mister Christian. Mister Kaw no have nice legs like you."

Blushing, Christian turned back to the issue at hand. "This is really going to blow you away, Parker. I've got half the Federal government wanting to lock me up for their own agenda, and that's only because the other half hasn't found out about me yet."

"What do you expect after flashing those legs around on national TV?"

"Cute. Seriously though, this is rapidly spiraling out of control. I just spent half an hour with a couple of suits from the CIA solving cases going back to JFK. They've got a private jet sitting at the airport preparing to take me to Langley. Although a cross-country trip with that lovely agent wouldn't be that much of a hardship."

"A fed in a skirt, eh? Single?"

"Forget it, stud. She's way too smart to be fooled by you. Besides, aren't you sticking with the married variety for a while?"

This was the first time since Stephanie he had heard Christian speak with any interest about a woman. Parker figured he'd better sit up and pay closer attention. "Okay, okay. I've had a few dealings with these Agency types. Once you're in their custody, there's not much I'm able to do, regardless of what legal grounds they don't have to stand on."

"And don't forget our friends from last night. They're right behind them."

"Did you ever figure out what's going on?"

"Better put on your Twilight Zone soundtrack for this one, buddy," Christian began as Parker settled down and focused on the conversation.

"Remember that thermal that thrashed me around while we were hang gliding?"

"Let's see," Parker pondered. "Hang gliding? Erratic thermal? Naw, not ringing a bell." Snapping his napkin at Christian he laughed, "Duh, how could I forget it? What does that have to do with all this."

"Turns out that wasn't thermal turbulence after all. It was a retrovirus-laden gaseous cloud that was released during a spaceship collision."

"A spaceship collision?"

"Yup. Two thousand, eight hundred and thirty-seven light years from Earth."

"Give or take a few light years, I trust?"

"No, exactly two thousand, eight hundred and thirty-seven," Christian responded, oblivious to Parker's sarcasm. "Took a bit longer than that to find its way here though."

"What the hell is a retrovirus, anyway?"

"It gets into your DNA and inserts its own genetic code."

Parker contemplated for a moment as Christian anxiously awaited Parker's thoughts. "A cloud, eh? Well, I guess it could have been worse."

"Huh?"

"It could have been a meteor. That would have really hurt!"

Nothing much fazed Parker. As a Nevada attorney, he got to see all kinds of crazy stuff and he had learned to isolate any initial emotions he may have when first hearing just about any story, although he had never heard anything quite as outrageous as this.

"Parker," giving his friend a disapproving look, "I'm dead serious here. I now have the ability to know the truth, as well as every detail, about anything I take a moment to think about."

"Let me understand this. Your DNA now has a gene that gives you some sort of sixth sense?"

"Exactly. I guess you'd call it a 'knowing gene'."

"So, what you're telling me is that you've become some sort of 'super psychic' or something?"

"That's pretty much the general idea. There's an area of the brain that can tune into another energy dimension. What we generally think of as psychics, and there actually are a few genuine ones around, have some very limited ability to access it. Mankind just hasn't evolved that far yet. With this gene, I'm fully tapped into that part of my brain."

"That's actually pretty cool, Christian. So, what's the problem? Can't you just help them out?"

"Sure, I'd love to. There are all kinds of things I can tell them that would solve all sorts of world issues. The problem is that they couldn't care less about curing cancer or finding solutions to poverty and disease or solving other world problems that I care about. They want the truth to be revealed only to the degree that it helps their own political agenda. The agencies are vying against each other to secure me first. Neither one of them wants me to reveal their secrets to the other. Not only that, but the political cronies that run the agencies don't want anything uncovered that is counter to their political goals. It's a real quagmire. You realize we're talking about the highest levels of the FBI and CIA?"

"Well, you certainly don't mess around when you finally do decide to get into a little trouble, do you?" Parker asked as he began to think it through. "Okay, let's start by getting you somewhere they'll never look for you and you can take your mind off things at the same time. I need to figure out our next legal move to keep them from screwing up your life." Parker stood up from the table, "Let's go."

Christian followed Parker into the house as his friend gathered his wallet, keys, and mobile phone. Raising his phone to his ear he announced "Moneypenny" and awaited as he is connected to his secretary. "Looks like we're going to have to put everything on hold today, young lady." He continued into the garage with Christian behind him as his secretary reminded him of an important meeting later in the day. "Tell him I've got to save the universe today."

Parker had an all afternoon meeting planned with one of his clients to get ready for court the following week and his client was nervous. Rich and nervous, that's the way Parker liked them. "No, tell him that I've come across some new very credible information that is going to blow this case wide open for him. We'll be negotiating a hefty settlement for him within a week. I'll need today to get everything in order. Tell him to go play golf and plan his victory dinner. If either the FBI or CIA try to reach me, tell them I've gone out of town with a client, am unreachable, and will be back in touch with them in a couple of days. Anyone else just put off with your usual charm."

Parker's law practice catered to a very high-end clientele that all too often had more money than sense; another way he liked them. Parker had started his legal career by stumbling into a legal situation with one of Nevada's largest land developers and made an impressive series of slick legal maneuvers which saved the corporation millions of dollars while opening up extensive areas that had been previously inaccessible. Parker's clever legal maneuvering provided the developer with a greater revenue opportunity than he had ever imagined. Between his charm and continued legal successes, his reputation grew to legendary proportions not only throughout Nevada, but the entire West Coast; providing him access and introductions almost anywhere in the world.

He never had to look far for clients; the referrals that started from his first client only snowballed, catalyzed by Parker's own self-promotional skills. His practice had grown to four partners and fifteen associates which handled a broad range of personal and corporate law. His firm's biggest clients were in the gaming and development industries, both of which have been booming throughout the duration of his practice.

"Sunye," Parker called to his maid before going into the garage. Sunye quickly entered, anxious for her next command.

"Listen, Sunye. If anyone comes looking for me today, the story is that I've gone to Vegas with a client."

"Yes, sir, Mister Parker."

"And this guy," Parker motioned towards Christian, "you haven't seen him since he was last here a couple of weeks ago." Parker then gave her an extra intense look, "He has not been here this morning. Right?"

"Right, Mister Parker. I no see anyone else here."

Parker winked at her before he turned, and the two men headed out to the garage. He knew that intentionally befuddling a couple of Agency or Bureau agents would be child's play for Sunye.

The three bays in Parker's garage housed his Porsche convertible, a Harley that he often rode with Christian, and his respectable business car, a Bentley Flying Spur.

"We better take the Bentley so you can duck down in the back," Parker noted. He pressed a button on his key and the car started and the garage door opened.

"Where are we going?"

"You'll see," Parker replied as they got in the car. Handing Christian a digital recorder, "Don't make a liar out of me with the morning appointment I just cancelled. Give me all the information I need to blow my client's opponent out of the water."

Another disapproving look, and Christian inquired, "Who's your client and what's the case?"

"You're the psychic, you'll know."

Christian smiled as he accepted the challenge. Settling back, he closed his eyes for a few moments. "Damn Parker, where do you come up with these scumbags?"

Parker replied, "That's the one. Remember now, I need whatever will win him a big settlement."

Christian lay down on the back seat and began thinking as Parker pulled out of the driveway. "You know, if the guy your client is suing wasn't even more of a scumbag, I wouldn't be doing this," he commented after a few minutes.

"If such scumbags didn't exist, I'd be out of business," Parker replied. "And oh, when you're done, grab a piece of paper from that pad back there; I've got another special assignment for you."

≈

It had been fifteen minutes and Marcus West had long given up waiting outside for Christian. Although at first engrossed in Langley's directive and planning the trip to Washington, he eventually decided to go into the house and investigate Christian's whereabouts. Not having a warrant was of little concern to him in this case. The situation was highest national security priority; the Director was at that very moment being briefed by West's superior.

Having scoured the entire house, including garage and basement, they found no sign of Christian, or any clue at all as to where he had gone.

"Damn it, Heather," West snapped as they joined up in the entrance foyer. "If this guy slips through our fingers, it's both of our necks. What in the hell do you think happened to him?"

"I suspect he needed some time to clear his head. There's an awful lot of confusing things happening to him today, he's probably over-whelmed."

"What did you two discuss in the kitchen?"

"There's no doubt he wants to help us, Marcus. He's a little skeptical of our motives, though. Trust is a big issue for him. It also wouldn't surprise me if he knew the content of your conversation with Langley."

As always, Agent West respected Heather's training and judgment in such matters. "So where has he gone? Off to a cave to meditate?"

"His vehicles are obviously still here, and there's not much out here except hills and woods. He most probably snuck off to one of his neighbors," Heather suggested as she looked out the large glass window overlooking the neighborhood.

"Find out what operatives we have in the area, and I'll see if I can stall Langley," Marcus ordered as he grabbed his phone. "We'll use this as base until we track him down."

"Looks like we'll be having company." Heather nodded her head towards the front window where Agents Dawson and Carver could be seen pulling their car into the driveway.

"Damn," Marcus said. *What else could possibly screw this operation up?*

Agent Carver had been instructed by Marcus to delay their arrival as long as possible, but the urgency Waymon had put on the mission made it difficult for Carver to stall Dawson very long.

"I recommend we throw them off until we can isolate Christian," Heather suggested.

"You're the persuasive one. Come up with a good story and con-vince them. Carver will go along with whatever you come up with."

West went out on the patio as the doorbell rang. Heather opened the door to greet them.

"Good morning, ma'am. I'm Agent Dawson with the FBI. This is Agent Carver."

As the men held up their badges, Heather reached in her pocket and retrieved hers. "Special Agent Heather Johnson, CIA. Good to meet you, gentlemen."

Overcoming his initial surprise, Dawson responded, "You wouldn't be interfering with an ongoing FBI investigation would you, Agent Johnson?"

"On the contrary, Mister Faraday contacted us with some critical terrorist related information. Of course, we got here as soon as we could." Heather stepped aside, "Please gentlemen, come in."

"Thank you," Dawson replied as he stepped in, followed by Agent Carver, who made brief eye contact with Heather. She smiled and winked at Carver as he passed.

"However, we seem to have a problem. Shortly after we arrived, Christian had to excuse himself and the next thing we know he was hopping in someone's car at the end of the driveway."

"Any idea who it was?"

"None."

"What kind of car?"

"Looked like a green Camry, but I couldn't tell for certain. It was just before you got here."

"We'll get right on it. Carver, check with the guys on stakeout and see if they saw anything, and get that vehicle description to local authorities."

"I wasn't aware the place was under surveillance, Agent Dawson."

"If you were, they wouldn't have been doing their job very well. But given that they didn't make me aware of your arrival means they probably weren't doing it all that well anyway."

"Don't be too hard on them, Agent Dawson; this place was awfully busy this morning with news crews. I'm sure I just looked like another harmless reporter to them."

"Did he give you any idea what was going through his head?"

"I think he is a little overwhelmed by all the attention. Probably just clearing his head for a little while."

"So, he just left with you two sitting here in his house?"

"Doesn't make much sense to me either," Heather replied, beginning to put a naïve woman act on. "Didn't you guys wrap up that missing children's case last night, Agent Dawson? What do you still need with Mister Faraday?"

"Oh," Dawson slightly caught off guard, "we still have a few loose ends to tie up."

"I can imagine. Is there anything else I can tell you before you head out looking for him?" Heather encouraging them to leave so they could get to the business of locating Christian in the neighborhood.

"We'll be outside getting resources lined up for a thorough search."

Neither of the teams of agents trusted the other, as they knew Christian's whereabouts was not something either organization would take lightly. They were both well aware that the real question was who would locate, and secure, Christian first.

"Great. Let us know if we can help in any way, Agent Dawson." Heather watched as he went outside to confer with Carver, then called the local office to inquire about sources.

≈

Outside on the patio, Agent West contemplated the amazing view as he awaited a call from Langley. By now they should have been wheels up on their way back to Langley with Faraday. West had never lost an asset before, much less one of this value, and he knew this was not going to be a pleasant conversation.

Once Heather finished her calls, she joined him on the porch and filled him in on her progress. "We've got three operatives on the way over now and I've kicked off a rundown on everyone in the neighborhood." They already knew everything there was to know about Christian via the top-secret file Carver had emailed them early that morning through a non-Bureau system they used to communicate.

"How about our Bureau friends?" West asked.

"I gave them a song and dance that we saw him hop in a car and take off. Unfortunately, they apparently had the place under surveillance; I doubt it will throw them off track for long. They're out front now trying to get their act together. How are we doing with Langley?"

"Blanton is in with the Director as we speak. I'm waiting for a call back any moment." Deputy Director of Operations Jacob Blanton was both Marcus' and Heather's boss and had once reported directly to Admiral West back when he was in Naval Intelligence. It was Jacob that recruited his former boss's son to join him in the Agency. Blanton had watched Marcus grow up and used his inside knowledge of Marus' intelligence and discipline, as well as his personal relationship with his father, to time the recruitment process perfectly.

Agents West and Johnson were two of his finest agents, and Blanton trusted their ability to pull off any mission he assigned them. It was with this confidence that he just spent twenty minutes throwing off the Director's schedule with the high priority briefing of Christian and his planned arrival later that afternoon.

Just then Marcus' phone rang, and Blanton's secretary informed him that the Deputy Director was ready to speak with him. "Patch in

Johnson first, will you, Sarah?" Marcus knew that Heather's psychological diplomacy would probably be helpful on this call.

After a brief moment, during which Heather sarcastically mouthed the word, 'Thanks', Heather's phone rang and she joined the call. "The Deputy Director will be with you momentarily."

They waited until Blanton's voice boomed across the line. "Let's hear some good news, Marcus."

"Didn't I give you enough this morning, sir? I would think fifty-nine terrorists, three double agents, a few smuggling operations, and a billion or two in illegal financial transfers, all before lunch, would be a pretty good day." West answered, attempting to keep things in perspective for Blanton given the bad news he was about to deliver. "Not to mention the truth behind the JFK assassination."

"Hell, we knew about JFK, but otherwise, not at all a bad morning. We've already checked out and rounded up a few of the folks Mister Faraday identified and the rest should be secured within the next forty-eight hours."

Blanton's excitement was obvious to both of them, and quite uncharacteristic for the Deputy Director. "The Director is thrilled and on his way to brief President Beucler now. Operation Holy Grail has been activated."

'Holy Grail' was a code name that the Agency had in reserve, although no one ever expected they'd actually see it activated during their lifetime. The mere mention of an active operation named such would cause anyone, all the way up to the Director, to stop and marshal any resources necessary to support the mission. Initiating it was the first thing Blanton did after his briefing with the Director. By now, every conceivable communication device in the CIA's network had received an alert that it had been activated.

"I trust you guys are on your way. What's your ETA?"

"We've got a little problem on our end, sir." There, he got it out. Now he just had to wait for the reaction.

"How little?"

"This is Agent Johnson, sir," Heather knew it was time for her to step in. "It appears our friends at the Bureau spooked him pretty bad overnight. He snuck out as we were getting ready to head to the airport."

"What?" Blanton's voice boomed louder than normal. "You guys should be at thirty thousand feet by now. Instead, he's somewhere in the Nevada desert?"

"We understand your concern, Jacob. This is a temporary setback which we should have resolved shortly. We've mobilized the local operatives and initiated all standard investigative and tracking protocols," West replied.

"Screw standard protocols!" Blanton yelled back. "Break every rule in the book if you must. I want exceptional measures taken. I'm setting up a task force here with full satellite and comms. They will be reaching out to you shortly."

"Yes, sir."

"And I want hourly updates through Kristine. Christ, Marcus, do you have any idea what this means? Especially if the Bureau gets him first. And heaven help us if anyone outside the government gets their hands on him. Our own secrets aren't safe unless we've got him contained. And I'm sure you know how embarrassing some of those are."

"We're on it, Jacob."

"Then get off the phone and make it happen!"

≈

In front of the house, Agents Dawson and Carver had just received a similar chewing down from Samuel Waymon. Every FBI agent within a hundred miles, regardless of specialty or current assignment, was on alert to help with the search. Warrants were being issued. Drones were already scouring the area.

The surveillance team had not seen a Camry, or any green car for that matter. Fortunately, they had also not seen the Bentley that had exited the development without passing by Christian's house.

Waymon had played these games with his Agency brethren before and rarely won. However, never before had so much been at stake.

Chapter Eleven

Still lying on the back seat of Parker's Bentley, Christian was finishing up his dictation when he saw the distinctive downtown skyline of Reno come into view. *I thought we'd be heading out of town*, Christian pondered.

"Jules!" Parker exclaimed into his phone. "Think you're ready for another one of my high rollers?"

Christian shot up in the back seat and whispered to Parker, "Are you nuts?"

Parker held up his hand, motioning for Christian to stay down. "Stay down. There are cameras everywhere!"

Christian rolled his eyes and lay back down. Parker had pulled many an outrageous scheme before, and although usually a bit hair raising, they always managed to pull through the adventure, with many a fond memory and unusual tale to tell. Christian had learned to trust his friend, get ready for a wild ride, then simply go along with the flow.

By virtue of his gaming clientele, Parker was extremely well connected in all the casinos not only in Reno, but all of Nevada. Many of his non-gaming clients provided a great deal of revenue to the Reno casinos in and of themselves. He figured that last year alone he increased their collective bottom lines upwards of fifty million dollars. *I'm gonna have fun this morning,* Parker thought to himself with a smug grin on his face.

"Sure, sweetheart," responded a sweet southern accent on his phone. "The last two alone allowed me to pay off my Jag and funded a nice Hawaiian getaway."

"You didn't take that bum Nico, did you?"

"Someone's got to appreciate the long-term potential of a pretty girl, Parker."

Juliette Prioleau and Parker had quite a passionate history, although they were now just very good friends. Juliette was one of the industry's most sought-after casino hostesses. Standing 5'10" tall and looking as if she had just casually strolled out of a Paris fashion magazine, Juliette had the polish and personality to make just about any man unconcerned with how many chips he had gone through. It didn't take her long, however, to figure Parker out and beat him at his own game, dumping him at the peak of his interest.

Parker actually had to recover from that relationship; the first, and only, time that had ever happened to him. The nearly two-year relationship with Juliette was the only one that caused him to think about giving up the bachelor life; a weak moment that fortunately didn't last terribly long. Nonetheless, long enough to alarm him. He tried to swear off women altogether after Juliette, lest such a close matrimonial call happen again. While celibacy didn't last long either, there had yet to be another woman that touched him anywhere near as much as Juliette had.

Juliette had since moved from Parker to a much more stable partner in Nico, who was the Vice President of Operations at the Mediterranean. Reno's answer to Vegas' spectacularly glamorous Bellagio, the Mediterranean had just opened two years earlier. In Nico she found the dapperness and charm of Parker, but with a healthy respect for long term relationships that Parker lacked, and Juliette, like most women, longed for in a man. Nico really enjoyed the man's man that Parker was, not to mention the business he meant for his casino, but he never quite trusted him around Juliette. This was the case with most men whose woman had ever been involved with Parker.

Glad to be free of Juliette's spell, Parker continued to be close friends with her and saved his highest roller friends for her and the Mediterranean. In return, they treated Parker like royalty and passed more than one wealthy businessman in the direction of Parker's law practice.

Parker knew Juliette and Nico would eventually catch on to his plan this morning, but he had a plan for when they did, he was very much looking forward to that moment. What Parker really wanted to do was to hide out somewhere that the Feds wouldn't think to look for Christian while he worked out a legal strategy for him. That he was able to find a way to enjoy the hideaway was simply a bonus.

Unfortunately, it had slipped his mind that there were often many visits to the casinos by FBI agents. Fortunately, Waymon had them all reassigned to look for Christian in other places and none of them were in the casinos today.

"I think you'll find this gentleman a little luckier than most."

"Bring him on, big fella."

"You're gonna regret that statement, young lady. Care for a little wager?"

Parker always offered side bets with Juliette, with the implication that something naughty was to be at play if he won. Juliette was never one to fall for it though, although she often thought she should put something monetary in play with Parker. His whales almost always walked away with losses that might have been petty cash for them, but left the Mediterranean quite happy. Juliette's personality, coupled with the lavish comps she showered Parker's associates with, assured her that they never regretted the experience.

"Get over me, big boy," Juliette knew he was right but couldn't help reminding him of her conquest. "So, when are you coming in? Tonight?"

"How about ten minutes?"

Monday mornings were not the norm for Parker to bring his clients in; Juliette was a little taken aback. "What? Are you guys still up partying from last night? And why wasn't I invited?"

"In a way, yes. Just get a hundred grand from my account and have the chips ready. I think we'll start with a little roulette."

Christian sprang up and waved his hands to indicate for Parker to stop. "Not roulette—I can't tell the future," he whispered.

"Better make that blackjack, in a private room. We'll need complete discretion; the player needs to remain anonymous."

"Anything else, Your Highness? If you'd like I can even have Janis here for the slaughter."

Janis was Parker's favorite blackjack dealer, and Juliette and Janis were quite the dynamic duo themselves. Every bit as stunning as Juliette, albeit a few inches shorter, the two had previously worked together in several other casinos and were the first to be recruited as a team by the Mediterranean—unquestionably two of the Mediterranean's greatest assets.

With her blazing natural red hair, Playboy-worthy body, and outrageous, yet charmingly flirtatious, personality, Janis had a way of keeping players at the game tables long after they normally would have given up and cut their losses. As a team, Juliette and Janis had a well-earned national reputation for attracting and keeping whales. Their reputation grew even greater once the duo was featured on the cover of High Stakes Gaming magazine. Many aggressive attempts at recruiting them to both Vegas and Atlantic City had failed; their love of the Sierra Nevada and dislike of the mega gambling towns trumping anything anyone had to offer them elsewhere.

Being the big fish in the small city of Reno suited them perfectly.

"Sure," Parker smiled, as he accepted her challenge. "But even the two of you don't stand a chance this time."

"So, just who is this superman and how come I didn't know he was in town?"

"You'll find out, sweetheart. We'll see you shortly." Parker impishly smiled as he disconnected the call. Back at the casino, Juliette brandished her own smug smile, rushing off to make arrangements while visions of the funds for her next vacation excited her further.

≈

The face of the seven-iron was wide open as it hit the ball from the left-side rough of the third fairway at North Tahoe Country Club. "Damn. I just can't get into my game today," Benny moaned as the ball sliced well into the woods on the other side of the fairway. Frustrated, he grabbed his already lit cigar from his caddie.

"It's okay, boss. Take a mulligan. I won't count it," the caddie reassured him.

"You're damn right you won't count it," Benny responded as he signaled his caddie to tee up another ball. "It wasn't my fault—it was Christian Fucking Faraday's fault."

Benny Malone was a man possessing little patience to begin with, and this morning's news didn't make his mood any more forgiving. Benny was not a tall man, standing no more than 5'8", but stocky and quite rough looking. The fine golf clothes looked out of character on him; indeed, ten years earlier he was seen in little other than cheap dark suits, cut wide enough to accommodate the handguns strapped to his chest. A series of profitable deals, combined with timely 'accidents' of key rivals, enabled Benny to take over all underworld activity in western Nevada and everything north of San Francisco in California.

While most of the manpower of his organization labored from the docks of Oakland to the halls of power in Sacramento, most of the real deals went down in the Reno area, so he made this his base. Ever wanting to obtain a respectable image, Benny began to try fitting into the mainstream of the leisure upper class of the area, getting involved in legitimate business activities, local charities, and of course, joining a prestigious country club and learning golf. He had actually done quite well in golf, although it didn't appear so this morning.

Benny lined up and took another swing. This time the ball landed in the sand trap to the right of the green. "We are not posting a score today. I'm not letting some damn psycho screw up my handicap."

"That's psychic, boss. Not psycho." The caddie reminded him.

"Whatever. I worked hard to get it down to fifteen and he's not gonna mess it up for me."

As Benny and his partner, followed by their caddies, headed towards the green, a golf cart with two men raced their direction.

"Do you have him?" Benny inquired as the cart pulled up beside them and the driver slammed on the brakes.

"No, boss. Nobody does."

"What the hell do you mean? If nobody does, why don't we?"

"The place is crawling with reporters all morning, and the CIA pounced on him the minute the reporters left. We couldn't get near the place."

"Yeah, I saw him on TV. Nice legs. So, he's with the CIA?"

"No, boss, apparently, he gave them the slip. The CIA and FBI have half the law enforcement resources in Nevada looking for him right now."

Earlier in the morning Benny destroyed the evidence Christian had told the FBI about, thanks to his own informant in the FBI. He was still too much of a danger to Benny if he continued talking to the authorities. Besides, he'd like to tap into Christian's ability himself. If he was unable to achieve this, Christian simply had to get whacked to avoid any further disruptions to Benny's operations.

"So, no one has any idea where this psycho is?"

"That's psychic, boss," the caddie once again corrected him.

"Whatever. He's somewhere, but not with us. What else did we find out about him?"

"He's a widower, has a fifteen-year-old daughter, Tatum. She goes to school south of town, a private place called Laurel Ridge Academy. No other family we could find out about."

"Okay. Pick her up and take her to the lodge. Have some boys watch the Feds. If they find Faraday, take him away from them, I don't care how ugly it gets."

Benny returned to walking towards his ball. "Damn psycho," he mumbled to himself as he strolled down the fairway.

Chapter Twelve

Juliette had made all the necessary arrangements for the arrival of her new VIP. The table and chips were ready, and a limo had been sent to pick up Janis.

Having just awoken and showered, Janis was surprised to hear her phone ring so early in the day. She was relieved to hear Juliette's friendly voice.

"We've got a hot one on the way in, girl. Jorge's ETA to pick you up is in five minutes."

"Good thing I didn't work last night. Where did you find this one, Juliette?"

"Courtesy of Parker."

"Oh, I like his friends. I might be able to get that new TV this month after all. I'll have my makeup on by the time Jorge arrives. I haven't had anything to eat yet though." Not that Janis needed much in the way of cosmetics. She was one of those natural beauties that putting more than some basic highlighting on was doing nothing more than messing with perfection; never having to spend more than a minute or two, and that was due more to that inexplicable magnetism between females and cosmetics than anything to do with her appearance.

"No worries. There's OJ, coffee, berries, and muffins in the limo. See you soon."

Juliette stood anxiously on the red carpet at the grand entrance of the Mediterranean, checking and double checking her hair, her dress, her shoes, and just about anything that would keep her busy. As Parker's Bentley pulled up, she clapped her hands quickly to get the valet's attention and then made one last adjustment to her dress.

"Parker, darling!" she exclaimed as he stepped out of the car. She walked over to give him a hug as he approached her, all the while glancing around for her target. Juliette smiled when she noticed her old friend get out of the back seat. "Well, hello, Christian. We don't get to see you down here too often. How have you been, sweetie?" she asked as she gave him a warmer embrace and a soft kiss on his cheek.

It was Stephanie who introduced Juliette to Parker. Stephanie and Juliette had been very close friends, becoming acquainted during modeling gigs. Juliette adored Christian and was always trying to find someone to fill the void in his heart, although she knew that would be near impossible.

"Hi, Jules," Christian returned the kiss, "You're looking lovelier than ever." Christian then whispered in her ear, "This is not my idea."

"So, Parker, where's your Mister Moneybags?"

"You've just been groping him."

"Christian? You've got to be kidding. He couldn't gamble if his life depended on it. Besides, I wouldn't take his money if he could. He's way too sweet." She turned to Christian and winked. Juliette turned back to Parker with a more serious look. "Just what are you up to? I've had this place turned upside down with a whale alert. And you bring me, Christian?" Juliette turned back to Christian. "No offense, Christian."

"None taken, Jules." Christian was clearly embarrassed that his dear friend had to be involved in this ordeal.

"If I were you, I'd be a little nicer to Christian. He's about to take you guys to the cleaners."

"Parker, do you know what a fool I'm going to look like after this false alarm?"

"There is no false alarm." Parker put his arm around her shoulder and directed her towards the casino entrance. "You just treat Mister Faraday here as if he has just flown in from Dubai."

Juliette hustled to keep up with Parker's pace as she glanced back quizzically at Christian, who just shrugged his shoulders and followed along.

"You do have my usual Bloody Mary ready for me, I presume?" Parker had a standing arrival drink of pepper vodka Bloody Mary if he were ever to arrive before noon. In the afternoon it was a Sam Adams draft, and in the evening, Laphroaig single malt on the rocks.

"Have I ever not been perfectly ready for your arrival? And what would my whale like?"

"Sparkling water is fine, thanks. Really, don't go to any trouble for me." Christian never liked to put people out or have a fuss made over him.

Inside the Mediterranean, it was odd that the same environment would provoke such totally different reactions from two such close friends.

The ornate casino was a class of exquisite design, architecture, quality materials and craftsmanship the likes of which were extravagant even by Vegas standards. The outlandish displays of wealth and pretension, all enclosed in an endless sea of rows of flashing lights, spinning wheels, and green felt topped tables with all sorts of intimidating designs on them, transported any visitor to a completely overwhelming world.

Within this arena, scantily clad women distributed complimentary alcoholic beverages as their double-D breasts were challenged to remain contained in their uniforms. Flirtatious dealers managed to keep anxious customers intensely stimulated while awaiting their next card. Sharply dressed floor managers kept an eye on every movement of every person in the place while people of all ages, from all walks of life, emptied their wallets and bank accounts to feed the ravenous beast of coin and bill slots that existed on just about every piece of furniture in the place.

To the average person, this scene evoked dreams of easy money and fast riches, and they kept coming back for more of it, whenever possible. To Parker, this was an integral part of the universe he was the master of, and as such, he felt a certain self-satisfaction whenever he observed the pawns of his playground play out his carefully laid game of wealth redistribution.

To Christian, however, he could not help but shake his head as he simply didn't understand how all those people didn't realize that all this extravagance was being paid for by their cumulative dollar bets—as well as keeping Parker's clients obscenely wealthy. One might as well just send them a donation and save the trip.

Christian rarely visited the casinos, and when he did, it was for a professional reason, such as client entertainment; although he was never one to pass judgment on those who did enjoy them. It was their money, and if people wanted to blow it on ringing bells, bouncing metal balls, and the luck of the draw, they were welcome to it. Christian on the other hand, had mountains to climb, rivers to raft, and fresh air to enjoy; all of which of course was also a part of Parker's universe, one which they enjoyed together quite often. This casino was not at all a natural environment for Christian, but his bud was on another harebrained adventure, one which they would no doubt laugh about for a long time to come.

As they made their way through the seemingly endless maze of slot machines, Juliette put her arm through Christian's and asked, "So what is this system you think you have? This isn't at all like you."

"No system, Jules. Your boy here just seems to have a great deal of faith in me today."

"You know as well as I do that Parker would never go this far out on a limb on 'faith'. I'm not sure he even knows what the word means." Juliette turned to Parker and grinned.

Just then, Christian stopped in his tracks, opened his wallet, and pulled out a crisp one-dollar bill. "Mind if I try something?"

"Sure, that's what they're here for."

Walking up to a specific slot machine, he put his dollar in the slot and pulled the lever.

As the wheels inside the machine spun around, Parker watched with a huge grin on his face. *What are these two up to?* Juliette wondered to herself. The wheels came to a stop one at a time. Seven. Seven. Seven. Suddenly bells started ringing and lights began flashing faster than normal. Christian's winnings clanked noisily in the payout slot below.

"Congrats, Christian!" Juliette exclaimed with a big smile on her face. Looking at Parker, Juliette's smile turned serious, and she asked, "All right, what exactly are you up to?"

A little surprised himself, Parker calmly replied, "I told you, Jules, the guy is hot today."

As the coins continued to fall from inside the machine, Christian picked up a coin bucket from a nearby stack and handed it to an elderly woman sitting at a nearby machine, motioning to the machine still spewing out coins. "Here you are, ma'am. This should help with your husband's medical expenses."

The old woman wasn't quite sure what to make of the gesture, but cautiously reached out to accept the bucket.

"Really, it's okay. Go ahead," Christian reassured her. "Just take good care of your husband. He loves you so."

"God bless you," she finally managed to get the words out. "There's a place for you in Heaven, young man."

As Christian continued on his way, Juliette rushed to catch up with him, with Parker right behind. "What are you doing?" she asked him, "That was a ten-thousand-dollar payout."

"She needs it more than I do, Jules. Besides, our friend here tells me I have real money to take from you at the tables."

"Don't you wish? I'm just glad this is Parker's money you're playing with. I would never take yours."

On the other side of Christian from Juliette, Parker whispered in Christian's ear, "I thought you couldn't tell the future."

"I can't, but apparently, I could tell the machine is primed to 'hit'," Christian whispered back.

Parker smiled broadly as they continued on their way to the VIP room, scheming how to best leverage Christian's ability.

The activity in the Casino was remarkably brisk, at least from Christian's perceptive. Although barely approaching ten o'clock, there were already many people sitting in front of the slot machines, coin buckets in hand, busily pulling levers. Many of the tables were already well attended and money and chips freely passing between dealers and players. Even the gals in the tight outfits were hustling to and fro with trays of drinks. *What is going on here?* Christian looked perplexed. *Don't these people have things to do at ten in the morning?* Never having been to a casino at this time of day, he always assumed they'd be vacuuming and otherwise cleaning up from the night before while getting ready for the day ahead. It never occurred to him that the new week's crowd would have arrived the night before and they would be anxious to begin exercising the gambling bug that had been building up since their last visit. Thus, the weekly, never-ending, round-the-clock cycle renewed itself in the magical land of casinos.

Having crisscrossed through the field of gaming tables, including poker, craps, roulette, and blackjack, Christian was escorted into a private VIP room where Janis waited to greet him.

"Christian, I believe you remember Janis."

Janis had just rushed to the table after arriving at the casino moments earlier. Janis was quite familiar with Christian, as Juliette had more than once attempted to set the two of them up. Christian was totally oblivious to the subtle suggestive introductions Juliette tried, and he all but ignored her more direct approaches; with Janis or anyone else. He did that to everyone that attempted to introduce romance into his life. For her part, Juliette never took it personally, but she was always ready to try again.

"Great to see you again, Christian," Janis greeted him with a warm smile and hug. Being a flirt for this customer was not going to be a problem at all, although she was more than a wee bit confused by the sight of Christian as her high roller.

"Good morning, Janis. You're looking lovely." Although he did genuinely mean it this time, he was gentleman enough that it was almost a habit to say that, regardless of how bad a woman looked.

"Do we have Mister Faraday's chips ready?" Juliette asked Janis as she approached Janis's side of the table.

"Right here, Juliette," Janis replied as she scooted a stack of chips across the table to Christian.

"The limit at this table is a ten-thousand per hand with a thousand minimum. Are you sure you want to do this, Christian?" Juliette wanted to make sure Christian wasn't feeling pressured by Parker.

"Sure, why not? It's Parker's money."

"Always happy to get out of bed—or into it—for this sweet hunk," Janis whispered to Juliette. "But what gives? Where's our whale?"

"Not sure what Parker is up to this morning, Janis. But keep an eye on him," Juliette whispered back. "Parker, that is. Christian doesn't have a sneaky bone in his body."

"Sure you're not in for a side wager, Jules?" Parker made one last attempt.

"Please, Parker. Besides, you never offer me anything if I win."

"Well, I figured you'd be thrilled about the same deal either way."

"You wish."

"Okay then, how about I throw this in?" Parker reached into his pocket, retrieved his keys, and removed the distinctive key displaying the Porsche logo. Parker held the key up and flaunted it in the lights above, as if it were the Hope Diamond.

"The new 911 Turbo S convertible you bought yourself for Christmas?" Juliette asked in disbelief. How she'd love to snag that from him. This was definitely cause for a moment of thought. "And what do I have to put up in return?" finally making him be explicit about his intentions.

"Hmmmmm. What say a weekend in Cabo?"

Ouch. That hurts. Cabo San Lucas had been one of their favorite getaway spots when they were a couple, usually staying in a prime oceanfront Jacuzzi suite at the luxurious Palace San Lucas. After a weekend at the world-class spa, pristine beach, and culinary decadence, it would take Juliette weeks to get back to the reality of the working world. Parker knew how to treat, not to mention tease, a lady.

Juliette looked at Janis, who didn't know which way to advise her. On the one hand, Nico was definitely the best thing that ever happened to her. On the other—well damn, this was a two-hundred-forty-thousand-dollar car. Besides, it was only Christian that she had to worry about.

On the other side of the table, Christian took a break from quizzically examining the card shoe and gave Parker a clear look of disapproval. But he trusted Parker, so the glance was only momentary before he got back to the matter at hand.

"I'm not sure what you're up to stud, but I don't think I want to fall for it. Let's get this show on the road, shall we?"

Christian picked up a thousand dollars in chips and placed them on the bet mark in front of him.

"Just a thousand? I thought we were talking real money, Christian?" Juliette teased.

Christian just smiled at her as Janis began dealing the cards. She placed a card face up in front of Christian, an eight, then a card face down in front of herself, the next card face up in front of Christian, this one a four, then another face up in front of herself, a seven.

Although he knew a five awaited him at the top of the shoe, Christian tried to make sure he didn't give away his secret too early and paused, while pretending to think. After tapping the table, indicating a hit, Janis dealt him a five of clubs, giving Christian a total of seventeen. He waved over the cards, indicating he'd hold.

Janis reached for her face up card and slipped the edge of it below her face down card and flipped it over, exposing a three. Rules require dealers to hit anything sixteen or below in their hand. Janis dealt herself a nine. "Nineteen. Dealer wins." Janis gave Christian a sympathetic look as she removed the chips in front of him followed by the cards, which went into the discard rack. Christian placed another thousand in chips on the bet spot in front of him.

"Not off to a promising start here, Parker." Juliette gloated.

"There's still time for you to really take advantage of the situation, Jules," Parker replied as he held up and twisted the Porsche key around in his fingers.

Juliette tried to keep a look of disinterest, "You really are awful, Parker." Inside, however, she could barely contain herself from jumping at his deal.

Janis began the second hand. An eight for Christian then a card down for herself. The next card up for Christian was a five, followed by a nine for Janis.

Christian waved his hand.

Juliette tried hard not to make any expression. Even the most amateur of players knows that a thirteen, especially facing a dealer's nine, was a hit situation.

"Would you like a strategy card, Christian?" Janis suggested, referring to the little card available in every casino's gift shop showing when to hit or stand based on the cards showing on the table.

"I'm fine, Janis. Thanks anyway, though."

Janis flipped her face down card over, displaying a Jack.

Once again, Janis cleared the chips and cards from in front of Christian.

"What were the details of that bet, Parker?"

"Christian's up a hundred by noon," Parker replied as he teasingly played with the Porsche key.

He's got to be kidding, Juliette thought. Christian would have to play almost flawless blackjack to pull that off, and thus far he's headed in the opposite direction. Janis held off as she saw Juliette pondering the challenge. What the hell, Juliette thought, if this turns into a disaster, Nico is probably going to dump me anyway for taking such a risk. May as well get a little pampering out of it. Besides, the odds are way in my favor. Juliette couldn't resist the challenge any longer and nodded her head towards the table, "Throw it down." The bet was on.

Parker gave her a wink and a grin as he gently placed the key on the table and slid it across to her.

Janis took a deep breath, shook her head, smiled, and continued dealing as Christian slid out five thousand dollars in chips.

Once the cards were dealt, with two kings exposed for him and a five exposed for Janis, Christian separated his kings then slid another five thousand next to the first.

Janis glanced at Juliette, before giving Christian a big flirtatious smile. "So brave this early in the morning, sweetie?"

Christian smiled back at her. "I don't get to abuse Parker's bank account that often so I might as well enjoy it."

Janis placed a four on the first of Christian's kings. Christian pretended to spend a moment thinking, before waving a pass on that hand. Juliette had become slightly tense, holding her breath after Christian split and doubled his bet. With Christian holding on a fourteen, she let out a sigh of relief, while Parker stood there with an ever so confident smirk on his face.

Janis then dealt Christian an eight on the second king. Christian waved his hand, passing on another.

Janis flipped over her down card, exposing a nine; her hand now totaling fourteen. Dealing herself a nine she announced, "Nine makes twenty-three. Dealer busts." Janis cleared the cards and slid over five thousand in chips to each of the two stacks in front of Christian's hands.

"If it will make it easier, I'll throw in a new set of Louis Vuitton luggage for the trip," Parker smiled as he goaded her, then took a long sip as he stared at Juliette over his Bloody Mary glass.

"Don't you have something you're supposed to be doing, Parker?" Christian looked sternly at Parker. "And whatever you do, don't use your mobile phone."

"Jules, can I get a phone and a little privacy?"

Glad to no longer have to put up with his gloating, Juliette quickly complied and set Parker up nearby so he could begin figuring out Christian's legal strategy.

Chapter Thirteen

The front of Christian's house looked like a dark sedan parking lot as every FBI agent within reasonable proximity had rushed to deal with the current crisis. Several more sedans cruised the neighborhood, and a helicopter searched from the air. Inside, Samuel Waymon had arrived and turned the kitchen table into his command center. Agents West and Johnson were quite satisfied with the comfort and beauty of the patio for their planning.

Both agencies had tremendous resources allocated for this effort, with the FBI's being primarily manpower and the CIA's more intelligence-oriented—solving the problem with advanced data gathering and analysis then quickly and quietly swooping in to close the case. While Samuel Waymon orchestrated searches and coordinated local and state agencies inside, West and Johnson spent their time on the phone with various analysts at the Langley headquarters on drone feeds and other tools.

"Where in the hell could Faraday have gone?" Waymon remarked as he looked at a blueprint of the Sierra Vista neighborhood. "How many teams are out there now?"

"We've got cars at all the neighborhood access points, four vehicles roaming the neighborhood, and six teams on foot searching the woods in all directions," Carver replied.

"Any information on the neighbors yet?"

"We're waiting for reports now, but I've just sent out three more teams to interview them."

"Anything from the chopper, drones, or satellites?"

"No, sir."

Waymon glanced up and saw his CIA friends disappearing out the front door. "Find out what they're up to."

Outside, Marcus and Heather got in their car and drove off. Soon afterward, Agent Dawson approached Waymon. "I think I know where he is. Remember that friendly attorney of Christian's?"

"Yeah, and?"

"Turns out he lives right," Dawson looked down at the map, oriented himself, then put his finger on the lot belonging to Parker, "here."

"That explains a lot. That's adjacent to where we are now. We should probably be able to get there through these woods before West can drive around the neighborhood and find it through this maze of roads. Get a few teams in cars there right away and the ground teams covering the rear and sides of the property. Have the drones focus on that area. Let's go."

Agent Carver began giving directions on his walkie-talkie, as Waymon and Dawson headed out the back door of the house and started running in the direction of Parker's house.

≈

Just as Agents West and Johnson pulled into Parker's driveway, they saw several FBI cars converging to the same spot as well as the helicopter hovering overhead. The caravan pulled up to the front of the house as Agents Waymon and Dawson approached the front door from the side of the house, quite a bit out of breath.

"I can't believe the Bureau lets their guys get so out of shape," West remarked to Heather as they got out of the car.

"Fancy meeting you here, Samuel," West commented to Agent Waymon.

"You didn't think we were going to let you have all the fun, did you, Marcus?"

The four key agents approached the front door together as several FBI agents exited their vehicles and cautiously surrounded the house.

West reached out to ring the doorbell, but Waymon beat him to it. "Allow me."

"By all means," West smirked back.

After about two minutes of waiting, the agents growing increasingly uncomfortable with each other, Sunye finally answered the door. Both West and Waymon held out their identification and asked for Parker at the same time. West held up his hand, interrupting Waymon. "Allow me."

"Oh, of course," Waymon replied, none too happy about it though.

"Ma'am, we're looking for Mister Parker Farr. Is he available?"

"Oh, no, sir. Mister Parker he no here."

"How about this man?" Waymon asked as he held up a picture of Christian.

"Ahhh, Mister Christian. Very nice man."

"Yes," West responded. "But is he here?"

"Oh, no. Mister Christian no here."

"Was he here?" Waymon interjected.

"Oh, yes. Mister Christian was here."

"When? Do you know where he has gone?" Waymon finally felt as if they were getting somewhere.

"Mister Christian here often. He here two weeks ago. He and Mister Parker watch basketball. That Mister James, he very big man."

"But this morning, ma'am," West felt like he needed to take back the interrogation. "Have you seen Christian Faraday this morning?"

"Oh, yes. I see Mister Christian this morning."

"He was here this morning?" West repeated. Both West and Waymon were getting a little frustrated with the language barrier.

"I see Mister Christian on TV. He on news and everything. Nice legs, no?"

"Yes, ma'am. Very nice legs," Waymon replied, giving up on the questioning. "Do you mind if we have a look around?"

"I don't know. I not sure Mister Parker like that."

Heather interjected; her diplomacy clearly needed at this point. "There is a very important case involving Mister Faraday and we are worried about him. It's possible he's in danger. We'd just like to take a quick look to see if there is anything that can help us locate him." Heather herself didn't believe that, and it was clear to her that Sunye was playing with them.

Sunye pretended to look skeptical, but she knew there was nothing they could find, and this might give her boss and Christian more time to do whatever it was they were doing.

"Okay, but please, I just now clean. No make mess. Okay?"

"Yes, ma'am," West responded. "We'll be very careful."

Sunye stepped out of the way and allowed the men and Heather to enter the house. Agent Dawson signaled to two of the men out front to join them inside to help with the search. As Heather, Agent Dawson, and his men began looking around the house, Waymon made sure West was always in sight, not wanting to miss anything he might stumble across.

"Has Mister Farr gone to his office, ma'am?" Agent West asked Sunye.

Remembering her instructions, Sunye repeated what Parker had instructed her to. "Oh, no. Mister Parker no at office. Mister Parker go to Vegas this morning."

"Was he going alone?" Waymon interjected.

"Mister Parker say he take client to Vegas."

"What time did he leave?"

"I think Mister Parker leave maybe hour ago."

That was a little longer than it had been since Christian disappeared, but close enough that West figured that she might be off a little bit; she was, only deliberately.

Dawson came downstairs and shook his head at Waymon as the two other agents converged, returning from the other levels, also indicating no success. Immediately afterwards, Heather returned from the patio.

"Nothing here, Marcus," Heather reported to Agent West.

"What kind of car was Mister Farr driving, ma'am?" Waymon continued with Sunye.

"Mister Parker have two cars. I no know which he drive today." Sunye knew exactly which car Parker had taken, but she figured the longer she stalled, the better it was for her beloved boss.

"There is a Porsche and a motorcycle in the garage sir," reports one of the agents.

"What is his other car, ma'am?"

"Oh, big car. I no know. It big and blue."

"Do you have his mobile number?"

Although Sunye had it memorized, she wanted to delay them as long as she could for her Mister Parker, "I have here somewhere. Me go look."

The agents looked at each other, totally exasperated, but trying to remain patient as they knew they had no alternative. Sunye went into Parker's office and pretended to look around, opening drawers and looking at papers. After about five minutes, Waymon and West entered Parker's office and Sunye pretended she had just found the number. "Here it is. Mister Parker number," she said, handing a piece of paper to Waymon.

"Thank you, ma'am," Waymon retrieved the number before West could reach for it. Retrieving his phone from his pocket, he dialed the number and was immediately connected with Parker's voicemail.

"Mister Farr, this is Special Agent Samuel Waymon, with the FBI. We met last night. It's imperative that we talk to you immediately. Please call me at 775-555-8804 as soon as you receive this message."

"Well, thank you, ma'am," Agent West said to Sunye as he handed her his business card. "If you hear from or see either Mister Farr or Mister Faraday, will you please contact us?"

Samuel Waymon scrambled to get one of his cards out and handed it to Sunye, as well. "Same here. Please let us know right away."

"No problem," Sunye responded as she showed them to the door with a big smile on her face. "I call right away I see Mister Parker or Mister Christian."

≈

As the agents headed to their cars, Agent West turned to Samuel Waymon and commented, "You know Faraday is that 'client', don't you?"

"No shit, Sherlock. They train you well at the Agency, don't they? Someone else must have picked Christian up and met up with Parker. I'll get the road to Vegas covered, as well as the airports. Given the resources this Farr fellow has, I wouldn't be surprised if he has chartered something." Waymon was quite pleased with himself, knowing that the resource game gave him a huge edge over the Agency in closing in on Faraday. *I'm gonna beat them this time,* he couldn't help thinking to himself.

West knew this too, so he had to keep himself in Waymon's loop to make sure he was in for the capture. "My helicopter is ready to go. I'm heading there right now. Once we get a fix on them, we can head to wherever he is and pick him up. Want to come along?"

Waymon wasn't wild about the idea of sharing with West, but he had already given his jet to Bragg, and it would take some time to get a pilot and ready another helicopter. West might have Faraday by the time Waymon got things together. Basically, they needed each other, although neither was happy about the situation.

"That would be great, thanks." Waymon turned to Dawson who had been huddling with the two other agents, "What do you have on that car, Dawson?"

"2024 Moroccan Blue Bentley sedan. I've alerted the state police and choppers and we're mapping out a roadblock strategy now. Units are currently on the lookout, and several units have been deployed to each of the commercial airfields."

"Anything on private or commercial flight activity?"

"Nothing yet. They aren't listed on any passenger manifests. There were several private flights this morning. We're reviewing those flight plans, and we've alerted agents at all the destination cities."

"If you identify their flight and it's still airborne, secure a military jet to escort them back. I'm going to meet our Agency friends here at the airport."

Agents West and Johnson got in their car and backed down the driveway. "Drop me back at Faraday's house, Marcus."

"What's up? We're going to need you when we meet up with him."

"Something isn't right.   That housekeeper wasn't completely straight with us. This might just be a diversion."

"What do you mean?"

"Her answers were calculatingly vague and deceptive. Christian was there this morning. There are two chairs on the patio table that had been used, judging from their positions, along with two coffee cups and juice glasses in the sink. It's unlikely that a maid would have left her own dishes in the sink by this time of day. I think you've been sent on a wild goose chase. I want to do a little more investigation at Faraday's place."

"Okay, but I'm going to cover this FBI chase anyway, we can't afford to miss out in case it pans out."

≈

"How on earth did you get away with that?" Nicki exclaimed as she and Tatum got out of earshot of the classroom they had just left. "Mr. Brown hates you."

"It was all subjective grading anyway. He just changed his mind I guess," Tatum responded as she looked at a paper with a red "C" crossed out and an "A" written next to it. She was dying to tell Nicki, but figured she better not.

"No way. Two minutes after you marched up to his desk, he changed the grade up to an "A". That never happens. What did you say to him?"

"Nothing, I swear."

"Bull. Besides, I don't think I've ever seen such a pissed off look on the man's face before."

Tatum just smiled back, still holding back her desire to clue Nicki in.

"Girl, I swear, if you don't tell me I'm going to tell Joseph you like him."

Giving in to temptation, Tatum stopped walking, and turned to her friend, "Okay, but you can't tell a soul. Pinkie swear?" Tatum held up her closed right hand, with the pinkie extended.

Nicki shook pinkies with Tatum and began to giggle. "Okay, so I'm telling my dad this morning about how much of a pain Mister Brown is, and how he hates me. He grabs a piece of paper, writes something on it and tells me to give it to Mister Brown next time he is unreasonable. And that was a damn good paper. I think he was very unreasonable with that 'C'."

"Cool. What did the paper say?"

"Dad told me not to look at it."

"Yeah, right. Since when did that stop you?"

"Okay, maybe I took a little peek."

"And? What did that little peek reveal?"

"Nothing much, just something about his master's thesis and plagiarism."

"Shut up!" Nicki exclaimed. "This new power of his is awesome. Can I borrow your dad for some of my teachers too?"

"I'd first worry about the pop quiz we're about to have in Latin if I were you."

Realizing the implications of this, Nicki's eyes lit up. "I think I like your dad even more than I did before."

Chapter Fourteen

"Dealer busts. Christian wins with eight showing."

"Who holds onto an eight?" Juliette whispered to Parker. "What is going on here?"

Juliette was long past nervous; not only did Christian pass the hundred-thousand mark long before noon, but the stack of chips in front of him was now over four times that amount, and it was only one o'clock.

"Good, isn't he?" Parker smiled at Juliette. "I meant to ask you, in what color would you prefer that Louis Vuitton? Brown or white?" Parker had been teasing her about their bet since Christian hit the fifty grand mark at shortly after eleven.

"You're incorrigible," Juliette blurted back. She still didn't have any idea how she was going to explain all this to Nico. "You do know that I can't make it to Cabo if I'm buried in the middle of the desert, don't you?"

Overhearing the exchange, Christian reassured her, "Don't worry, Juliette. Parker was just kidding about the bet." Christian couldn't stand to see his dear friend feeling so uncomfortable.

"I was?" Parker responded with a surprised look on his face.

"I think he meant the weekend was for you and Nico."

"I did?" Parker nearly choked on his Bloody Mary. Christian gave him a cross look, and Parker knew his friend was serious. "Why, of course I did. You and Nico have a good time, compliments of Christian and me."

Breathing a sigh of relief and knowing her good friend Christian just saved her neck, Juliette stuck her tongue out at Parker then hugged Christian around the neck from behind, giving him a kiss on the cheek. "Thank you, Christian." *I still have to explain this to Nico,* Juliette thought to herself. *It's a good thing he's in a meeting all day.*

Suddenly, Nico appeared from the general casino area and marched into the VIP room, with a less-than-pleasant look on his face and an intense urgency in his stride. Nico stood an even six feet tall, and the unlimited access to the hotel spa kept him in excellent shape. Nonetheless, he was dwarfed by the casino security men flanking him at the moment.

"Okay, Parker—how do you plan on saving me from this?" Juliette whispered to Parker.

"Don't worry, sweetheart. Have I ever let you down?"

"More times than you can possibly imagine."

"Parker, this is going way too far," Nico's voice bellowed out as he and his security men approached. "Juliette, do you have any idea what's going on here? Have you not been watching the news today?"

As his face reddened with anger, Juliette stepped back and moved slightly behind Parker, who smiled as Nico set his target on him. "And you, Parker, what kind of scam are you trying to pull on us? Why, twenty years ago we'd already be on our way out to some abandoned mine for you to spend eternity in."

"What is he talking about?" Juliette whispered into Parker's ear, to which Parker shrugged his shoulders. Juliette had gone to bed late the night before, straight from work. Back at the casino first thing in the morning, she had not seen any television at all, news or otherwise.

"Listen, Nico, I can explain," Juliette began.

"You can explain how you let a man known to have extraordinary psychic powers have free rein at one of our high-limit tables and is sitting up over two hundred grand? How can you possibly explain that?"

"Christian? Psychic?"

Now that Juliette was totally confused and Nico was as mad as even Parker dare let him get, Parker decided it was time to step in. "Yes, Nico," Parker began in a casual and confident voice. "Jules realized the potential of Christian's new power right away and contacted me first thing this morning, begging us to come down here."

"I did?" Juliette whispered to him.

"And what a deal she made for you," Parker continued.

"I did?" quietly Juliette repeated just as she realized she had best play along. She hated trusting Parker, but knew she had no choice. His explanation was bound to be better than anything she could come up with, especially since she had absolutely no idea what they were talking about. "That's right, Nico. As soon as I heard about Christian, I got them down here right away so we could—" Juliette paused, giving Parker a slight nudge to have him continue.

"So Christian and I could get some invaluable information for my two favorite people."

"What the hell are you talking about, Parker? And what does it have to do with your trying to skim my casino profits?"

"Calm down, Nico. Jules was just letting Christian practice his new skill a little bit. Small price to pay for the information she negotiated out of him."

"Absolutely. You wouldn't believe what we got out of this, Nico," Juliette played along, giving Parker another nudge.

Christian had thus far pretty much ignored the entire conversation; busy concentrating on the play, adding several thousand more dollars to his cache of chips. Nonchalantly, Christian pulled out of his pocket the piece of paper he had worked on in the car for Parker, subtly slipping it into Juliette's hand behind Parker's back. Slightly startled, Juliette unfolded the paper and Parker indicated for her to pass it over to Nico.

"I think this will explain it all, Nico," Parker started as Nico, continuing to project his anger by staring down Parker, reached out and snatched it from Juliette's ever so slightly trembling hand.

"If this is another one of your tricks, Parker, you're gonna find that my boys still know a few virgin pieces of dirt just east of town."

Nico slowly opened the paper, not looking at it, but continuing his stare-down with Parker. He couldn't help but like Parker; a suave man's man that most men longed to be. Just the same, he was aching for an excuse to bring down the great Parker Farr.

"If you're not thrilled with your girl in thirty seconds, I'll bury myself. How's that sound?" Parker had no idea what was on the paper, but he knew that the information Christian would have written was unquestionably some powerful corporate intelligence that could save and/or make substantial amounts of money for the Mediterranean.

Nico was even less amused now. *God, I hate that man's overconfidence,* Nico thought to himself as he casually moved his eyes away from Parker's, making sure Parker knew he wasn't about to fall for any flimsy tricks.

Parker really enjoyed Nico's little show. Becoming one of Nevada's most prominent attorneys doesn't happen without being a master of one-upmanship. Watching Nico take himself so seriously, knowing that in just a few moments he'd have his own foot halfway down his throat, was a simple sort of amusement that Parker truly enjoyed in life.

As Nico began reading, Christian stood up from the table. Shaking out his legs and stretching from the extended period of sitting, Christian announced it was time that he and Parker get a move on.

"Janis, as always, it's been fun. You've been lovely company." Turning to Parker, he continued, "Parker, we really need to get going. There's a game afoot out there that you've only diverted for a little while. Folks are beginning to get a little anxious and we don't have much time to make our next move. Whatever it is that you've planned out, that is."

"Christian!" Nico blurted out as he suddenly looked up from the paper. "Please stay. Play as long as you like." Turning to one of the nearby servers, Nico snapped to her, "Will you get Mister Faraday another drink? Now!" Turning his attention to Juliette, Nico turned on all his charm, knowing that he might just have been perceived as overreacting, "You thought of this darling?" Nico reached both hands out and cupped her cheeks, then gently pulled her to him for a gentle kiss on the lips. "That was a sheer stroke of genius!"

Juliette, still clueless as to what was going on, just played along, suddenly feeling a massive sense of relief.

Nico had been ignoring Parker as he summoned the strength to eat crow to the man he finally thought he had bested.

"Thanks Nico, but we really have to go," Christian shook Nico's hand before turning to Janis. "Could you do me a favor and cash these in? As quickly as possible if you wouldn't mind," Christian slid his now substantial pile of chips to her. Picking out a small handful of five-thousand-dollar chips, Christian handed four of them to Janis with a sheepish grin. "This should cover a couple of really nice flat-panel TVs for you. Most probably a few other goodies as well."

Janis had a half-thrilled, half-shocked look on her face. *I didn't tell him about that TV I wanted,* she thought to herself as she leaned over, deliberately exposing her cleavage again, and gave him a kiss on his cheek. "Thank you so much, Christian. You'll have to come over and watch it with me sometime. Still have my number, I trust?"

Christian smiled back, suddenly remembering just how oblivious he can be about how charming women find him. He really didn't mean to lead anyone on, and he certainly hoped he hadn't led Janis on in any way. "That would be nice. But something tells me my life is going to be in a little turmoil for a while," Christian replied, hoping that he wasn't being too obvious in putting her off.

Turning to Juliette, Christian gave her a kiss on the cheek and slipped the remaining chips into her hand. "This should take care of the Cabo trip for you and Nico," Christian whispered to her. "Have fun and forget about our friendly stud over there."

Turning to Parker, Christian informed his friend they needed to leave. "Come on, Parker, we have to hit the road. Tatum has only a half-day at school today and we have plans to make."

"Parker—," Nico began, realizing he had to clear the air before they left.

"Don't worry about it, old pal. Just glad we could help the Mediterranean out," Parker replied. *God that felt good!*

Janis returned with her hands full of straps of cash and handed them to Christian, reaching up to give him one more kiss on his cheek, "Don't forget to call sometime, handsome."

Christian turned again to Juliette, "Could you do us one more little favor, Jules?"

"Sure, Christian. Anything."

Handing her two of the straps of bills totaling twenty-thousand dollars, Christian asked, "You wouldn't mind renting us your car, would you? I'm pretty sure this will cover it."

Chapter Fifteen

The young man looked oddly out of place as he lingered on the side-walk leading from the doors of Laurel Ridge Academy to the student parking lot. His slicked down hair, crisp black jeans and a blazer, dark brown silk T-shirt, and shiny alligator cowboy boots ruled him out not only as a student, but as either academic or athletic staff as well. If all that didn't catch anyone's attention, the cigarette dangling from his lips was a dead giveaway that he didn't belong. Fortunately for the man, this was the "quiet before the storm" of pre-dismissal moments, just prior to the end of the school day. No one was around to notice his odd behavior as he anxiously paced the sidewalk, occasionally reaching into his jacket pocket and glancing at a small photograph of Tatum Faraday.

Out of the quiet of the early afternoon, a loud bell pierced the silence. Dropping his cigarette on the sidewalk, he ground it outwith his heel, then made his way to a strategic point near the exits where he could observe the students as they left the building. Within a few minutes, the doors of the school burst open and a flood of teenagers began pouring out to meet their rides. At first the crowd was just a trickle, but within a few minutes, the two sidewalks became quite crowded with kids in various states of urgency and social interaction, causing the man to wish he had brought one of his colleagues to ac-company him. If he didn't spot this Tatum chick, he wouldn't be in much need of these fancy alligator boots, or any clothes at all for that matter.

Fortunately for him, he did not go unnoticed as many of the even most self-absorbed teens turned their heads out of curiosity, wondering what such a strangely out of place man was doing at their prestigious school. Oddly enough, that which would normally cause him difficulty during such a stakeout actually helped him out, giving him ample opportunity to view as many of the kids' faces as possible as they gawked at him.

Nevertheless, picking out a pretty brunette in a sea of them wasn't going to be terribly easy, especially since they were all wearing the same uniform.

Damn. Where's the little bitch? He anxiously pondered as the minutes ticked by. Now his scouting not only included the two exits, but scanning the parking lot as well, to see if he had missed her.

Continuing to ignore the stares he received as the students passed by him, his level of urgency increased as he walked to different vantage points, anxiously looking around and occasionally pulling Tatum's picture out of his jacket pocket to compare it to anyone closely resembling her image.

That's her! His anxiety turning to relief as he recognized the girl walking towards him with a girlfriend, engrossed in conversation only to the point that they couldn't help but notice the man, glancing over at him momentarily.

"Is there a creepo circus in town or something?" Nicki laughed as the two inseparable friends walked towards Nicki's car. "Don't we have campus security around here anymore?"

Tatum rolled her eyes, "Maybe *that is* the headmaster's new idea of campus security. Now that would be scary."

"Yeah, I wouldn't put anything past him. Oh, by the way, thanks for the heads up on the Latin quiz, I managed to catch up just before class.

I think I got them all right. There's no way I would have passed it if you hadn't clued me in."

"You mean Mister Mitchell's rendition of 'It's A Small World' didn't throw off your concentration?" Tatum was referring to their Latin teacher's trick of humming 'It's A Small World' as he handed out quizzes to destroy anything in short-term memory that might be there from last minute cramming.

"You've got to be kidding; I've been able to tune that out since second semester last year."

"Something tells me that you and I are going to do pretty well in school this year," Tatum replied as they threw their backpacks and lacrosse sticks in the back seat of Nicki's convertible.

"I love your dad, you know that?"

"But this is our secret. If word of this gets out, we are big time busted. Don't even tell him that I told you, I'll never get another thing out of him."

"No worries, sis, this is definitely our little secret," Nicki reassured her as she pulled her car out of the parking space and towards the lot exit.

The man, now at his black Lincoln Town Car, watched as the girls drove off. Reaching into his jacket pocket, he pulled out a mobile phone and pressed a speed dial button, "Hey Jacko, she's in the passenger seat of a blue convertible."

"The Volvo that's pulling out now?" replied the voice.

"Yeah, that's the one. I'll be right behind you." The man hopped into his car and began driving in the same direction Nicki and Tatum had just gone.

≈

"You mean to tell me with all the resources the Agency has given you, you're still clueless?" Blanton's voice boomed out of Marcus' mobile phone. Marcus pulled the phone away from his ear for a moment.

"Jacob, the reason this guy is so important to us is because of the advantage his ability gives him. Knowing what we are doing and how we're trying to find him is no doubt keeping him one step ahead of us."

"Regardless, you've got satellites, electronic tracking, and every other possible technology available to you. There isn't a rock in the Sierras that we shouldn't be able to find him under."

"We're looking into ways we can get him to come in voluntarily. We've got a team heading over to his daughter's school now to pick her up."

"Great. What about other family members? Wife, parents?"

"Nothing. She's it, and they're very close."

"Do what you need to do. Fly her to Langley and make him come get her if that will do it. Regardless, I want him in your custody within the hour, or I'm coming out there myself."

That was the last thing Marcus wanted. Having to compete with Waymon and the Bureau was bad enough, but adding more Agency higher ups would create more of a political quagmire. Bringing in 'Holy Grail' would be the crowning moment in his career, making him one of the most visible field agents in the Agency. He'd be damned if some-one from Washington was going to interfere and take away his glory.

"It's only a matter of time, Jacob. We'll have him on his way to Washington shortly, I'm confident of it," Marcus reassured him. Unfor-tunately, Marcus was not quite as confident himself. *Damn—for all we know, he's reading our minds and knows all our plans.*

≈

The two attractive teenage girls in the flashy convertible were the picture of carefree existence as they drove down the rural road be-tween the highway and the general area of Sierra Vista. The majestic

Sierra background on the beautiful spring day gave little indication of just how drastically the girls' lives were about to change.

Tatum and Nicki were so busy scheming about the possibilities available to them with Christian's new ability, they hadn't noticed the black SUV that had been discreetely following them since they pulled out of the school parking lot.

"Certainly, he won't mind giving us all the social 411 so that we can stay ahead of the game?" Nicki suggested.

"There's no way I'll have any trouble getting him to help us out there. He loves mischief like that. I'm not sure I'll be able to get much academic stuff out of him though."

"Don't underestimate how much you've got him wrapped around your little finger."

"Maybe so, but he gets pretty pissy about me earning my own grades."

"What the hell?" Nicki screamed as the black Lincoln passed then quickly braked in front of them, causing Nicki to slam on her brakes to avoid a collision.

The girls composed themselves after being thrust forward in their seats during the rapid stop. Watching the man emerge from the car in front of them, Tatum recognized him. "That's the weirdo that was outside the school this afternoon."

"I don't know what the hell he wants, but I think we'd better get out of here," Nicki responded as she turned to look behind her while shifting her car into reverse. As she started applying pressure on the accelerator, she realized that the black Suburban that had been follow-ing them had stopped immediately behind her Volvo, forcing her to slam on her brake pedal.

"*What is this shit?*" Tatum yelled to no one in particular as she unfas-tened her seat belt and Nicki put the car in Park. Neither Tatum nor

Nicki were ones to back down from confrontation and both jumped out of the car to find out what was going on.

"You don't think this has anything to do with how those kids disappeared do you?" Nicki asked Tatum.

In unison, all four doors of the Suburban opened and four men, dressed in dark jeans and jackets, emerged from the vehicle.

"Just what is going on here?" Nicki began as she marched towards the driver of the sedan. Stopping and turning to the driver of the Suburban, she continued, "What kind of goon squad are you guys part of, and why are you blocking us in?"

"We've got to get home and would appreciate you getting out of our way," Tatum added as she began to reach in her backpack for her mobile phone.

Completely ignoring her protests, Jacko, the driver of the Suburban, reached Nicki and grabbed her right arm, twisting it behind her back and spinning her around, allowing his partner to easily place a chloroform-saturated cloth over her nose.

Nicki struggled for a moment, but then became limp and she quickly fell backward into Jacko's arms.

On the other side of the convertible, Tatum had pressed the power button on her phone and awaited it to start up, expecting to watch Nicki give them a piece of her mind but ready to jump in if her friend needed assistance. Instead, Tatum watched her friend's misfortune in horror as the two men from the passenger side of the Suburban rapidly approached her.

"Hey, let her go!" Tatum screamed at them as she jumped back into the convertible, escaping the two men that prepared to jump her. She had no idea what she was going to do with five big men and an unconscious friend, but she wasn't going to run and leave Nicki at the mercy of these goons.

As Tatum climbed her way across the convertible, the two men that held Nicki headed back towards the Suburban, dragging Nicki with them. One of the other men jumped onto the trunk of the convertible, grabbing Tatum's ankle. Not one to be intimidated, Tatum twisted out of his clutch, and grabbed her lacrosse stick which had been lying on the back seat. Rolling over and reaching it as far over her head as possible, she swung the stick as hard as she could. The head of the stick struck him squarely on his temple, creating a three-inch gash which immediately began gushing blood, causing him to release her ankle as he screamed in pain.

Tatum's resistance clearly surprised all the men just as much as they had surprised the girls.

Tatum reoriented herself and stood on the trunk of the car, taking aim at Jacko. Reaching up to block her swing, he prevented the stick from landing another headshot. However, the edges of the aluminum handle caught his forearm at full force, chalking up another bloody gash for Tatum while nearly breaking the man's arm.

As the man doubled over in pain, the uninjured man on the passenger side of the car drew a gun from the small of his back and pointed it at Tatum.

All the excitement caused the men still dragging Nicki to speed up and get her to the Suburban. Max, the man from the Town Car, rushed towards Tatum, yelling "Don't shoot her, she's the one we need."

Jumping down from the convertible, Tatum again raised the lacrosse stick into attack position as she charged towards the men carrying Nicki. Landing the base of the stick hard on the back of one of the men's skulls, she felt her knees give out below her and she fell to the road, followed by the man and Nicki.

After tackling Tatum from behind, Max wrestled to get her under control as she wriggled wildly to escape his grip, smacking him with the lacrosse stick with what little power she could muster, but causing no significant physical damage.

"Get over here, will ya?" the man yelled to the last uninjured man on the other side of the convertible. "Who's got the damn chloroform?"

"Right here," yelled Jacko. "Use this," he said as he crawled over to them reaching out the chloroform cloth. He was still in severe pain from his encounter with Tatum's lacrosse stick.

"Get it over her damn face, will you?" Max ordered as he struggled to keep the girl from causing any more damage to the men.

As the other uninjured man made his way over and held Tatum's shoulders down, Jacko attempted to position the chloroformed cloth over her nose.

"Do you guys have any idea what's going to happen when my dad catches up with you?" Tatum protested as she shook her head from side to side, fighting with all her strength to get the men off of her.

"Don't worry, sweetie. We'll be seeing your daddy real soon," Max replied.

Although shaking her head back and forth kept the cloth away from Tatum's face for a few moments, Jacko was eventually able to secure it firmly on her nose, despite his injured forearm. Tatum held her breath, still wriggling; she stared at him with a look that made the obviously hardened man wonder if she had another trick up her sleeve. Within a minute, Tatum had no choice but to breathe, which quickly rendered her unconscious.

As Tatum fell limp, the men relaxed and those that Tatum had left her mark on tended to their wounds. Fortunately for the men, it was the middle of the afternoon on a relatively isolated rural road, and no one had driven by to see the fiasco.

"Get your asses up and get the girls into the Suburban," Max snapped at them all. "And Jacko, get in the girl's car and follow us to the house."

The men, some stumbling and one attempting to orient himself, gathered themselves and the two girls, shoving them into the back of the Suburban. One of the injured men picked up Tatum's lacrosse stick and informed Max, "If she gives me the slightest excuse, she's gonna get a little of her stick back."

"Benny isn't gonna like that. I wouldn't lay a hand on her, unless you want another cut; the kind across your throat," Max replied as he returned to his sedan and led the caravan away.

≈

"Did you see the look on his face?" Parker laughed as he counted out the one hundred eighty-seven thousand dollars Christian had netted from the morning's adventure. "I'm pretty sure that there was actually some smoke seeping out of his ears."

"It was the groveling at the end that I particularly enjoyed," Christian grinned as he steered Juliette's car into Sierra Vista.

"By the way, what's with you giving away my weekend in Cabo with Jules?"

"And deny all those girls that haven't had a chance with you yet? I believe there's still a long line of ladies in waiting."

"Thanks, champ. You really are too considerate."

"No problem. Now listen. Tatum should be home shortly and we're going to need to get into hiding quickly until you can figure out a way to protect us. They've abandoned our places to focus all their manpower on the wild goose chase you sent them on this morning."

"What's your plan, Christian?"

"I need to get our stuff together and think of a good hiding place for Tatum and me while you negotiate whatever legal strategy you've figured out for our friendly government. I really don't relish the idea of being locked up in a basement in some super-secret government facility for the rest of my life."

"Sounds like a plan. I'll drop you off and come back for you in say, half an hour?"

"Don't you think you should be negotiating from your office while we hide?"

"Are you kidding me? They'll haul me off for obstruction of justice and a dozen other things for helping you disappear this morning. They'll make sure we have no contact until you're found, if ever. If I'm going to be able to negotiate on your behalf, I'd better be with you, and figure out a way to contact them securely. I've worked up some good strategies that I think will ensure your security."

"Fair enough. See you in a half an hour," Christian agreed as he pulled the car into his driveway.

Christian parked the car and both men met at the front end of the car, where they shook hands. "I don't think you know what we're going to be up against, Parker. The government has me on highest priority. President Beucler is briefed hourly on the progress of catching up with me. The fun is just beginning, my friend."

"You and me against the 'ole U.S.A., eh? Not even a contest," Parker replied with his usual bravado. "See ya in a half hour."

As Parker drove off, Christian rushed inside and dashed up the steps to his bedroom, not even noticing the mess that the FBI and CIA had left behind.

Grabbing his suitcase from his closet and throwing it on his bed, Christian wasn't giving any thought to anything other than what to pack for himself and Tatum. *She's not going to be happy about all this.*

When she heard the door security alarm chime as Christian entered his house, Heather knew her hunch had been correct. Christian had indeed sent them off in the wrong direction, only to return. Maybe now she could make some headway bringing him in.

Making her way quietly up the stairs, Heather found Christian's room. Leaning against the door frame watching him gather items to pack, Heather calmly confronted him, "Going somewhere, Mister Faraday?"

Startled, Christian looked up at her. "Damn, I thought you were all down at the airport looking for me."

"I guess you should have thought about me just a little harder."

Oh my God! I was just flirting with him! Heather was not a flirt by nature, especially when it came to anything to do with work. Quickly recomposing herself, she returned to the issue. "Christian, we really need to work out some kind of arrangement. I understand your concerns, but you know you can't hide from all the resources we have for very long, don't you?"

"Listen, Miss Johnson—"

"Heather," she corrected him.

"Listen, Heather, I love my country, and want to help any way I can, but I know exactly what the CIA and the FBI have in mind for me, and that's before any political infighting over me. I have no intention of being locked up in a Langley basement being a perceived security risk, regardless of being a valuable source of information."

"I'm sure we can work something out, Christian. We aren't unreasonable and evil people."

Continuing to throw things in his bag, Christian continued, "Don't you understand, Heather? It's not up to you. As we stand here talking, there are Cabinet-level people and the Joint Chiefs of Staff trying to figure out how to outsmart each other and leverage me to their advantage. Not what might be best for the country, not what's best for humanity, but what is best for their political agendas. It's a shame too, but that's the way Washington works. I hate to say it Heather, but this is way above your pretty little pay grade."

"So, what do you plan on doing? Running from the U.S. government? That's not going to get you anywhere for very long."

"Tatum and I will be disappearing for a few days while my attorney negotiates an agreement with your people, one that keeps politics out—," Christian suddenly stopped in mid-sentence and a terrified look appeared on his face. *"Tatum! They've got Tatum!"*

"What are you talking about, Christian? *Who's* got Tatum?"

Just as he realized that Tatum was not on her way home, but had been kidnapped, his mobile phone rang.

Knowing exactly who it was before he even answered, Christian angrily shot into the phone as he answered, "You lay one hand on her and you'll regret the day you were born."

"Mister Faraday," returned Benny's Brooklyn accent, "your daughter is fine. All we want to do is discuss a little business. I'm sure you'll find I'm a reasonable man."

"I'm not reasonable when it comes to someone messing with my daughter. I'm on my way and she better be telling me what a wonderful time she's been having."

"She's just fine, happy as can be. I trust you know how to find us?"

"I know exactly where you are. I even know what color skivvies you're wearing. And if you harm Tatum in any way, I promise you'll be wearing nothing but orange for the rest of your natural life."

Benny was amused by Christian's angry humor. Very few men had the balls to stand up to him, much less in a way that left Benny chuckling. "Orange never did suit me. I'm sure we will be able to work together just fine. Oh, and Mister Faraday, don't be bringing any of your Federale friends."

Christian disconnected the call and curtly informed Heather, "I've got to go. It's been a lot of fun, Miss Johnson. Tell your boss he'll be hearing from Parker." Rushing down the stairs, he left behind the bag he had been packing, as well as the stunned CIA agent.

Heather was not going to let Christian escape again and began rushing down the steps after him. "Who was that? Where are you going, Christian? You're just going to make this worse."

"My life was fine until you and your friends decided that I'm some sort of circus freak and have been trying to take away my life since. I'll take my chances, and be just fine, thank you."

With Heather right behind him, Christian rushed into the garage, heading straight for his motorcycle. "Besides, there's only room for two on this bike."

Shit. They have Nicki too. I'll have to take the car, Christian realized as he went to the garage wall in front of the Volkswagen SUV, his everyday car, and pressed the automatic garage door opener.

Hopping into his SUV, Christian started it up quickly and began backing out of the garage. Rushing after the rolling car, Heather jumped through the open rear window as Christian turned the car ninety degrees, stopping briefly to put the car into drive.

"Whether you believe it or not, Christian, I can help you with both Tatum and the Agency," Heather continued as she pulled herself into the car, not letting the physical challenges bother her in the slightest.

Christian wasn't paying any attention, however. He simply pressed the gas pedal and left a trail of rubber on his driveway as he rushed off to retrieve his daughter.

At Reno Airport, where the FBI had taken over a section to make it their command post while stopping all air traffic, an FBI technician looked at his computer screen and called over to Agent Dawson.

"He's back at his house."

"What do you have?" Dawson responded as he leaned over the man's chair, looking intensely at the monitor.

"He received a call on his mobile phone about five minutes ago and we tracked the signal to his house."

Samuel Waymon stepped up behind them and immediately formulated a plan. "Get air and ground support out there immediately. I don't want anyone in or out of that area without a full vehicle search. No one. Not little old ladies, not flower trucks. No one. Have the air support cover every path, river, creek, and flock of birds to make sure he doesn't leave."

Chapter Sixteen

As Heather climbed into the front seat, Christian took a hard left at the end of his driveway, throwing her up against the passenger door. While still attempting to catch her breath, she continued trying to convince him to stop running. "Christian, you've got to accept the fact you'll have to work with us."

"I've accepted that. You'll have to accept that it's going to be on my terms, not yours. Until my terms are worked out by my attorney and agreed to by the government, you'll just have to do without me," Christian replied, almost nonchalantly. He was not interested in a debate with Heather at this point, but more focused on driving his SUV as fast as he possibly could without running off the winding roads of Sierra Vista.

Slowing down at the gatehouse of the community, Christian leaned out of his window and smiled at the elderly man standing at the door. "In case anyone asks, I wasn't here, Charlie."

Smiling and waving back to Christian, the old man replied, "Haven't seen you all day, Mister Faraday. Have a good one. And hey, by the way, nice legs."

"Thanks, Charlie, I've long admired yours as well."

As Christian floored the car and headed out of the neighborhood, Heather tried to get him focused back on her issue at hand. "You know you really don't have a choice. Let me work something out with the Agency before you make this any worse."

Still little more than ignoring her, Christian responded only for the sake of having a diversion. "And exactly what do you think you can do, that I can't? With all due respect, Agent Johnson, do you really think in this Holy Grail situation you've got any negotiating power on my behalf?"

"Holy Grail. How did you know about Holy Grail?" Catching herself, she gave her forehead a little smack. "Duh, never mind."

"And why do you think I'd trust you anyway? You're a black suit through and through. When it comes down to it, you'll be a good soldier and follow your orders, no matter how much disdain you might have for them."

"Listen, I don't like what they're up to either. I've been around long enough to know what these boys are up to, but the reality is that we're the only game in town, and you'll have to deal with us. You might as well have an insider like me protecting your interests. I might be a 'suit', but I'm one of the good ones. Let me bring you in."

"Nothing doing, sister. I'm not coming in until I know that I'm not going to be the subject of political manipulation. And I would know, you know."

Just then, Heather's mobile phone rang. Christian gave Heather a look that she took exactly as he meant it. "Okay, let's just see how you're going to help me," he challenged her.

Initially caught off guard, Heather knew she had to accept his challenge and prove to Christian she could be trusted. Her respect for him grew with each exchange they had, knowing deep down that he was right.

Heather answered the call and gave Christian a reassuring look, "Johnson."

"Is he at the house?" Marcus' distinctive voice replied. "Waymon's boys just picked up a mobile call from there."

Heather knew she would have to use all her psychology training to keep them both convinced that she was putting their respective priorities first, "What did they pick up?"

"Just that a call had been made to his mobile phone, and it was answered. They're on their way back to the house now."

"He's not there any longer. He just took off."

"What? To where?" Christian heard Marcus' voice over the phone from across the car.

"Don't worry, Marcus, I'm an uninvited guest in his vehicle at the moment. I'm trying to negotiate his turning himself in before the situation gets any worse."

"This isn't a negotiation. There is nowhere to go, and nowhere to hide. Where are you?"

"He has some very legitimate concerns, and if we don't work with him, we're going to lose him altogether. Don't underestimate this man."

"We're not going to lose him, and I want him in now. I've got some men on their way to pick up his daughter from school. Tell him he can meet her here at the airport and we can get on our way to Washington."

Although he hadn't been able to hear the other side of the conversation, Christian knew exactly what Marcus had been saying to Heather. He couldn't help but interject into the conversation at that point. Marcus apparently had no idea that it was a half day at Laurel Ridge Academy, or that the mob already had her. He may as well send them off on another dead end.

Grabbing the phone from Heather, Christian replied to Marcus' demand. "I've been meaning to trade her in for a while now anyway, Agent West. If you think you can tame that stubborn teenager, she's all yours."

Ending the call before Marcus had a chance to respond, Christian handed the phone back to Heather. "That should keep him busy for a while."

"What's going on, Christian? Just where is your daughter?"

"I think you people call that 'need to know'."

As Christian turned a hairpin curve so fast Heather feared that she was going to be thrown out the window, she replied, "Considering you're about to kill me, I think you could at least extend me a little 'need to know' courtesy."

"I didn't invite you along. You're welcome to hop out at any time."

"You're not getting rid of me that easily," Heather replied as she was thrust into him as he made a hard right curve.

In the distance, they could see what appeared to be several dark sedans racing towards them with grille lights flashing. As the vehicles neared, Christian pushed Heather's head down out of sight and warned her, "We've got company. Hang on." He abruptly made a sharp right turn onto a side road.

Recognizing Christian as he passed them in the middle of Christian's turn, Agent Dawson slammed on his brakes and turned his steering wheel as far counterclockwise as he could. The two cars behind him were caught totally off guard and slammed on their brakes as well. The car immediately behind Dawson's veered to the right to avoid Dawson's car. The one behind that had nowhere to go, skidding into the rear passenger side of the middle car. The force knocked it into a ditch with its rear end sticking up and tires spinning.

As Christian sped away, Dawson yelled out the window to the agents behind him, "It's Faraday!" Waving his arm he added, "Follow me!"

The car with all four wheels still on the ground backed up, turned around and sped off after Christian.

Dawson pressed a button on his steering wheel. "Dawson here. In close pursuit of Faraday. Need all available air support."

"We've got your location," a voice returned. All FBI vehicles were equipped with advanced GPS units allowing them to be securely monitored over the internet as well as from one another's vehicles.

"Don't lose him this time, damn it," Waymon's voice joined into the conversation. "What the hell is Williams doing just sitting there?"

"I suspect he's trying to crawl out of his vehicle about now, sir. You might want to send an ambulance to his location just in case."

"Thanks for the concern, Dawson," Williams' voice came over the system. "I'm okay, but I will definitely require a tow."

Waymon, in one of the helicopters involved in the air search, signaled to his pilot to change directions. "I'm on my way to join you now. All air and ground units to the vicinity of Agent Dawson."

While accelerating SUV to its limit, Christian grabbed his phone and dialed Parker.

"Where the hell are you, Faraday?" Christian was greeted by an annoyed Parker who was at Christian's house, looking for him.

"Listen, Parker. Get out of there, now. I'm being chased out here in the boondocks by the Feds. I've got to shake them so I can save Tatum from a bunch of even worse crooks."

"Gambling. Practically exposing yourself on national TV. Toying with authority. You haven't gotten into this much trouble since that rugby tournament in Colorado during third year. What's gotten into you today?" Parker replied as he backed out of Christian's driveway.

"And the day is barely half over. No doubt the fun is just beginning. Now listen, I need you to take the money, go down to West Reno Custom Auto & Electronics on Evermore Street."

"West Reno Custom Auto on Evermore. Got it."

"Ask to speak to Alex, he owns the joint. Tell him you want the green van he just finished customizing."

"And what makes you think he'll part with it?"

"He's putting it up for auction this weekend. Offer him eighty thousand. That's ten grand more than his best hope from the auction. At that premium, he'll sign it over to you on the spot with no questions asked. And throw in another five for his silence."

"And what do I do with it? I never was a van kind of guy, you know."

"Well, buddy, you are today. Just take it and hide away with it until I contact you. Don't go anywhere they might think to look for you." Christian was beginning to get into his groove; becoming skilled at learning what he needed to know and how to piece everything together. "And ditch your phone. Now! Don't worry about me finding you. I'll know where you are and how to reach you. Just stay well hidden."

Ending the call, he tossed the phone out the window into the brush on the side of the road. "So much for tracking my frigging phone calls."

Still out of sight of Dawson, Christian was aware of the converging FBI and police and knew that he had to lose them in order to get to Tatum and Nicki.

While his SUV had still had plenty of distance ahead of Dawson, he knew the souped-up FBI sedans would quickly close in on him if he didn't take evasive action.

Approaching the entrance of a small dirt road on the right, Christian slowed the car and pulled onto it, being careful not to leave any telltale tire marks on either the asphalt or the dirt. Pulling behind some bushes, Christian hid the car from the approaching FBI vehicles.

"Pretty slick, Christian. What now? I told you, there are no places to hide. The minute you think you're safe, they'll be right on your ass. You're fighting the inevitable."

Christian sat back, clasped his hands behind his head, and closed his eyes, not acknowledging Heather's comments. After a brief moment, Christian began slowly counting, "Five, four, three," and the sounds of sirens were heard, quickly increasing in volume, "two, one," at which point the two FBI sedans could be heard speeding past them.

"You were saying?" Christian looked at Heather with a smirk. He started the engine, and began driving down the dirt road, fully aware that the air patrol would soon spot his car.

This guy is out of his mind! We're on a road that doesn't appear to go anywhere but further into the backwoods of Nevada. The road was cut into the grade of a modestly sloped hill, which was reasonably well vegetated, yet not well enough to completely hide the car from aerial view on any sustained basis. Fortunately for Christian, the road, which led to a small reservoir dam, was mostly straight for the several miles to its destination.

"Well, that's just great, Christian, but what are you going to do when this no doubt dead-ends in the middle of nowhere?"

"The first thing on my agenda is to determine if you're really interested in helping me," Christian stated as he accelerated to forty-five miles per hour, then pressed the cruise control button on the steering wheel. "Mind if I borrow your bra?"

The sound of several helicopters could be heard coming from a distance and it was clear that one of them was quickly gaining on them.

"This is the FBI," a loudspeaker from the helicopter directly above blared. "You are ordered to pull over and stop immediately."

"My bra? Don't you think we ought to get to know each other a little better first?"

"Do you believe in me or not, Heather?" Christian challenged her with a very serious look.

Heather knew she had no choice. Christian was making her prove she was indeed committed to doing the right thing. She had enough psychology training to realize she wasn't going to be able to debate her way out of this with a man of such strong character and conviction. He was clearly making her prove herself. If she didn't show a significant level of faith, she could blow the opportunity to show him that he could trust her.

Heather had no idea what Christian planned for her bra, but she removed her jacket and lifted her blouse out of her skirt. As she began reaching up under the blouse, she nonetheless felt the need to put up at least a semblance of a defense regarding her modesty. "Don't get too full of yourself just because you're the only man that's been able to get me to do this. It's only 'cause I believe in you, Christian."

Heather began manipulating her bra under her blouse the way women seem to have a naturally inborn ability to do. However, to the male observer, the maneuver had all the magic and mystery of one of Houdini's more amazing secrets.

"You've forgotten your senior prom date, already?" Christian couldn't help tossing out that little tidbit. This comment definitely took the serious look off his face and almost caused him to begin laughing.

"Okay, buster. Let's not even go there," she replied in protest as she pulled the elegant white silk lace bra out from under her blouse. While the exchange was amusing even to her, she maintained a serious look on her blushing face in an effort to retain some dignity. He was definitely going to be the biggest professional challenge she'd ever had to deal with. *Heaven help any woman that gets involved with him!*

"Nice taste, young lady. Never would have expected this from a CIA agent." Christian knew good quality in general but was particularly versed in women's lingerie as Stephanie's taste in this area was also for the finest. Stephanie had acquired her appreciation of fine lingerie from her career, which included an extensive amount of lingerie modeling as she looked so damn good in it. Christian was just thankful for his budget that she received most of her collection gratis from her clients.

Not one to spend much on herself either, Heather had been socking a substantial amount of her pay into retirement investments, planning a comfortable early retirement by the age of forty-five. A tough challenge, but she had no children, lived modestly, and the CIA took care of most of her day-to-day living expenses due to her extensive travel. Her only real expenses were on her adventure vacations and fine lingerie; her only notable weakness.

During her worldly travels, Heather always sought out the highest quality pieces made of the finest materials. As a child, Heather had been deprived of so many things. Once she discovered, quite by accident, the decadent feel of an outrageously expensive bra, she was hooked. She had a taste of the opulence she wished for as a child yet had been completely out of her reach. She had no desire to show any pretensions publicly. This was her private luxury and lifted her out of the otherwise all too often sleazy world she lived in. It was very rare for a man to see them at all, and unheard of within just hours of meeting someone.

"I'm not your typical CIA, or haven't you figured that out yet? And don't be expecting any more where that came from, I don't care how much you think I need to prove myself."

Christian winked at her and accepted the bra. Tapping into his extensive rope knotting experience, Christian secured the steering wheel in position so it would remain straight without any human assistance.

As the car entered a heavily shaded area, Christian slowed the car to idling speed. Although they could hear the helicopters overhead, the vegetative canopy would hide them from the FBI. "It's time to contin-ue on foot, Heather. I'd take off those heels, if I were you."

This was an important moment for Heather; she knew she had at least partially won him over as he was inviting her along as opposed to making her chase him. Removing her heels and grabbing her suit jack-et, Heather followed Christian's lead and opened her door, jumping out of the barely moving car. Heather caught up with the car enough to close the door then stopped, awaiting Christian's next move.

On the other side of the car, Christian reached in through the win-dow and pressed the 'Resume' cruise control button on the steering wheel and watched the car rapidly accelerate down the road.

"Quick, it's only a matter of time before they catch up with it and figure out what I've done with the help of your unmentionables," Chris-tian yelled to Heather as he reached out his hand to her. This was an even clearer sign of acceptance. Heather was beginning to feel that Christian might just possibly be considering them a team.

Taking his hand, she followed him down the hill, being careful to stay in a course covered by trees in order to avoid visual contact by those in the choppers. They heard the helicopters pass, and when they reached a ravine near the bottom of the hill, they watched Dawson's car speed by at the point they had left Christian's SUV.

As they crouched in the ravine to avoid being seen, Christian asked for Heather's phone.

"Ordering some take-out, I hope. I'm starving," Heather smiled as she handed her mobile to him.

"I was thinking Italian. Does that work for you?" Christian replied as he dialed a number on her phone.

≈

In the large, walnut-paneled office of his home, Benny Malone was surprised when his mobile phone rang. Benny shared this number with very few, and everyone who had it was in the room with him for the impending interrogation of Faraday.

"Who the hell is this?" Benny barked into the phone. With three of his men wounded, not to mention two belligerent teenagers that had been threatening them all since they woke up, he was in no mood to deal with any more difficulties.

"I'm going to need a ride, Malone." Benny immediately recognized the voice as that of Christian. "We've been a little sidetracked. Pick me up where Riverbluff and Skyline Canyon Roads meet. Better make it quick as the FBI is pretty anxious to find me as well."

"Damn it, Faraday," Benny barked into the phone. He was losing his patience with all the delays. "Fine, I'll have a car there in ten minutes. And no more bullshit."

Benny called out to two of the men sitting on a sofa in the next room tending to their wounds. "Get off your ass and get over to Riverbluff and Skyline Canyon Roads. Faraday is waiting there."

The two men looked at each other, wishing they had more time to recover from their encounter with his daughter. They certainly were not looking forward to dealing with the old man.

"Don't worry, you wussies, he's not going to risk any harm to his precious little girl. I think you'll be safe enough. Now get your asses out of here. I want you back in twenty minutes," Benny ordered.

As the two men got up and headed towards the front door, Benny glanced at the girls, tied up in chairs in opposite corners at one end of the room. Turning his attention to the remaining men, Benny ordered, "Get the daughter ready."

Tatum was scared but was not going to let these thugs see it. "As if you guys have any chance with my dad. He hates your type and is smarter than the bunch of you. By the time he gets through with you, you're going to wish you had never messed with us."

Lighting his cigar, Malone stared at her for a moment then turned away, ignoring her protests. Two of his men went to Tatum and picked up her chair, moving her through a pair of French doors leading to a deck overhanging the cliff on which the house was sitting. The third man followed with a three-foot wooden rod.

≈

Crouching in the ravine, Christian pointed to a specific point on the road to the east. "See where those two roads meet, Heather?"

Heather looked, then nodded her head.

"We've got to get there quickly. It looks like the only safe path that has sufficient cover is over there on the right, through the trees." Christian paused and gave Heather a concerned look, "Do you think you can keep up in those bare feet on this terrain?" Christian noticed that she had been examining her feet, most likely out of concern that her hose were getting torn up pretty badly.

"I'll tell you what, Christian. The day you've outsmarted a leopard who's in hot pursuit while climbing mountains in Tibet, you can question my ability in environments like this." Her look changed from that of serious to a playful smile, "The real question here is, can you?" With that, Heather winked at him and took off into the trees.

Christian was completely caught off guard by Heather's resilience, as well as her playfulness. Watching her make her way through the ravine, he couldn't help but admire her spunk; not to mention the undeniably awesome figure the athletic woman displayed as she masterfully coordinated running through a maze of small, ragged boulders. He caught himself and his obvious attraction for her, something he hadn't experienced for anyone since the death of Stephanie, then quickly began the trek after her.

Chapter Seventeen

Samuel Waymon ordered his pilot to pull ahead of Christian's car. "We'll set down in the large clearing up ahead," he said into the microphone of the helicopter radio. "Unit two, do you see the break in the trees up ahead?"

"I see it, sir," returned Agent Carver's voice over the radio.

"I want you to drop some spikes there. I think you have enough time to get there ahead of Faraday, if you hustle."

"On our way, sir," Carver responded, motioning his pilot to the area Waymon had indicated.

"Drop the spikes as soon as we're in position," Carver yelled to the pilot.

Christian's SUV continued to stay straight on the road at an even forty-five miles per hour while Dawson's and another vehicle rapidly gained on it.

"Careful, Dawson, we're about to spike the road. Best keep your distance," Carver warned him.

As the two ground vehicles began to slow down in order to avoid the spikes, Samuel Waymon's helicopter was setting down about a quarter mile ahead of where the spikes would be dropped. Hopping out of the helicopter, he began running towards the location he expected Christian's SUV would come to a halt.

Carver's pilot carefully positioned himself as close to the road as possible, without danger of the propellers clipping the trees, and pulled a lever on the instrument panel. Simultaneously, an exterior double latch opened near the rear of the craft and hundreds of sharp jumping-jack-shaped tire deflation spikes fell onto the dirt road.

Dawson watched from behind as Christian's SUV entered the field of spikes that had just been dropped, a few bounced off the SUV before continuing to fall to the ground.

As Dawson pulled up to the field, careful to avoid the spikes, he watched as the tires on Christian's SUV started tearing apart; pieces of rubber pulling off the wheels and dropping onto the road.

Inside the phantom car, the steering wheel was shaking hard from the forces placed on the wheels and the tearing rubber. Even the combination of Heather's high-quality bra and Christian's formidable knotting skills couldn't handle the forces exerted by the conditions now in play.

When tire deflation spikes are deployed, the driver normally realizes there is nothing more he or she can do and brings the car to a halt; usually staying and giving up, but all too often making a run for it on foot. The FBI agents in pursuit watched in amazement as the SUV did not slow down and began to lose control.

Suddenly, Heather's bra snapped due to the physics in play—the steering wheel no longer able to keep the front wheels straight. The SUV began swerving wildly and within a few moments veered off the road and lunged down the hill, knocking over brush and bouncing off small boulders and trees before finally coming to rest at the trunk of a large pine tree.

Holy shit! If Faraday is injured, I'll be in some serious career jeopardy. Running towards the scene of the crash, Waymon yelled into his radio, "Ambulance to the scene, immediately!"

Back at the spike field on the road, Dawson turned to the driver of the other sedan, "Get these spikes cleared up and move our cars out of the way. An ambulance will need to get through." He and Waymon ran towards the edge of the road where Christian's car went over.

Both Waymon and Dawson reached the scene at the same time and ran down the hill to Christian's vehicle.

≈

With the FBI's full focus on the crash site, no one noticed as Heather and Christian came out of the brush and headed towards the black Suburban that had just arrived at the intersection a couple of miles away. The two men saw the pair approaching and got out of the vehicle to greet them in their own personal way.

Pulling their pistols from behind their backs where they had been tucked in behind their black jeans, they motioned Christian and Heather against the car.

"Who's the broad?" asked Jacko, looking none too happy about the complication. "We're only to pick up you, Faraday. Benny didn't say nothing about no babe."

Positioning himself in front of Heather to shield her, Christian looked at them coldly. "But he did tell you to pick me up, and that I had better get there quickly and safely. If you don't do those two things, your lives won't be worth your weight in pond scum." Pausing, he gave them a moment to reflect on their position. "Now, unless you want me to make a run for it and screw everything up for you, I'd suggest we get in your car and start driving."

The men looked at each other, realizing they had no leverage, even with their handguns. "Okay," replied the driver of the car, "Let's get going then."

"Not so fast," Christian replied. "Toss the guns. Now." he instruct-ed while nodding off to the side of the road. "I never feel comfortable when people have those things around."

"We ain't tossin' our guns, mister. Now let's go. Get in the car."

"Have it your way then," Christian replied as he took Heather's arm and started walking away from the Suburban. "Feel free to explain to Benny how you couldn't do a simple task like pick me up and get me to his house—unless you're planning on shooting us, of course."

Realizing that if they didn't cooperate with Christian's demand, he was going to make this far more difficult than it need be. If he was half the headache his daughter was, they were certainly going to be in trouble with the boss if anything complicated getting Christian to the house. Besides, he was sure Christian wasn't going to do anything to jeopardize them getting him to his daughter.

"Okay, Faraday, whatever you say. Let's just get going."

Christian turned around and waited for the men, who hesitantly flipped their guns off to the side of the road into the brush.

"Are you happy now, Faraday? Can you get in the damn car now?"

"Works for me," Christian replied as he slowly started towards the car, still arm in arm with Heather.

Feeling comfortable that they were finally getting underway, the men approached the car. Christian looked straight ahead while moving his head a bit closer to Heather's. "Think you can take the shorter fel-la?" he whispered.

"Before you can take the other, I'd bet," Heather whispered back.

After a brief smile and look of challenge in each other's eyes, they rushed their respective targets from behind. Before either man could so much as turn their heads, their attackers were upon them.

On the driver's side, Christian's right fist caught Jacko's jaw just as he turned his head in response to the sound of Christian rushing him. Stumbling forward with his back still towards Christian, Jacko quickly regained his balance. As he turned to confront his attacker, he found Christian in midair headed down upon him.

On the other side of the car, a kick to the back of the knee, followed by slamming the man's head against the side of the car as he fell, made quick work of Heather's task. After running to pick up one of the tossed pistols, Heather rushed back to the scuffle between Christian and Jacko.

Christian, who had been knocked back against the car by his opponent, scrambled to his feet. Just as Christian was about to body slam him again, Jacko suddenly put his hands up in surrender. A look of satisfaction came over Christian's face as he asked, "Had enough already?"

"I think it's me he's worried about, big boy," Heather interjected.

Turning around, Christian saw Heather pointing the pistol directly at Jacko.

"I'd of had him in a minute, you know."

"I have complete confidence you would have. Would you like me to let you continue your thrashing?"

"That's sweet of you, but we've no time to waste. We've got to get to Tatum." Turning to Jacko, Christian ordered, "Up against the car." Turning back to Heather with an impish grin, Christian asked, "Heather, you wouldn't mind parting with a little more of your lingerie, would you?"

"You know, they're going to have a fit when they see the expense report from all this, don't you? What in the world could you need now?"

"Since your hose are already shredded from the run through the woods, certainly we can get a little more use from them before they get trashed."

"Sure, Christian. Three hundred fifty euros in French silk is already ruined, I might as well get my money's worth, huh?"

"Your wrists are in for quite a treat. Agent Johnson doesn't use this stuff to tie up just anybody." Turning to Heather with a perplexed look, "You actually paid three hundred and fifty euros for one pair of stockings?"

"My only real weakness, I'm afraid."

Infuriated that Christian had tricked them so, Jacko hit his head against the side of the Suburban. Heather pulled off her stockings, one leg at a time.

"He's all yours, Heather. Have your way with him," Christian said.

Retrieving the limp body from the other side of the car, Christian couldn't help but comment on their obvious wounds to Jacko. "You boys had a little trouble already today, I see. Those cuts look awfully fresh."

"The little bitch that did this to me didn't turn out quite so clean," he replied, hoping to piss Christian off, not yet fully understanding the depth of his ability.

Christian couldn't help but laugh, "Nice try, Gotti, but had you put so much as a scratch on that girl, I'd have put you face down in the creek over there by now. Just be thankful that it was five of you big strong men against her. I'm pretty sure just the two of you punks wouldn't have stood a chance. Quite a girl, isn't she?"

Once the men had their hands secured behind them, Christian opened the passenger door and indicated to Jacko to get in the front. The man snarled, but reluctantly climbed in the front of the Suburban. *What the hell is Benny going to do about this?*

Closing the door, Christian opened the rear door and motioned to the other, now conscious, man, "Now you."

"Watch these boys for a moment will you, Heather?" Christian went around to the other side of the vehicle, opened the back door and climbed in. As he leaned over the back of the back seat reaching for something, he added, "You boys comfortable? Anything I can get you before we head home?"

"Benny is expecting us now. If we aren't back soon, your daughter will not be among the living for long," Jacko replied.

"We'll be getting on our way in just a moment, just one more thing to deal with." Christian leaned over the seat with one of the chloroform cloths the men had used on the girls. Before he could react, Christian had the cloth firmly over his nose until he fell limp. Just as Jacko opened his mouth to object, Heather placed the gun against his temple through the open window. Jacko immediately shut up and accepted his treatment.

"This is for my little girl. Sweet dreams, Gotti!" Christian put the cloth firmly over the man's nose and watched as he slumped over. Hopping out of the car and getting in the driver's seat, Christian called over to Heather, "Come on Heather, we've got a couple of girls to tend to."

Christian started the SUV. Looking in the direction of the crash scene, he saluted and drove away.

Just as the ambulance appeared at the crest of the hill, Waymon and Dawson reached Christian's SUV. Waymon went around to the driver's side while Dawson headed to the passenger side. Not noticing the bra tied onto the steering wheel due to the deployed airbag now draping the steering wheel, the first thing Waymon noted was that Christian was not inside.

"Shit, he must have taken off on foot," Waymon proclaimed as he pulled his head out of the car and began looking around the surrounding area. "That must mean he's okay. Any sign of him that direction?" he asked Dawson.

"Nothing here, sir."

Samuel Waymon pulled out his radio, "Suspect on foot. All ground units report to the crash site to begin a ground search. Air units form a search pattern of the area." Putting the radio down and turning to Dawson he added, "No way he could have gotten too far."

As Waymon began to survey the scene for signs of disturbance to the natural area, Dawson took a closer look inside the car for signs of blood or other injury. Leaning in over the passenger seat, Dawson lifted up the airbag and caught sight of the white lace bra tied onto the steering wheel.

"Hey, boss. Check this out."

Waymon leaned into the car and watched as Dawson lifted up the bra, exposing the knots on the steering wheel. "I don't think he's anywhere down here."

Livid, Waymon slammed his fist on the roof of the car, "Son of a bitch threw us off again." Calming down, he raised his radio, "Carver, Faraday wasn't in the car, we'll need to expand our search area. Look around and see where he could have jumped out of the car without being seen from above."

"Yes, sir," Carver responded as he signaled the pilot to turn around.

Waymon needed to calm down so he could get back in control of the situation. Never in all his years had one individual given him the slip so often; in such little time, no less. "All air units grid search a half mile off this dirt road all the way back to the beginning. I want all roads within a mile of here closed and all traffic fully searched."

Throwing the radio to Dawson, he instructed him to coordinate a ground search once Carver had worked up a starting point. "Get K-9 units out here and cover every inch of the area."

"Yes, sir. Where are you off to?"

"Probably to a basement desk job in Alaska," Waymon replied as he headed up the hill to report the latest to Washington.

≈

Well outside of the search area by now, Heather and Christian remained anxious to get to Tatum. "Just what happened to these guys anyway, Christian?" Heather asked.

"Let's just say they found out just how feisty my little girl can be when she's pissed off," Christian laughed. "Even I'm not that brave."

"Is she okay?"

"Sure, she's fine. Her ego is a little bruised and she has a little chloroform hangover, but they're smart enough not to mess with her if they want anything from me."

"Who is this Benny guy, anyway?" While the FBI was closely engaged with investigating the Malone organization, the CIA had little to do with the situation and Heather was totally unfamiliar with the man.

"He's a Brooklyn transplant from the old country; brought here years ago to keep an eye on some mob family activities. He's head of his own family now, controlling a huge territory from here to northern California."

"And I take it he wants you to provide him with privileged information to help him avoid problems with Federal agencies?"

"That and he's hoping I can supply inside information on the other families."

"Now do you see why you need the CIA's assistance?" Heather thought she'd have one more go at it.

"And who is going to protect me from the CIA?" Christian asked back.

"Touché." Heather was through debating him on the subject. "You win, Christian. Sign me up on your team."

"And for some reason you think you'll have an easier time getting those expense reports past me?" he smiled.

Pulling up to the entrance gate of Benny Malone's compound, Christian pressed a button on the dashboard and the gate began to open up. While they waited, Christian and Heather were viewed through a pair of binoculars from a sedan across the street.

Christian drove up the steep winding driveway leading up to a rustic, yet expansive cliffside house. Pulling off at a spot just out of sight of the house, Christian stopped and closed his eyes for a few minutes. He looked at Heather with deep concern. "You don't have to come in, you know. There's a bunch of real scumbags in there."

"You can't even imagine some of the scum I've had to deal with, Christian." She stopped and corrected herself, "Well, maybe you could. At any rate, there is no way I'm going to miss another real-life episode of Superman."

Christian continued to be impressed with her spunk and chuckled, "I'd rather be in a few real-life episodes of Gilligan's Island right now. Okay. Here's the situation. Benny and his bigwigs are in his office. Two of the goon squad are in his living room, just inside the front door. Nicki is safe in a corner, but they've rigged Tatum up in a dangerous situation on the deck to make sure I'll cooperate. He's got one of his goons out there with her too."

"I've got an idea for neutralizing the guys in the living room so we can get in and secure Tatum and Nicki," Heather said.

"You're the pro; I'll follow your lead. Hang on. Let me give this cloth another dose." Christian went to the back seat and saturated it in more chloroform to keep it fresh.

"Looks like our boys are pretty secure here," Heather noted as she lifted up the limp head of one of the men by his hair then let it fall back down. "Shall we go save the damsels in distress?"

"I'd bet good money that Benny is the one in distress from having to deal with her," Christian replied as he placed the cloth in his rear pocket. "Hell, it's usually me in distress, and she loves me."

As the two cautiously approached the front door being careful to stay out of sight of any windows, Heather felt she had to remind Christian of one additional thing, "You do know that I'm down to my last undergarment."

"I know. And a fine one it is, too. Not to worry, I'm sure I'll find something useful for it."

≈

As Waymon sat in the cab of the helicopter, thinking of how he should break this to Washington, his mobile phone rang.

"Waymon," he answered tersely.

"Morris here, sir." Morris was one of only a few FBI agents not working on the Faraday case. Morris was assigned to keep an eye on Benny Malone, another high priority case; made more so by Christian's revelations the night before. He would be rejoined by the rest of his team once they were free of the current crisis.

"Morris, I don't have any time for Malone today. I'm right in the middle of the Faraday crisis."

"I understand, sir, but you'll never guess who just pulled into Malone's driveway."

Waymon jumped up from the helicopter seat. "Faraday?"

"Yes, sir. He just drove up in one of Malone's vehicles. One of Malone's men was passed out in the passenger seat and there appeared to be another unconscious man next to a woman in the back seat."

Waymon was ecstatic; Morris might just have saved his neck. "Pull your car up and block anyone from exiting that driveway until we get there. Not a soul leaves, is that understood, Morris?"

"Yes, sir."

"And, Morris. Thanks."

Grabbing the helicopter microphone, Waymon broadcast the latest step in the cat-and-mouse game that the Faraday case had become.

"All units to the Malone compound. Carver, coordinate closing the roads in and out of Malone's neighborhood. Dawson, meet me over at the compound with whatever units Carver doesn't need. Make sure you get the SWAT teams in place, too. Give me the signal when you are ready to go in, I don't want to arrive ahead of you and give them a chance to scatter."

Spinning his finger, Waymon indicated to the pilot that they needed to take off. "To Malone's compound, as fast as you can get us there."

Chapter Eighteen

Parker's mind had been in overdrive all day, but particularly so since his last conversation with Christian. Not having the luxury of Christian's insight, Parker felt as if he were in the dark. He was usually the one making plans and sending out his minions to carry out his instructions. Now he was running errands while not knowing what was going on with Christian and Tatum, let alone whether they were even safe. Parker didn't like being in this position, but just as Christian had learned to unconditionally trust Parker, Parker never questioned Christian. He had to have faith, now more than ever.

Parker always hated driving down to the industrial sections of Reno. It wasn't too bad ten years earlier, but the growth the city had experienced in the last decade left so much of it a traffic nightmare; getting from one side of town to the other had become a major pain.

Following the directions being dictated to him from the navigation system in Juliette's car, Parker pulled onto Evermore and began looking closely for a sign leading him to West Reno Custom Auto & Electronics. Evermore was right in the heart of this particular cinderblock-constructed industrial park. It was populated by various businesses, such as large-scale print shops, body shops, and distribution warehouses.

Parker had never personally dealt with West Reno Custom Auto & Electronics. However, being one of Nevada's premier auto customization shops, many of his clients had relationships with them. Parker had certainly dealt with their attorneys from time to time on contractual issues, fortunately nothing of a contentious nature. One casino client had their stretch limo fleet practically built from scratch, from the stretching to the luxury interiors, outfitted with everything from custom massaging seats to satellite television and internet. Other high-end businesses used their services for executive vehicles of all types. One client had a personal party van created for nights on the town.

Finally spotting the distinctive signage for West Reno Custom Auto & Electronics, Parker turned into the parking lot in front of the rather nondescript glass door with an 'Open' sign hanging in it. To the left there were several oversized garage doors from which loud, and often very strange, noises emerged.

Parker entered the building and was surprised to find a very clean and high-tech reception area; much larger than he would have imagined. About the size of a couple of garage bays in and of itself, the reception area was primarily a series of displays of high-end automotive parts and electronics. There were displays of shiny spinning wheels, custom exhaust systems, automotive satellite TV and navigation systems, and many contraptions Parker had absolutely no idea what they were.

Off to one corner sat the modest reception counter. Approaching the counter Parker noticed brochures describing their ability to customize any automobile to any specifications with the latest high-tech accessories.

"Can I help you, sir?" the very beautiful and scantily dressed young blonde greeted him.

"Yes. I need to see Alex Gutierrez about an urgent matter."

"I'm afraid Alex is in a meeting right now. Probably won't be available for at least the next hour," the girl replied.

Leaning over the counter towards the handsome, dapper, and most probably wealthy, man in front of her, she continued, "Is there anything *I* can do for you?"

Attempting not to be distracted by the girl's penetrating blue eyes, contagious smile, stunning blonde mane, and deliberately exposed cleavage, Parker lifted the nylon bag he was carrying and placed it on the table. Opening it up, Parker intentionally exposed to the Daisy Duke look-alike the straps of cash from the casino. Pulling a hundred-dollar bill from one of the stacks, Parker placed it on the counter in front of the girl. "I don't think you understand, Miss. This is a *very* urgent matter. I need to see Alex immediately."

Retrieving the bill, the girl smiled even more broadly as she stood up straight, folded the bill, and slipped it beneath her blouse and into her bra. "I'll see what I can do, sir. Could I tell him who's asking?"

"Farr. Parker Farr." Parker never could resist the Bond act.

With that, the girl flirtatiously walked to, then disappeared behind, a door leading to the office area of the building.

Parker began pacing around the showroom. Once he shook the thought of the girl from his head, he began to ponder just what Christian had in mind with this van. *And what kind of van is worth eighty thousand dollars? I hope she comes with it!* Parker really hated being out of the loop and not in total control. He simply wasn't used to being the good soldier, blindly following instructions.

After a few minutes, a rough biker looking man in his mid-thirties emerged from the office door and approached Parker on the showroom floor as he admired some automotive contraption, having no idea what it was. "Alex Gutierrez," the man outstretched his hand to Parker. "I understand you have an urgent need of some sort."

"Good afternoon, Mister Gutierrez. Parker Farr," he replied, while returning the handshake.

Alex was quite familiar with Parker's reputation as Reno's most no-torious man about town. He had also seen his name on many a letter-head and contract that had crossed his desk over the years. Alex was surprised by a personal visit from the great Mister Farr himself. Fortu-nately for Parker, Alex had been in his office since the early morning hours and was not aware of the massive search for Parker and Chris-tian.

"Well, Mister Farr, this certainly is an honor. How can I help you?" Alex ushered Parker over to a table in the corner of the showroom.

"You have a vehicle that I'd like to purchase," Parker replied.

"I have several that are for sale, I like to tinker and make new toys all the time," Alex replied. Pointing to the chairs at the table, Alex sug-gested he have a seat. "Which one did you have in mind?"

"I believe you just completed a very special green van."

Alex was obviously surprised. The van Parker referred to had been a top secret vehicle until recently, when it was announced within the cus-tom auto community. Alex hoped to drum up interest for this week-end's auction. While Alex certainly expected the van to create a buzz within the community, he never expected someone like Parker Farr to be beating down a path looking for it.

Getting over the initial intimidation of having Reno's most powerful attorney in front of him, Alex turned back to his business mode. "That van has been drawing a lot of attention. I've got it slated for auction this weekend. You're welcome to join the bidding if you like."

Reaching into the bag, Parker began pulling out the straps of hun-dred-dollar bills. "I'm prepared to pay you eighty thousand, cash. And I need it right away."

Clearly tempted, Alex figured that if this was Parker's opening offer, there was no doubt room for negotiation. "Mister Farr, there is an aw-ful lot of interest in this vehicle. I expect the bidding to be fierce on Saturday."

Parker smiled. *Who does this guy think he is, trying to out-negotiate me?* "Do you mind if I make a quick call?" Parker asked as he reached over to the phone on the other side of the table.

Thinking he was calling a client to get permission to raise his offer, Alex slid the phone to him. "Sure, take your time."

Parker dialed a number and pressed the speakerphone button on the phone.

Over the speaker came the voice of a chipper young lady, "Miss Cano's office."

Regina Cano was the closest thing to a female version of Parker Farr that existed in Reno. Long-legged and often described in the society pages as 'luscious', Regina was a single socialite with looks, brains, and power. Although she and Parker might have seemed a perfect match in so many ways, both of them knew that would be dangerous territory, so neither one ever once acted on the idea. One of them was bound to get hurt. Privately, each of them thought that the other was capable of breaking their heart. They confined themselves to being active participants in the Reno social scene; seen at the same parties and other functions on many occasions.

After completing Georgetown Law School twenty-two years ago, Regina came out to visit a friend in Reno and never left. Beginning her career as an assistant in-house counsel for a modest-sized casino, Regina navigated her career through several mergers to become the president of the second largest casino in Reno. The Fleur-de-Lis had been Reno's largest, until the Mediterranean opened.

"Good afternoon, Angel," Parker said in his usual charming voice. "Is she in?"

Recognizing his voice immediately, the secretary on the other end became even perkier, "Mister Farr! How are you today?"

Alex was visibly impressed. The Fleur-de-Lis was an account he had been trying to get for years but was securely locked up by his main competitor in the custom limo business. He was unaware, however, that Parker was the Fleur-de-Lis' primary outside counsel and that he and Regina were the best of friends. Alex was also not privy to the knowledge that Parker was just about to finalize canceling the contract with Alex's competitor due to some significant disputes with their last several orders. This was not public knowledge, but Parker saw no harm in using the information to his advantage.

Alex leaned forward to more clearly hear the conversation.

"Great, Angel, how about you?"

"Wonderful thanks, but I'm afraid Miss Cano is not in right now, she's down on the floor with some VIPs. I'm sure she wouldn't mind if you called her on her mobile, though. Would you like me to forward you over to her?"

Alex would never have the chance to have a conversation with Regina Cano, and he knew it. The chance to listen in on a speakerphone call with her was something he had to control his excitement about.

Knowing he had Alex's interest piqued, Parker smiled and shook his head. "That's okay, no need to disturb her. Could you just tell her I'm with a friend that can help with that fleet expansion issue we discussed the other day?   I'd like to continue our talk as soon as she has the opportunity."

"Sure, Mister Farr. I know she's been anxious to follow up with you on that issue."

"Thanks, Angel."

"My pleasure, Mister Farr. And oh, can I ask you a favor?"

"Sure, Angel, anything."

"I have a friend from LA visiting for a few weeks; would it be okay if I brought her with me to your party next Saturday?"

"Angel, any friends of yours are always welcome."

"Thanks, Mister Farr. Regina and I have been raving about your parties to her; she'll be really excited. We'll all be coming together."

"Great, see you then, Angel."

"Bye, Mister Farr."

Alex sat in stunned amazement. Not only did he get to see the legendary Parker Farr in action with a woman, but he demonstrated that he could make or break Alex's plans for getting into the Fleur-de-Lis with a single phone call.

"Now, about that eighty thousand?"

"Eighty thousand will be perfect, Mister Farr," Alex replied quickly, almost jumping from his chair to shake his hand.

Parker just loved blowing people's minds, and he now had Alex's total attention.

"Great, I'd like to conclude this as quickly as possible."

"We weren't planning on detailing it for a couple of days yet, but I can reassign some people to get it done now."

"No detailing will be necessary. It's only important that it's fully operational." Parker had no idea what 'fully operational' meant in this case, but whatever it was, Christian would be expecting it.

"Not a problem, Mister Farr. Bring the van, or any other car you like, anytime, and we'll detail it for you at no charge."

Picking up the phone, Alex dialed an extension and waited a moment. "Jim, bring up the green van to bay two, right away, and make sure it's ready to go." Without waiting for a response from his worker, he hung up the phone and turned back to Parker.

"You do have time for a demonstration, I trust."

Demonstration? What the hell does this van do, anyway? The mystery grew more intriguing for Parker, but he couldn't let on. Nor did he have any idea how much time he did or didn't have so he figured he'd better get on his way.

"That won't be necessary," Parker replied. "If you don't mind, I'd like to just collect the van and get going."

Alex insisted that it was a complex operation, but Parker simply pulled out the cash and counted it out, causing Alex to quickly cease with objections.

"Here's an extra ten grand for you and your staff for everyone's utmost discretion in this matter, regardless of who asks." Christian had only instructed five, but with all the attention their case was getting, Parker figured a little insurance was probably in order.

"Thanks, that's very generous," Alex replied as he accepted the cash. "We always respect our customer's privacy, Mister Farr."

"This time it's going to be a little more difficult for you. If any word of this transaction leaks, or that I was even here, you'll never have the opportunity to meet Miss Cano," Parker added with a very serious look on his face. "I hope we understand each other, Alex."

"Perfectly. But the paperwork?"

"Just sign the title and I'll take care of it from there. Forget you ever saw me or that van. Clear?"

"Absolutely. Let me show you your purchase now," Alex led him behind the counter and towards the door that led out to the shop floor.

"Nice to meet you, Mister Farr," the girl behind the counter smiled as she waved goodbye to him with a perky and flirtatious smile.

Just for the fun of it, and since Parker cannot help being a constant flirt, he reached into the bag and pulled out another hundred-dollar bill. With a wink he tucked it in her blouse himself. "Was a pleasure meeting you too, sweetie."

The girl giggled as he walked through the door.

As they entered the shop area, Parker watched as Alex's man drove a green Ford utility van up to one of the open bays. It looked like any other panel van—no windows on the sides, two doors in the back, a door on the passenger and driver's side. *Pretty regular van. Nice if you're a plumber, I guess.*

Alex excused himself, returning a few moments later with a shiny, briefcase-sized metal case.

"You're sure you don't want a demonstration?" Alex asked as he handed the case to Parker.

"Positive. I really have to get going. We'll have no problem with it."

"Good luck with it, Mister Farr. Don't hesitate to let me know if I can do anything else for you."

"Yes," Parker pulled out Juliette's car keys and threw them to Alex. "Would you mind keeping this car somewhere, completely out of sight, for a few days?"

Chapter Nineteen

Benny Malone and five of his men sat in Benny's office discussing the issues that Christian would help them with. These men were his senior 'executives', essentially 'underbosses', each managing different territories and activities for Benny's comfortably-sized fiefdom. Benny never wanted his organization to grow too large. He was well into his fifties now and wanted to enjoy himself with the ample operation he had built. He'd seen too many of his Mafia brethren get greedy and then killed for not recognizing their limitations and being happy with what they had.

In the adjacent living room, two of Benny's 'enforcers' kept an eye on Nicki, who remained tied up in the corner, while the other waited out on the porch with Tatum.

"My priorities are what's going on with our cocaine pipeline and who's got designs on our port monopoly, including what politicians they're starting to pay off," Benny informed his men. "I also want to know who's been cutting into our loan sharking business in Sacramento." Turning to one of the men he asked, "What are your needs from this psycho, John?"

While each 'executive' individually discussed what he needed from Christian, on the other side of the closed door to the living room, two of his men awaited the return of their colleagues, and the famous Mister Faraday.

"So, what's the boss gonna do with Faraday and the brats once he's through with 'em?" one of them asked Max.

"You can bet they aren't gonna be allowed back out where the Feds can get to them and screw with us, like he tried to do last night," Max replied. Looking over at Nicki who had been observing the men, he added with a snicker, "Don't worry sweetie, you'll get used to us. And if you don't, off to a Mexican whorehouse you go."

As the men laughed, they heard a thump outside. It wasn't the sound of a car arriving, but nothing so unusual that they would worry too much about it.

"Go see what that is," Max ordered the other man.

The man on the sofa rolled his eyes and got up. "You know, I can barely see out of this eye thanks to that little bitch."

"I don't want to hear about your damn eye. Just go find out what is going on while I check these girls one last time."

As the man stepped outside, closing the door behind him, he heard the unmistakable sound of a pistol cocking. Before he could react, he felt its cold steel on his neck.

Heather, having stood to the side of the door as it opened, spoke quietly, yet firmly, "CIA, don't make me reach my daily quota for whacking scumbags. Okay?" As the man slowly clasped his hands behind his head, Christian came from behind Heather and pulled the man's pistol from his shoulder holster.

"Calmly now, ask your friend to come out," Christian ordered as he indicated for him to step off to the side.

Already in enough pain from Christian's daughter, the man realized he could only expect worse from her father, so he quickly complied. "Hey, boss, you gotta see this," he yelled into the house.

Inside, Max was visibly irritated. Send him out to do a simple task and the idiot can't even handle it on his own. "What the hell is it?"

"Just come out here, boss. You *really* gotta see this."

"I'll be right back for another chat with you, sweetie," Max informed Nicki, sneering at her as he headed to the door.

Christian heard Max coming and pistol-whipped the man. Tucking the gun in his belt, Christian quickly dragged the man off to the side.

As Max stepped outside, looking for his colleague, Heather stepped up behind him from the side and pulled the door closed. Realizing something was up, the man instinctively reached for his gun as he turned around to see first Christian and his unconscious colleague, then Heather. Before he could get the gun to his front, Heather made it quite clear that taking it any further would be a bad idea. With both hers and Christian's guns pointed directly at his face, she warned him, "Unless you want to be the dumbest of the lot, slowly hand your piece to my friend."

"She really isn't one to be toyed with right now. So far today I've destroyed her wardrobe and completely disillusioned her entire patriotic belief system. Probably best to do as she says," Christian suggested.

"So, you're the famous Mister Faraday. You do know your daughter sits inches away from a two-hundred-foot drop onto ragged granite?" he replied as he held the grip of the gun by two fingers and passed it over to Christian.

"Yes," Christian replied as he accepted the gun. "I also know that the only people that can make that happen are a bit self-absorbed at the moment, not to mention just a little overconfident that you and your men are doing your job." Adding with a bit of self-satisfaction in his voice, "How's it feel to let your boss down so badly?"

"Don't you have something else for him, Christian?" Heather interjected.

"Oh, yes. Max, thanks so much for providing us an ample supply of chloroform," he added as he pulled the cloth from his back pocket and shoved it in Max's face. "That's for Tatum, you scumbag."

Max had a look of near horror as Christian lunged towards him, then succumbed to the chloroform as quickly as everyone else, collapsing to the ground.

"Wow! Something tells me you enjoyed getting that out of your system," Heather commented as she tucked the gun in the back of her skirt.

"Tatum and Nicki might have a slight headache from it, but I sure am glad they left that stuff in the car for us," he commented nonchalantly as he piled the two men next to the edge of the house.

"After you," Heather said as she stepped away from the door.

"I'm going to go straight for the patio door to see what I can figure out for Tatum. You go free Nicki. The door to Benny's office is closed so we should be able to get in unnoticed."

"I'm right behind you, Superman."

Christian slowly opened the door and peeked around. It was exactly as he knew it would be—closed door to Benny's office, Nicki in the corner, and Tatum out on the deck in a very precarious position with the last of Benny's goons standing by. Christian quickly opened the door the rest of the way and rushed out to the deck door while Heather headed for Nicki.

The chair Tatum was tied to had been placed over a trap door in the floor of the deck. Benny used this trap door from time to time to rid himself of enemies and remind anyone that got out of line exactly who was in charge. The house itself sat at the edge of a two-hundred-foot cliff, with the deck extending fifteen feet out over the cliff. Anyone going through the trap door wouldn't touch the ground until after a very long drop. While the front two legs of the chair were securely on the deck, held from sliding forward by a stationary 'stop' in the deck, the rear legs were not resting on anything, and sat directly above the open latch. Tatum's entire life depended upon a rod secured at the bottom of the deck and at the top of the chair's back. Any inappropriate jarring of that rod would cause the chair, and Tatum, to free fall to their demise.

"Da—" Tatum began in excitement as Christian lifted his finger to his lips, indicating for her to keep quiet. Christian crouched at the door to the deck to see just how visible she was from Benny's office door and what position her guard was in. Fortunately for Christian, the man was halfway down the fifty-foot deck, leaning over the railing, smoking a cigarette, paying no attention whatsoever to his charge.

"Don't move, sweetheart," Christian whispered, "we're going to get you out of this. I promise. Just stay still."

Although she was trying to be as strong as she had been with Benny and his gang, having her father here caused her to slightly lose her grip on herself. Christian could see a small tear or two beginning to streak down her cheek. "I'll be okay, Daddy," she whispered, followed by a brief pause, she added, "I love you, Daddy." She wanted to get in that last part just in case it was the last opportunity she had to say it to him.

"I love you too, precious. Don't worry, I'm not going to let anything happen to you," he reassured her.

As Heather began cutting Nicki loose with a knife left on the coffee table, she introduced herself, "Hi, Nicki. I'm Heather, Mister Faraday's personal CIA agent."

Before saying anything, Nicki started to cry and jumped up to hug Heather, "Oh, God. Thank you, thank you, thank you!" Nicki had tried to remain strong but gave in to a tremendous amount of pent-up emotion. As tough as she was, nothing had prepared her with facing the very real possibility of being killed, or of being sent to a Mexican whorehouse for that matter.

Just then, Benny marched into the room, beginning a sentence as if he was talking to his men, not realizing that there was now an entirely different audience. "Haven't they gotten—"

Assessing the scene, he was taken aback but quickly figured out what was going on. "I see you've made yourself at home, Mister Faraday. I trust my men have taken care of everything you need?"

"They were a little tired and went off to take a nap, Benny. But we're doing just fine anyway, thanks."

Visibly angry, but not shaken, Benny made the best of the surprise situation. "I see you've managed to catch up with your daughter." He then called out to her guard, "Damn it Jinx, we've got company, will you please take care of Miss Faraday—now."

"Yes, and we'd really like to get going. If we could get a move on, I'd really appreciate it."

"You see, it's come to our attention that you have access to information that me and my associates might find somewhat valuable."

"Just how did you know about Mister Faraday's capabilities, Malone? And what makes you think he's willing to cooperate with you?" Heather cut in.

"Who's the dame, Faraday? I told you to come alone."

"This is Heather, my fashion coordinator. I never go anywhere without her. We're a team, so deal with it," he informed Benny. Turning to Heather, he added, "The CIA isn't the only one with moles in the FBI, Heather."

"Gambling debts can be a heavy load to bear, Mister Faraday," Malone added.

"Especially if Agent Clemens didn't know that the deck was stacked and the dice were loaded," Christian quipped back.

"Minor details," Malone replied. "Anyway, back to the matter at hand."

"We'll be back to nothing until Tatum is untied and by my side." Christian interrupted him.

"You see, Mister Faraday, hickory is indeed a very strong wood, but I couldn't vouch for how well that balancing act is constructed. I'd say the sooner we get our business concluded, the sooner we can minimize any danger to your daughter."

Christian was furious, "Let me repeat this, Malone. If my daughter is not released and brought to me immediately, we will not be discussing any business. Do I make myself clear?"

Malone boldly stared back at him, clearly knowing he had the upper hand. "Let's talk a little business. Then we can discuss furniture arrangements."

As the men from the office began to make their way into the living room, Christian realized he needed to give Malone a few nibbles of information so that he could get Tatum from her precarious position.

"Fine, you win, but I warn you, if I can't concentrate, I'll have no information for you at all."

"Let's give it a try. We've got a whole slew of things we want to go over with you, but why don't you start by telling me anything you think I ought to know about."

Christian composed himself, closed his eyes and concentrated for a moment. The room was silent as everyone's attention was on Christian, breathlessly awaiting what his gift will bring to them. Suddenly he opened his eyes.

"Well, where to start? The shipment of cocaine that is to arrive tomorrow is cut fifteen percent more than what was agreed to, one of your Vegas guys has been skimming an extra five percent of the take for himself over the last year, and your wife is screwing," pointing to one of the men that came in from his office, "your Sacramento under-boss! If you want any more information, release Tatum."

"That was all very interesting, Faraday," Malone said as he pulled out a gun, aimed it at the man Christian had singled out, and nonchalantly shot him in the chest. "I think that has earned a little trust between us, but we have a lot more work to do," he commented as the man fell dead on the floor.

Turning to Tatum's guard, Malone nodded his head, indicating that he was to position Tatum on the deck away from the trap door. Walking across the room, he placed his arm around Christian's shoulder and led him to a sofa. Christian followed, keeping his eyes on both the man and Tatum to make sure that she was safe.

"You know, you're a bright guy, Mister Faraday. I'd really like to have you come to work for me. The hours are great, and the pay is out of this world."

"Maybe so, but the filth is intolerable. Let's just get this over with. The girls and I really have to get going."

"Patience, Mister Faraday. You should plan on being here for quite a while."

≈

After having the gate hinges blown, Agent Dawson led a dozen vehicles full speed up Malone's driveway. In addition to several FBI sedans, there were a number of SWAT vans, as well as state police cars. Dozens of additional vehicles covered the roads on all sides as back up and to ensure there was no escape from anywhere else on the property. Waymon wanted full coverage and no opportunity for either Christian or Malone to flee.

As the vehicles surrounded the three sides of the massive house, two of the SWAT trucks pulled up to the front door. Five men from each van quickly deployed in a very deliberate manner around the front door.

Surveying the scene, including the bodies draped on the left side of the door, Dawson gave the 'go-ahead-when-ready' signal to the leader of the SWAT team.

Hearing the commotion outside, everyone inside began to flee from the room and Malone, thinking he'd been double crossed by Christian, turned to him, giving him a fierce look of disappointment then yelled to his man outside, "Ditch her!"

The double front doors burst open, and a large squad of fully armed SWAT officers rushed in, Heather dashed out on the deck and leaped towards the trap door as Malone's man pushed Tatum into the opening. Tatum let out a blood-curdling scream. Malone aimed his gun at Christian as he rushed after Heather. Before he could fire, he was hit in the shoulder by a bullet from one of the SWAT team members.

Although having learned earlier that she was definitely out of her league, Nicki nonetheless realized that she needed to help in whatever way she could, so she jumped in front of the French doors leading to the deck, to keep the SWAT team from firing at Christian as well.

Diving onto the deck with fully outstretched arms, Heather managed to grab the back slat of the wooden chair with her left hand as it began dropping through the trap door. The man didn't hang around to ensure the order from Benny was completed but had turned and ran down the deck in hopes of escaping and saving his own skin.

Looking down the long drop to the rocks below Heather tried to comfort the girl. "I've got you, Tatum. Don't worry. I won't let go." Heather hung on desperately to the slat of the ladderback chair. Lying on her belly, Heather reached down to grab Tatum by the arm. She held on with all her strength. After Tatum realized that she was dangling with jagged rocks below, she looked up at the stranger who was saving her from a certain death. Tatum came to her senses, "I don't know who you are," she said with a trembling voice, "but I love you."

Reaching the trap door Christian stretched down to grab the other side of the chair back, just as Tatum began to squirm wildly, seeing something on the underside of the deck. "Spiders! Get me out of here, Daddy! There are spiders down here!"

Comfortable that he had a firm grip on the chair, Christian helped Heather pull Tatum up from the opening. "Tatum *really* doesn't like spiders," he commented to Heather as they pulled her up.

"Just get me away from them, Daddy!"

Yup, Tatum is just fine, Christian smiled with relief as they set the chair on the deck.

As everyone in the room quickly surrendered, Heather began cutting Tatum loose and Christian found the button to close the trap door.

"This is my daughter, Tatum. Needing to be bailed out of trouble, as usual."

"Hi, Tatum. I'm Special Agent Heather Johnson with the CIA."

Barely waiting for Heather to free her bound hands, Tatum jumped on Heather, hugging her tightly. "Thank you so much for saving me. I thought I was a goner."

"Hey, what about me? Don't I get any thanks?" Christian complained.

Tears down her face, Tatum turned to him, still half hugging Heather, and replied, "The man that let me dangle around with those awful spiders? You expect thanks?" Maintaining her act for as long as she could, which was only a moment, Tatum burst into tears and turned to give him a huge hug. "I love you so much, Daddy."

Nicki then rushed out and spontaneously the four melted into a group hug.

Pulling herself out of the group, Tatum turned to Heather and asked, "If I get my own personal CIA agent, can you make sure he's hot too?"

"If he is, you'd better share!" Nicki added as Heather and Christian laughed.

Waymon, who had landed the helicopter in the massive front yard and followed the SWAT team in, saw that the house was secured then stormed out onto the deck.

"God damn it, Faraday!" he bellowed, "Do you know what you've put us through today? Half of Reno is at a standstill, and the airports have been closed all day on your account. Do you know how many people you've put in harm's way?"

Trying to get a few words in, Christian gave up as Waymon continued, "And what the hell have you been doing with Malone and his gang of sleazeballs?" Turning to Heather he added, "And you, Agent Johnson, have you been aiding and abetting his illegal flight?"

That was quite enough for Christian. "Agent Waymon," Christian began as he put his hands up for the man to stop. "These goons kidnapped my daughter and as you can see had her in quite a dangerous situation. There is no way I was going to risk her life just so you could look good with headquarters. In fact, because of you, she was nearly killed— so don't give me any shit! As for Agent Johnson, she tried to stop me at every possible moment."

"Is that why her bra drove the getaway car?" Waymon smirked as he nodded down at Heather's clearly braless chest.

"I was in a lose-lose situation and Agent Johnson participated only when I forced her at gunpoint. She had no choice; now lay off her." Okay, so he lied a little bit, but it was nothing like the scam the FBI and CIA were trying to pull on him.

"Waymon," Heather interjected, "I can vouch for Mister Faraday's position. If you have a problem with that, I suggest you take it up with Washington. Maybe if you had been properly protecting his family, none of this would have happened, and we'd be halfway to Washington by now."

"Besides, we're here now and I can tell you everything you need to put everyone in this place away for the rest of their lives," Christian gloated.

Staring at Christian, realizing that it would be in his best interest to play ball with him in this situation, he finally responded, "Fine. But enough of your shenanigans, Faraday!"

As the FBI gathered and handcuffed all the men in the house, a paramedic attended to Malone's shoulder and a medic team carried the dead man out on a stretcher.

"Dawson, let's get all these guys lined up against the wall, and figure out who's who and what action we need take with each of them," Waymon ordered.

"There are a couple more by the door, and two others in the Suburban in the driveway," Christian informed him.

"Thanks, Faraday. We've found them. I take it you put them in that condition?" Dawson asked.

"Actually, you can thank Agent Johnson. She pretty much single-handedly tricked them all."

"Okay, Faraday," Waymon said as he indicated for Christian to take a seat, "let's get this mess figured out before we head to Washington."

Noting the dusk that had befallen the Nevada evening, Christian objected, "Don't you think Washington can wait until tomorrow? It's been a very long day."

"Don't worry, Mister Faraday, you and your daughter can sleep en route."

Fine, think what you like, Christian smirked to himself. *Stalling will just give me time to figure some way out of this.* Christian was becoming uncharacteristically cocky and self-confident with his new powers. It was definitely a new experience for him, although he hadn't had the time to contemplate whether or not he liked it.

"So, what can you tell me about these guys and their operation?" Waymon asked Christian.

Christian sat down and closed his eyes. He did this for several minutes, an unusually long time considering the knowledge he was seeking. Finally, he opened his eyes and smiled, "They'll probably be locked up in their next life, too."

Malone glared at Christian and sneered.

Christian started rattling off information of various files and vital evidence hidden in the office. He identified several domestic and international activities which could be halted in progress. He disclosed the location of a safe, then told them where they could locate a hidden munitions room in the basement.

Clearly elated, Waymon ordered several agents to join him and Christian in Malone's private office.

Turning to Waymon, Christian asked, "Can someone contact this girl's family and make sure she gets home? Hers is the blue Volvo out front."

"No problem, Mister Faraday. We'll take care of her right away," one of Dawson's men replied.

Christian walked over to reassure the girls that everything would be okay.

Nicki gave Tatum and Heather a hug and a kiss goodbye, "Thank you again. I so want to be like you when I get older."

"You just enjoy being a teenager. It's the best time of your life," Heather replied.

Turning to Tatum, Nicki reached out for a big hug. "Give me a call as soon as you can."

Returning Nicki's hug, both girls teared up just enough to be noticed by Christian and Heather, who looked at each other and smiled.

When the FBI agent led Nicki away, Christian told Heather and Tatum that they should probably go outside and get some fresh air. Christian gave the two of them a hug, whispering to Heather, "Once outside, head about twenty-five yards in the three o'clock direction. Wait there until I join you two."

As Heather now unquestionably trusted him, she put her arm around Tatum and they casually walked outside.

"What about you, Agent Johnson? Want to join us?" Waymon asked purely out of professional courtesy.

Turning around to him Heather replied, "Mafia activity is your territory. Besides, I need to check in with Marcus. I'll just take Miss Faraday outside for a little terra firma and fresh air."

Waymon and Christian led several agents into Malone's private office and Christian began rattling off computer passwords and pointing towards files. Waymon and his agents began searching the office's contents and uncovering a wealth of information on Malone's operations as well as other mafia gangs around the country. Christian picked up a note pad and wrote "15-3-57" on it and handed it to Waymon. Waymon looked puzzled and Christian pointed to a closet door. Waymon walked over and opened it to find the room sized safe that Christian had mentioned earlier.

"You won't need that safecracker now," he added.

While his men were engrossed in the trove of evidence they have just been given—a haul bigger than they could have hoped to obtain in five years of investigation, Waymon called the Director. While he gloated about their cache and bragged that they had both Malone and Christian in custody, Christian stealthily slipped out the office door and then through one of the house's side doors.

Trying not to draw attention, Christian casually walked towards Heather and Tatum. The full darkness of the evening had now set in; no one was paying attention to Christian as they were all busy loading up sedans and vans with prisoners and evidence. As he reached the two girls, he placed himself between them and with his arms around their waists, and directed them to the helicopter, about twenty-five yards away.

"Cool chopper," Christian commented to the pilot who was busy cleaning some of the glass that had gotten dusty after its recent flight. Heather held out her CIA badge so the pilot knew she was official.

"Thanks," the pilot responded, not paying terribly much attention to his visitors. "It's the latest FBI issue. Whoever this Faraday guy is, Waymon wanted only the best to chase him down with."

Christian positioned himself so that as the pilot moved along the helicopter he would have to come between Christian and the vehicle. At the perfect moment, Christian pulled the cloth from his back pocket, and quickly placed it over the pilot's nose.

Christian saw to it that the pilot fell to the ground gently and looked around to make sure they were not noticed. "Hurry girls—get in." He helped Tatum in the back seat as Heather ran around to the other side of the helicopter.   Christian climbed into the pilot's seat. After looking around and fidgeting with a few of the buttons and controls, Christian looked satisfied that he had set everything appropriately.

Tatum looked quizzically at her father, "You don't know how to fly a helicopter, Daddy. Do you?"

"An hour ago that was a very true statement, sweetheart. But do you really think it took all that concentration to learn a few passwords and file locations?"

"You know these helicopters can be tracked don't you Christian?" Heather interjected.

"Not this one anymore." Christian smiled back. "I've just disabled all transponders and lights. Fortunately for us, the FBI was considerate enough to let us borrow one of their stealthier choppers. Nice of them, don't you think?"

Starting up the helicopter was easy enough, but as Christian began to take off, it wobbled a little too much for the girls' comfort level.

"I thought you could fly this thing?" Heather asked.

"Oh, ye of little faith. Just relax. It will take a few minutes to get the fine points down. I'll have the feel of this baby in no time," Christian replied with a cocky smile. "Unless you'd like to have a go at it?"

Heather lifted both her hands up next to her head and bowed to him.

Tatum smiled as she observed the undeniable chemistry between them. Leaning over the seat, she gave her father a kiss on the cheek. "I trust you, Daddy. Just get us away from this nuthouse."

Waymon and the other agents didn't even notice the sound of a helicopter starting up outside. It was, after all, just a normal part of the commotion involved in such a big bust, and Waymon was busy with the personal ear of the Director at the moment.

As the agents went about their business, gathering evidence and processing Malone's men, the helicopter smoothly disappeared into the darkness.

Chapter Twenty

"Looks like that wraps things up for now," Waymon told Dawson as he went to collect his jacket. "Time to get Faraday off to Washington. Keep the estate secure and crews here as long as you need to wrap this scene up."

"The DA is on her way, so you'll have to deal with her, too."

"You two can handle her. Just make sure we have what we need to wipe this sleazy organization out. You're going to have your hands full with this haul, for longer than you can imagine."

"And you're going to be *where?*" Dawson inquired.

"Isn't this your baby?"

"I think I'll be relocating to Washington," Waymon replied with a self-confident smirk. "Now get the pilot to crank up the chopper and get Faraday and his girl in there. Find some excuse to separate Agent Johnson from the two of them."

"Yes, sir."

"I'll be in the kitchen scrounging for something. I'm starving. Let me know when we're ready to go."

Dawson headed out the door to make the arrangements, as Waymon headed down the hall to raid the kitchen.

≈

Waymon was sitting down finishing an apple when Dawson returned with the bad news.

"What do you mean he's gone?" Waymon barked.

"We found the pilot unconscious where you landed earlier," Dawson informed him. "The chopper is nowhere to be seen. Faraday, his daughter, and the CIA woman are nowhere to be found."

"Why the hell didn't anyone stop him?" Waymon was beyond furious. This was the third time today that Faraday had given him the slip. That would have been bad enough, but to have someone of this level of visibility escape three times in one day was simply unheard of in the history of the Bureau. Waymon could only imagine the consequences to his career.

"I think we were all a little preoccupied with the prisoners and the evidence gathering," Dawson replied.

"And no one bothered to secure him?"

"There were no instructions to that effect, sir," Dawson replied, feeling a little defensive. "You had us all busy on specific tasks."

Waymon knew it was his fault for not making sure that Faraday was under guard. He had all possible ground exits covered and never even thought of the helicopter being a possible method for Christian's escape. *What civilian knows how to fly a helicopter?*

"Get the ops center busy tracking that chopper and deploy all available resources to wherever the hell Faraday is," he barked to Dawson. "I want another full-scale search. We can't lose him again."

As Dawson grabbed his phone to get things moving, Waymon dialed a number from his own phone.

"Where the hell is your girl Johnson, Marcus?" Waymon snapped.

"Last I heard, she was clearing a scene for your army to come in and get all the credit."

"Cute. Well, she's disappeared now, and so has Faraday." Waymon really hated admitting that he lost Christian again, but catching up with Heather might be the only way to get him back.

"Let me understand this, you have him in a secure estate with probably dozens of units watching the place, and he slips away? Again?" West was so pleased. He'd been so out of the loop due to the sheer number of resources Waymon had at his command.

"Funny how your girl is always involved in his disappearances."

"She's just doing her job, Samuel. Don't worry, we'll get him to Washington if you're unable to."

"Marcus, the Bureau has first dibs on this guy, there's too much going on here."

"When I see a directive to that effect, I'll take it under advisement."

Waymon couldn't make out if the Agency had secured Faraday or not. There was no sense giving West any other information. "Let me know if you hear anything, okay?"

"Will do, Samuel. I'd appreciate the same."

West disconnected the call and dialed Heather's number. *Where the hell is she now?* he pondered. *Faraday had better not have hurt her.* As much of a chauvinist as he was, and as annoying as he could find her, Marcus' romantic feelings for Heather were clouding his otherwise superior objective and analytical judgment. Regardless, Marcus was none too pleased he hadn't heard more from her today. He had to give her credit, however, for managing to keep herself engaged with Faraday. Either that, or Faraday was holding her against her will.

≈

"Where in the world are we going, Daddy?" Tatum yelled to her father from the back of the helicopter as they appeared to be descending.

"We'll be there in a few minutes, sweetheart."

"You know, I'm probably on the ten most wanted list myself by now, Christian." Heather said as she felt herself resigning to the exhaustion from the events of the day setting in.

"Don't worry, Heather, I'll make sure you're taken care of. If they don't lock me up like Hannibal Lecter, that is," he reassured her with a smile. "You've been a great partner today, thanks for the help."

"Wouldn't have missed it. Definitely a lot more fun than being chased by that leopard," she smiled. "Although, the leopard didn't seem to have a thing for my underwear."

"Daddy! Are you collecting lingerie from unsuspecting beauties again?" Tatum piped in, quite stunned that her father was even remotely associated with something naughty. This was something new, and definitely very promising.

Smiling back at Heather, Christian wondered what Stephanie would think of his growing feelings for Heather. His face slowly became more serious as his attention turned back to flying the helicopter.

The landing spot he had been heading for came into view and Christian carefully guided the helicopter towards the ground.

"You really do like 'the middle of nowhere' don't you, Christian? Have a nice cave stashed out here for us?"

"I know it's not the Tibetan mountains, but it's the best I could do on short notice."

Christian had flown them about a hundred miles west; well over the border into California, deep into a remote area of the Sierras that was scattered with occasional vacation homes. Christian knew that this would be well out of standard search areas, and although there wasn't a very effective manner for hiding something as large as a helicopter, he had determined that this spot was the least likely to be searched.

Landing near a tree line to minimize visibility, Christian turned the engine off and announced, "We're here, girls."

"We're where?" a very concerned looking Tatum inquired, "It looks like a field next to a bunch of trees to me."

"Where's your imagination, Tatum?" Christian challenged her as he climbed out of the helicopter. "I see a world of possibilities."

Heather and Tatum gave each other a look clearly implying that Christian might have, in fact, lost his sanity.

"There is *nothing* here, Daddy! I am not going to sleep out in the woods."

"Hmmmmm, then where are you going to sleep?" Christian teased her as he started walking up the hill. "Besides, give me any more grief and I'll see if this cloth has any juice left in it."

As Tatum jokingly punched her father in the arm, Heather pulled her aside, letting Christian go ahead.

"Something tells me he's got something in mind. He's been surprising me all day. I find it best just to go with the flow."

"What have you two been doing all day? I've never seen him so ragged looking. And something tells me you started the day out a tad more fashionable yourself," Tatum joked. "Have you been corrupting my father?"

Heather laughed and the two girls followed Christian as he walked briskly ahead.

As they neared the crest of the hill and reached a break in the tree line, he turned to the right. Up ahead, they saw a very large, and very dark, house. There were no cars to be seen, and not a single light anywhere.

Approaching the house, Tatum whispered to Heather, "This is kinda creepy."

"True. But better than being locked up in a room in Langley. Trust me, *that's* creepy."

Reaching the front door, Christian stopped the girls and stepped into the bushes to a window well. Leaning down and reaching inside, Christian pulled something out. Coming back to front door, Christian held up a key and smiled broadly, "Voilà!"

As Christian opened the front door, the beeping of the alarm startled the girls, but Christian calmly walked over to the alarm system and entered the code, silencing the system.

"Does this place belong to a friend of yours?" Heather asked.

"Never met the man, but I'm reliably informed that the owner is a businessman that only visits the house during summer and ski season."

"So he doesn't know we're staying at his place?"

"No, but it's a safe place for the night and we need the rest. Besides, it's better than a cave in the woods. Isn't it, Tatum?"

Entering the house, the girls were in awe that such a beautiful home would spend so much of the year totally vacant. The moonlight filled the two-story great room from the oversized windows and skylights, enabling the three of them to easily find their way around without turning on any lights.

Tatum headed directly to one of the overstuffed leather sofas and plopped down. "I'm exhausted. I'm hungry. And I haven't been on Facebook all day!"

"Why don't you girls go freshen up. I'll see what I can scrounge up for dinner," Christian suggested as the he headed into the kitchen.

Following Christian into the kitchen, Heather grabbed him by the shoulders and turned him around, marching him back out and towards the open stairway leading to the second floor. "Maybe we should all freshen up and prepare dinner together," she suggested. "Come on, Tatum, let's get ourselves civilized. We'll feel much better."

Reaching the top of the stairway, they were even more impressed with the house. A very open floor plan, the house was clearly designed for entertainment and comfort. Christian went to the end of the wide hallway and opened a set of double doors. "This looks like the master bedroom. Why don't you two share this room?" he said as he stepped into the massive room. "I think you'll find it has everything you need."

"Where will you be, Daddy?"

"I've got a few other rooms down the hall to choose from. Whichever one has the biggest bathtub and a rubber ducky. I really need to soak for a while."

"Take your time, Christian. Tatum and I will get things going downstairs until you get down there."

"Thanks, Heather. I'm not usually so useless, I promise."

"Don't you worry about it. I'm just tired of smelling you," Heather said as she shooed him out of the room. "Now go relax and meet us downstairs when you can. Tatum and I will be just fine."

"You obviously don't know what my daughter is capable of," he replied as headed towards the door. Stopping, he turned and added, "There are plenty of candles lying around. Use those if you can. I really don't want to risk any house lights being seen by anyone outside.

Closing the doors behind him, Heather headed to the closet. "Check out the bathroom, will you? I'll see if I can dig up a change of clothes for us."

"Do you think the owner of the house will mind?" Tatum asked as she followed Heather. Tatum was still a little shaken, being alone in the room bothered her.

Inside the large walk-in closet, Heather continued, "One thing I've learned from being in this type of situation, it's often easier to get forgiveness than permission. Your dad is a good and honest man, I'm sure he'll make amends with whoever owns the house. If not, I'll make sure the Agency does."

"My mother used to say that. The permission, forgiveness thing."

"You must miss her terribly, Tatum. I'm so sorry you lost her so early."

"You two are a lot alike, I think. Beautiful, witty, athletic, outdoorsy, and not afraid of anything."

"Coming from you I'll take that as quite a compliment." Pulling out a couple of thick terrycloth robes, Heather held them up and asked, "What do you think?"

"God, they're decadently thick! Can I use the pink one?" Tatum replied.

"Sure, let's go get cleaned up. I'm feeling awfully filthy, and you need to get some of those spiders out of your hair."

Dropping the robe and beginning to shake her hair, Tatum began jumping up and down screaming, "Spiders! I've got spiders on me? Get them off, get them—" she stopped as she saw Heather beginning to laugh. "Oh my God. You're as evil as my dad!"

Picking up her robe, Tatum marched into the bathroom, followed closely by a still chuckling Heather. "Just for that, the agent you get for me better be *really* hot!"

As with the rest of the house, the bathroom was huge and luxurious, with picture windows and generous views. "These people are sinful," Heather remarked as she jealously admired the room.

"Isn't it great?" Tatum was clearly thrilled, "Mind if I take the bath?"

"Be my guest. I want to get through the shower quickly so I can get some food in our tummies."

Tatum began drawing her bath. Finding a bottle of bubble bath, she poured it in, as Heather examined the separate shower unit.

"What is this contraption?" Heather asked Tatum as she looked quizzically at a complex structure within the glass shower enclosure.

"Oh, they're heavenly. Daddy had one put in when he built our house. It shoots water at you from everywhere! My mom used to love it."

"Okay, but if I drown, you're going to have to explain it to the Agency," Heather warned her as she removed her clothes without even a modicum of the reticence which may have normally been present between two newly acquainted women. The exceptional circumstances of the day, the mental and physical exhaustion, their individual generally confident personalities, and, above all, their immediate intuitive closeness, all coalesced to eclipse any feelings of modesty between the two.

Tatum sat at the edge of the tub while Heather began washing her hair in the shower. "So, what is the story with your missing bra anyway? It's not like my dad to get into ladies' personals."

"Let's just say your father found another use for it which gave us the time we needed to get over to Malone's."

They continued chatting until Tatum's bath was ready. Tatum slid into the tub and turned on the Jacuzzi jets. "This is so perfect. Can I have dinner in here, please?"

"Like I'm going to prepare a meal for your father without your guidance? I think not," Heather informed her as she began drying her hair. "I'll see what we can make. You get down there before you start pruning up in that water."

"You and my dad seem to hit it off pretty well."

"I'm here on a strictly professional basis, Tatum."

"Yeah, right. Is that why you were being so careful shaving your legs in the shower?"

Heather crumpled up her hand towel and threw it at Tatum, giving her a wink in the process. Watching her leave the room, Tatum knew that the right woman for her father had finally entered their lives.

Returning a few minutes later in a pair of clearly too large men's silk pajamas, Heather placed a similar pair of folded pajamas on the sink. "I'm afraid the woman of the house sleeps in things that you aren't ready for, and I shouldn't be seen in. We'll just have to make do with these."

"Oh God, you're so cute! I love it."

"Thanks. I'll see you downstairs when you can drag yourself out of there."

≈

Christian soaked in a hot, heavily salted bath. His bathroom was not quite as luxurious as the girls' but did have an ample sized Jacuzzi tub. Unfortunately, no rubber ducky was to be found.

Christian attempted to relax and clear his thoughts, but his mind was overwhelmed with the events of the day and was continuously being flooded with new information; much of it he really didn't care to have. Clearly this newfound ability was going to need some harnessing.

The activities of the day were of particular concern to him. He had been responsible for so much chaos everywhere he went, and then some. His best friend was hiding at the sister of an old girlfriend that he figured the authorities would never trace him to. His dear friend Juli-ette had been grilled by the FBI and successfully played dumb about any knowledge of Christian's ability, as well as why Parker's car was still in the casino garage. Countless travelers had been inconvenienced. President Beucler was getting hourly updates on the status of the search and was planning to call the military into the situation if Christian wasn't in Washington tomorrow. His beloved daughter had nearly been splattered into bits at the bottom of a cliff. On top of all that, he had ruined two pieces of very expensive lingerie. Christian had a plan for ending the madness without being a political pawn, but it would take another day of extreme finesse to pull it off.

≈

Heather found a treasure of frozen meats and vegetables in the basement freezer, as well as other staples in the pantry and refrigerator. It was plain that the owner liked to be prepared for his visits.

"So, what are we going to whip up here, Miss CIA?" Tatum inquired as she entered the kitchen.

"Oh my God, you look so adorable in those things!" Heather greeted her.

"Thanks, but I don't think I'll be out shopping to add anything like this to my wardrobe anytime soon," Tatum informed her as she sat down on a stool and leaned on the granite countertop on the other side of the kitchen island. "How can I help here?"

"How does your basic steak, peas, and pasta sound?"

"Better than whatever breed of slugs and tree bark my dad would have suggested if we were out in the woods," Tatum replied as she rolled her eyes.

"Well, I did bump into a small container of chocolate-covered grasshoppers in the refrigerator. I guess you wouldn't be interested in those?"

"Shut up!" Tatum perked up with excitement, "You didn't? That would be a good dessert for him though!"

Heather chuckled, "That would be too funny, Tatum. But I think we should take it easy on him tonight."

The two ladies began preparing the meal in perfect unison. As Tatum thawed the steaks and prepared the water for the pasta, Heather chopped the onions and began making a marinade for the steak. At the same time, they shared jokes and secrets as if they had been longtime girlfriends. They worked so flawlessly together that Tatum had to stop for a moment and compose herself; this felt exactly like the fun she and her mother had together in the kitchen. *I swear, if Daddy screws this up, I'll never forgive him*, she thought to herself as she watched Heather orchestrate the meal.

"Keep an eye on these, will you?" Heather handed the steak tongs to Tatum, "I'm going to see what the wine collection looks like."

Just after Heather disappeared into the basement where the wine cellar was, Christian entered the room.

"Oh my, doesn't this smell good?"

Tatum marched over to her father with the tongs snapping and stuck them right in his face, trying to keep her voice down so Heather didn't hear, "If you chase her off, I swear, Daddy, I'm never going to talk to you again. Ever!"

"What are you talking about, sweetheart?"

"You know exactly what I'm talking about, Daddy. Only the most perfect woman in the world for you, next to Mother, of course."

Knowing she was probably right, but not wanting to let his guard down, he changed the subject. "Why don't I just set the table?" he quipped as he escaped her snapping tongs to find the dishes.

Just then, Heather returned with two bottles of red wine. "Merlot or Pinot Noir?"

"What are my choices?" Christian replied as he grabbed a few dish-es from the cabinet.

"You've got about twenty options of each. Whoever owns this place is quite the connoisseur. However, I've narrowed it down to a '95 Rutherford Hill Reserve for the former and—" giving him a very sassy look— "if you can handle it, an '01 Mommessin."

Wow, a wine lover too! "Sold!" Christian quickly replied. "Any more surprises like this and we might just have to stay here!"

"Here," Heather handed him the Pinot Noir, "You take care of this. I'll set the table."

Once Heather had left the room with the dishes, Tatum turned to her father, snapping the tongs in his face and whispering firmly, "I mean it, Daddy. Don't screw this up."

≈

"Wow! This is really excellent, girls," Christian said excitedly as he finished his first bite of the steak. "I recognize a few of Tatum's touches, but whatever you've added Heather, is superb."

"Thanks, cooking is my third passion. After outdoors and that other addiction you already know about," Heather replied, blushing. "But it was really the team that flavored everything so well," smiling at Tatum.

Christian raised his glass to the two of them, "Well done, ladies!"

As they continued through their meal, the girls wanted Christian to tell them more about his ability and explain what was going on. Christian detailed everything as he understood it. The cosmic cloud, the retrovirus, and how it modified his DNA.

"So, you have a 'sixth sense' of some sort now?" Heather asked.

"I guess you'd call it that. This gene simply unlocks a capability many humans have anyway. A run-of-the-mill psychic can access it to some degree, but I pretty much have free reign."

"Does this mean that you know the future, too?" Tatum quizzed him.

"No, I only know what is current or has been the truth, and sometimes it seems conflicting and really takes concentration to understand properly."

"It's the glowing thing I really like," commented Heather. "It could be an awesome party trick. Pretty sexy too," she added with a wink.

"This is really creepy, Daddy. I'm not going to be able to get away with anything, am I?"

"Well, considering the little details I've picked up on you so far, you're going to have a more challenging time than your typical teenager with her father."

Tatum looked at him innocently, as if she'd never done anything wrong.

"Don't give me that look, young lady. Where would you like me to start? Your summer dates with Keith, or perhaps the devious trick you girls played on Jessica at school?"

Tatum blushed, holding her head down. She had never wanted her father to find out about things like that. She was busted, and she knew it. No sense trying to talk her way out of any of it. "I'm sorry, Daddy. I'll be better."

"Don't worry, precious," he comforted her as he reached over and kissed her forehead. "Normal teenage stuff. I'm just glad you don't know about mine."

Heather, touched as she observed how understanding Christian was with his daughter, reached over and squeezed Tatum's hand.

As he finished up his dinner, Christian complimented the girls, "That was wonderful, young ladies. Thank you both very much. I'll take care of the dishes. Why don't you two go up and get some sleep? We've got another long day tomorrow."

"What do you have in mind, Daddy?" Tatum asked as she stood up from the table.

"Don't worry, Tatum, I've got it all planned out. We'll be just fine."

Tatum gave him a hug, "I love you, Daddy." Kissing him on the nose she added with a whisper, "and don't forget what I said."

As the girls started towards the stairs, Christian added "And Heather—"

The girls stopped and turned towards Christian and then Tatum released Heather's hand and continued towards the steps, hoping her father would take advantage of a little one-on-one time with the beautiful agent.

"I don't think I properly thanked you for saving Tatum's life."

Heather stepped closer to Christian, looking him straight in the eyes. "She's a good girl, Christian. She loves you so much."

Quickly pecking him on the cheek, she turned around and hurried to catch up with Tatum.

Damn, she looks cute in those jammies!

Chapter Twenty-One

Stephanie sits on a boulder with her left foot on the ground. Wrapping her arms around her right leg, she pulls it up to her chest and admires the unspoiled view from the Sierra peak; a spot which she and Christian so often hiked to. Her perfect strawberry blonde hair blowing ever so slightly in the gentle breeze as she radiates total peace and serenity. Smiling as Christian approaches her, he remains in total amazement of just how stunning one person can be.

Standing to greet him, Stephanie reaches out both of her hands at waist level to clasp his. Leaning forward, Stephanie gives Christian a gentle kiss on the cheek and whispers, "She's a beautiful soul. Perfect for you and Tatum. Take good care of both of them." Suddenly, her spirit begins to fade and distance itself from Christian, her arms still outstretched towards him; pure love radiating from her eyes. Christian wants to reply but can only stand in awe as a single tear makes its way down his cheek.

Christian jolted up in bed. After catching his breath and realizing where he was, he surveyed the room and regained his orientation. The occasional dream of his departed love was not that unusual. What was different this time is that he knew, without question, that it was in fact a message from Stephanie as she spoke to him from another dimension.

The clock read 5:32 and he heard a sound down the hallway. Even with the exhaustion of the day before, Heather awakened as usual in the predawn hours; in fact, this was a bit late for her. Her typical morning routine started at five with a five-mile run and a workout of at least forty-five minutes before making her ever-so-critical lingerie choices for the day. She stood and began stretching her muscles out as she made her way across the room to the bathroom.

≈

Outside, the moonlit night outlined the large house as several dark figures slowly encircled the building. The men were dressed head to toe in black, the long thin lens of the night vision goggles protruding from their headgear.

Stopping at the front door with two other men, Marcus West ensured that all men were in place. One of the men picked the front door lock, and the three of them slowly entered the house; silently making their way into the great room, handguns pulled up to their chests at the ready position. Unfortunately, due to his exhaustion, Christian had forgotten to turn the security system back on the night before.

≈

Christian slowly opened the doors to the girl's room and peeked around. Going over to the bed he saw only Tatum, still sound asleep, and worried for a moment before realizing that it was just the bathroom door that he had heard. Christian went over to the bed and gave Tatum a gentle kiss on her forehead.

Just as he began to head back to the door so as not to surprise Heather, although deep down he wouldn't have minded bumping into her, two of the black figures burst in the room, guns pointed directly at Christian and Tatum.

As Tatum startled awake, Agent West casually walked in between his two agents.

"Ready for your trip to Washington, Mister Faraday?"

How did they find us, and why didn't I know they were coming? Christian immediately thought as he assessed the situation. Equally as quickly, the answers surfaced—sharp, unwanted, immediate. Christian realized that he must be a little more disciplifned about how thoroughly he thought through things. He thought he would have learned his lesson when Heather surprised him at his house, although he's now glad that he hadn't known that she was there.

Christian realized that he was truly cornered this time, and no longer to be trusted by the Feds. He couldn't use the same 'you dare not hurt me' routine as he used with Malone's men, Marcus having taken the precaution of having his men load tranquilizer darts so they didn't accidentally hurt his prize. If Christian was knocked out, he couldn't ensure that Tatum and Heather were adequately taken care of.

Christian stepped back and sat down on the bed next to Tatum, who reached around and hugged him from behind. "I'm all yours, Agent West. Between running from you guys all day and trying to shake that pest of a colleague of yours, I'm totally exhausted."

"What have you done with Agent Johnson?"

Christian looked over at the bathroom door, "I've had to keep her locked up in there for the night. Don't worry, we haven't hurt her, and I was going to ensure she was plenty comfortable before we left her here."

Agent West nodded to one of his men to go to the bathroom and check for Heather. Hearing the commotion in the bedroom, Heather had put her ear up to the door and listened to what was going on between the two men. She had only known Christian for a single day, but by now they were already able to play off each other to an amazing degree. It was clear to her that Christian was attempting to distance Heather from himself to keep her from being in trouble, as well as ensuring her position with West, so she could continue to help them.

Hearing approaching footsteps, she drops down on the plush bathroom rug, pretending to be asleep.

The agent opened the door and Marcus went over as Heather pretended to be startled awake from her position on the floor.

"Marcus?" she leaned up on one arm, rubbing one of her eyes with the other hand.

"You okay, Johnson?" Marcus asked, although it was clear to him that she was. "Good move keeping your phone with you so we could track it."

Damn, I forgot about that! Heather thought as she remembered that the CIA could track almost any electronic device their agents were equipped with, even though they might be powered off. Heather hadn't wanted to be found since the moment they jumped from the phantom car.

Knowing that he had called several times, Heather replied to reinforce Christian's story, "Sorry I couldn't answer your calls, but I knew you'd be able to find us if I kept it with me."

Agent West, believing that Heather had indeed been acting in the CIA's best interest, walked over to her, extending his hand to help her up.

Feeling comfortable that West was not suspicious, she added, "What the hell took you so long? Do you have any idea how uncomfortable this floor is?" as she grabbed his hand and arose.

"What's going on, Daddy?" Tatum whispered to Christian. "Why are you and Heather saying those things?"

"Haven't you learned to trust me yet?" he whispered back, giving her a kiss on her temple.

"You don't mind being secured for the time being, do you, Mister Faraday?" West asked as he returned to the bedroom, nodding to one of his men to handcuff him. "You've been just a little too slippery for us."

Christian frowned at him, still not sure what he was going to do about the situation, and stood up, putting his hands in front of him as Tatum tried to pull him back down.

"My daughter stays with me."

"Not a problem, we just don't want to lose you again. You do understand, don't you?"

"Grab some stuff out of the closet for you and Agent Johnson to wear will you, sweetheart?" Christian instructed Tatum.

"We'll be downstairs when you're ready, Agent Johnson," Marcus informed Heather as she walked into the room. "I trust you can handle the girl on your own."

"Sure," she replied, as she observed Christian being handcuffed. "We'll be fine." Walking over to the closet, she signaled Tatum over, playing the part and speaking with a firm and professional voice, "Come on, Miss Faraday, let's get some clothes on."

After the men left, Tatum stepped away from Heather, shaking herself loose from the hand Heather had placed on her shoulder. "What are you doing?" Heather could feel the piercing of Tatum's eyes. "I thought you were helping us?"

"It's okay, Tatum. Your father wanted me to act like this. I had forgotten about the traceability of the phone. He has something in mind, and we just have to go along with him," she reassured her. "Between the two of us, we'll figure something out." Reaching her arms out to give Tatum a reassuring hug she added, "I'm on your side Tatum, all the way. Don't forget it."

Tatum fell into her hug, her strength dissipating from her as she broke into tears, "I can't keep going through this. Do we really have to run from our own government?"

"Trust your father, Tatum. He knows better than we do about what's going on back in Washington." Pushing her back slightly so she could look straight into Tatum's eyes, Heather continued, "I can tell you from experience with both the Agency and the FBI, your best interests are definitely not their key priorities. Your dad is smart and resourceful. He'll know what to do. You and I need to stay alert to help out if he needs us."

"I'm sorry, I didn't mean to doubt you," Tatum apologized as she wiped the tears from her eyes. "I usually don't cry like this. It's just all caught up with me."

"Don't worry, sweetheart," Heather smiled, "I know you're strong. You'll get through this just fine. I have all the confidence in the world in you."

"Don't leave us, Heather. If Daddy doesn't need you, I do."

Heather was taken aback, and deeply touched, giving Tatum a kiss on the cheek. "Let's go see where this woman has been shopping, shall we?"

≈

Downstairs, Christian was handcuffed and closely watched. He sat on the sofa, eyes closed and concentrating on the situation.

"Pull the cars around," Marcus ordered into his mobile phone, before turning to Christian. "Do you realize what a pain in the ass you've been over the last twenty-four hours?"

Coming out of his trance, Christian was not amused. "I assure you, Agent West, you've been a far bigger pain in my ass. Besides, it was a small price to pay for the help I've given you." Lifting up his cuffed hands, he added, "And this is how you repay me." He looked tersely at Marcus. "You wonder why I don't trust you people?"

Marcus didn't care about the terrorists captured, or the countless other nefarious activities the CIA and FBI had thwarted with the help of Christian's intelligence over the last twenty-four hours. His mission right now was to get Christian back to Langley. His career and reputation rested solely on that one task. Ignoring Christian, Marcus dialed another number on his phone.

In a dark bedroom somewhere in Washington, D.C., the phone sharply pierced the silence, and the man rolled over and answered, "Blanton."

"Holy Grail secured, sir. On our way to the airport now."

"Try not to lose him this time, Marcus."

"Don't think we'll have that problem, sir. I'll report in as soon as we're off the ground."

As Marcus ended the call, Tatum and Heather descended the steps. As soon as she saw her father, Tatum ran to him and gave him a big hug.

"Okay, guys. Let's get a move on," Marcus ordered as two black Suburbans pulled up to the front of the house. "Heather, take the daughter in the rear car, and I'll stay with Mister Faraday in the front."

"I don't suppose you have a third car do you Marcus, I'm kind of sick of them both," she replied, attempting to reinforce the perception.

"Hang in there, Johnson. We've got a long trip ahead of us. The fun is just beginning."

Walking across the room to Tatum, she firmly grabbed her upper arm and pulled her off Christian's lap, "Let's go, young lady." Making sure no one could see her face, she winked at the two Faradays.

Chapter Twenty-Two

As they sped their way down the highway, the two Suburbans were met along the way by several California state patrol cars, providing a caravan of sirens and flashing lights. A little further on, the escort was joined by two military helicopters. Marcus was not going to allow Christian any opportunity to escape yet again.

Continuing to put on an air of hostility in the back seat, Heather occasionally reached over and gently squeezed Tatum's hand, reassuring her that she was still on their side. Christian, on the other hand, laid back and closed his eyes, completely ignoring Agent West.

After a forty-five-minute drive, the vehicles approached the entrance of Beale Air Force Base, just north of Sacramento. The state police escorts peeled off the convoy as the Suburbans approached the gate. Having been ordered to allow the caravan to proceed without delay, the gates opened, and the guards saluted as the Suburbans passed.

West noted with interest the quantity of sedans and Suburbans in and near the hangar where an Agency Gulfstream G600 awaited them.

Driving straight into a large hangar where the jet took up only a quarter of the overall space, the Suburbans came to a stop next to the steps of the jet. Stepping out of the front seat of his Suburban, West opened up the rear door and waved Christian out. In the rear Suburban, once the agents in the front seat got out of the vehicle, Heather flashed a quick smile at Tatum, whispering, "Showtime." One of the agents opened Tatum's door for the two of them to exit.

West recognized several of his CIA field agents. He also was not surprised to see a small contingent of Air Force officers. He was, however, surprised to see many other suited individuals that he didn't recognize.

"Colonel Enzo Agudelo, commander of the 9th Reconnaissance Wing," the senior officer introduced himself as he approached Agent West with a salute.

Agent West returned the salute, "Special Agent Marcus West, and this," nodding over to Christian, "is our special guest, Mister Christian Faraday."

"Pleasure to meet you, sir." The Colonel reached his hand out to Christian, "it's an honor to have you pass through our modest home."

Smiling at the Colonel, Christian lifted his cuffed hands. "At least someone thinks I'm special," he said to Marcus as he attempted to shake the Colonel's hand.

Turning back to West, the Colonel continued, "Your jet arrived thirty minutes ago. We've had it fully fueled and all systems have been checked by our mechanics."

"Thank you, Colonel. Who are all the civilians here?"

The Colonel looked surprised, but Christian interrupted him as he began to speak.

"They're your friends from the FBI, Marcus. Weren't you expecting them?" Christian informed him with a smirk.

West contained his anger and walked up the steps leading into the jet, with Christian following closely. Heather introduced herself and

Tatum to the Colonel. West entered the luxurious jet to find Samuel Waymon sitting in one of the overstuffed swivel chairs speaking to someone on the phone. Seeing West, Waymon bid farewell, and disconnected his call. Standing up, he extended his hand to West, who totally ignored it.

"What the hell are you doing here, Waymon? This is an Agency op now. This baby is headed to Langley."

"I gather you haven't seen the memo?" Samuel responded as he pulled a folded letter from inside his jacket pocket and handed it to West.

Snapping the paper from Waymon, West began reading it. The memo was from Martin Mezzori, Director of National Intelligence; the principal intelligence advisor to the President. The DNI was responsible for coordinating all fifteen members of the Intelligence Community, primarily the CIA and FBI. The memo instructed all intelligence agencies to fully cooperate in the matter of Mister Christian Faraday. It also stated that a senior official from his office is being identified and would imminently be assigned to lead the management of Operation Holy Grail. Essentially, both agencies had lost exclusive ownership of Christian, although they would still gain an unprecedented amount of intelligence.

As Agent West finished reading the memo, Christian interrupted, "I could have told you all this in the car if only you had been a little nicer to me."

West looked at Christian angrily before Christian continued, "But don't worry, Blanton has arranged for you to get all the credit." Turning to Waymon he continued, "Sorry, Samuel."

Only slightly consoled, West turned to Waymon, "We're setting a flight plan for Langley, unless I hear from Mezzori personally."

None of this satisfied Christian to any degree. He knew that Mezzori was little more than a political crony; a huge contributor of President Beucler's and a law school buddy of the Speaker of the House. No action Mezzori ever took was done without the political implications being fully analyzed.

Heather and Tatum entered the cabin as Marcus approached the cockpit door, where the pilot had been waiting.

"We all set to go?" Marcus asked abruptly.

"Yes, sir, Agent West. Ready on your orders."

Turning to the Colonel, who stood at the top of the steps, West thanked him for setting everything up. "We really appreciate your assistance, Colonel. I'll make sure the Defense Secretary is aware of your support."

"Our pleasure, Agent West. Always glad to serve."

The pilot thanked the Colonel and closed the door. West returned to the group and instructed everyone to sit down. "We've got a long flight ahead of us, and a longer day once we get there."

Waymon wanted to keep an eye on Christian, and seated himself in one of the front seats, which faced the rear of the aircraft. Heather chose a seat on the opposite aisle, distancing herself, yet being able to read and signal Christian and Tatum, if necessary. As Marcus sat opposite Heather, he wondered why Christian remained standing. "You're going to stand during takeoff, Christian?"

Christian held up his wrists and raised his eyebrows.

"Not till at least twenty thousand feet, when I know it's safe. Now sit down, so we can take off."

Christian reluctantly sat down next to Tatum in the back as the three agents got comfortable in the group of seats closer to the front.

As the agents began talking, Heather started giving a totally fallacious account of the last twenty-four hours.

"I knew that you'd eventually catch up with us, Marcus," Heather smiled to West then leaned over to him whispering to him for effect, "If

I had to deal with another hour of their bickering, I'd have gone crazy. Those two are nuts!"

Christian and Tatum quietly snickered to each other as they listened to Heather's adventures in relentlessly attaching herself to Christian for the last twenty-four hours.

"She likes you, Daddy," Tatum whispered to him, "You two are perfect for each other."

"She's a special lady, that's for sure," Christian replied. "But what about your mother?"

"You know Mom would approve. They're so alike, it's scary."

Christian smiled and put his head on Tatum's shoulder, "We'll see, sweetheart."

"So, what are we going to do when we get to Washington, Daddy? Isn't it going to be kinda difficult to disappear once we're locked up in the Pentagon, or whatever dungeon they're going to put us in?"

"What makes you think we're actually going to land in Washington?" Christian winked to Tatum and closed his eyes. "Now let me rest for a little bit. Okay, sweetheart?"

As the jet taxied down the runway and took off into the rising sun, Tatum kissed him on the forehead, brushed his hair aside with her fingers, and watched as his body developed an ever so slight glow. Although the two men didn't notice it, Heather did, giving Tatum a subtle smile. Tatum smiled back while wondering what caper her father was scheming up for them now.

≈

"Yes, sir, we're airborne now. Our ETA is fifteen hundred hours," Marcus said into the plane's phone followed by a brief pause. "Yes, both Faraday and his daughter are doing fine. I'm sure he'll come around once he's confronted with the reality of the situation."

After a few more minutes of conversation, he hung up and began updating Heather and Samuel. "The White House has taken over a little corner of Langley for this joint intelligence mission. President Beucler himself will be visiting us and meeting with Faraday within the next forty-eight hours."

West was quite pleased with himself. Although the CIA didn't end up with exclusive access to Christian and a few Agency secrets were bound to cause embarrassment in the Intelligence Community, he personally would no doubt have a huge career boost and be positioned extremely well for the future. He never dreamed that he would ever see a Holy Grail scenario, much less be a central figure in it.

Waymon on the other hand was steamed about the situation. He had spent an entire day in non-stop pursuit of Faraday, while West was out of the loop most of the time. Waymon was subconsciously blocking the three occasions that Christian totally embarrassed him and his team. The Bureau was going to put a positive public spin on the two organizations working together, but all too many people knew the truth. Waymon was not looking forward to dealing with the internal ridicule he would undoubtedly face.

After Christian pretended to be asleep for twenty minutes, he 'awakened' and sat up. Turning to Marcus, he informed him "Twenty thousand five hundred."

"Huh?" Marcus replied, looking quizzically at him.

Christian lifted up his hands indicating that he would like the cuffs removed.

Marcus reluctantly stood up and walked back to Christian while removing a key from his pocket. "Well, I guess you're not going to jump out."

"It seems I've accepted the inevitable, Agent West."

"And your country appreciates it," West replied as he unlocked Christian's cuffs.

"Cheer up, Samuel," Christian turned to Waymon. "I've got some goodies to save your reputation."

"I don't think you understand, Christian. The FBI doesn't lose people like I did yesterday." Although Waymon was still entrusted to bring Christian back to the east coast, he had endured blistering abuse the night before, coming from as high as the Director himself. The only professional pleasure he had been able to salvage was being there to keep West and the Agency from obtaining full credit for bringing Faraday in.

"Listen, Samuel, I'm really sorry, and I know there are at least a dozen senior Bureauites back in Washington that are ready to skewer you, but I can fix that."

"The facts are pretty well known, Christian. I had you in custody three times, and you disappeared from right under my nose each time. That simply isn't tolerated in the FBI. It's as simple as that. Nothing even you can do about it, I'm afraid." Waymon really hated having this conversation in front of a couple of CIA agents.

"I'm not so sure about that, Samuel. Why don't you get the Director on the phone?"

Waymon himself was not very thrilled about his own performance, and definitely had reservations about putting Christian on the phone with the Director of the FBI. "You want me to put you on the phone with the Director? I don't think so."

Marcus watched in amusement as his Bureau colleague needed to be bailed out by a civilian.

"Listen, I'm going to be meeting with him in a few hours anyway. Besides, I really feel bad that you took the brunt of my foolishness. Let me fix this for you."

"What the hell," Waymon began as he picked up the phone and pressed a few buttons. "How much worse can it get?"

Once the secretary answered, "Director Allen's office," Waymon began to speak just as Christian snatched the phone from him.

"Could you tell Director Allen that there is an urgent call for him?"

Waymon looked at him quite disapprovingly, but he knew the call was out of his hands at this point.

"Director Allen is in a very important meeting right now, could I take a message?"

"This is Christian Faraday, Mrs. Nawlers. If you'd let him know it's me, personally, I'm sure he'll take the call."

"One moment, Mister Faraday, the Director will be right with you." The secretary knew that this was indeed a call the Director would accept.

Christian looked reassuringly at Samuel.

"Director Allen here," came the voice on the phone, causing Samuel to hold his breath in anticipation of just what Christian was going to say.

"Good morning, Director, this is Christian Faraday. I wanted to let you know what an excellent job Special Agent Waymon did collaborating with me yesterday."

"Thank you for the feedback, Mister Faraday, we are looking forward to meeting you upon your arrival."

"I'm not sure you appreciate what I'm telling you, Mister Allen. It was Agent Waymon's grasp of the bigger picture which allowed him to secretly work with me so I could clean up some personal matters before coming in. I made it clear that if I were to have some private time first, I could get my distractions out of the way. That would allow me to be more agreeable and productive with you guys. I was to contact him this morning, but your CIA friends caught up with me first. Waymon is a man of true integrity and deserves significant recognition."

"I wasn't aware of all that, Mister Faraday. I appreciate the input and will take the recognition part under advisement."

"Section Chief of Racketeering is probably appropriate."

"That is very generous of you, Mister Faraday."

"Otherwise, might I suggest putting him in charge of a special investigation of a certain deal negotiated between your old law firm and the EPA on behalf of one of your clients?" One aspect of Christian's newly obtained power that he was really beginning to enjoy was the ability to pull up dirt at a moment's notice to make sure people played nice.

"We look forward to seeing you soon, Mister Faraday. Could you put Section Chief Waymon on the phone now?"

"Mister Section Chief," Christian whispered to Waymon as he handed him the phone. Waymon reached up and took the handset, his eyes widening and jaw dropping in total shock.

As Waymon and Director Allen finished their conversation, West smirked and downplayed what Christian had just done. "The facts are still the facts, Christian. The FBI blew it, and the CIA had to close the case. As usual."

"I'm not sure facts are the most important thing here, Agent West. Perception, after all, is what Washington runs on. Facts are usually little more than background noise."

West really didn't care for Christian. He had been uncooperative from the get-go; he was smug about his ability and had almost single-handedly ruined a career Marcus had so meticulously laid out and executed for over twenty years. On top of that, although West couldn't put his finger on it, there seemed to be an undercurrent of a personal chemistry between Christian and Agent Johnson which he himself wished he had. It was perhaps his own interest in Agent Johnson that caused him to subconsciously ignore his own instincts and believe that all was as it was being portrayed between the two of them. Despite all that, the realization hit him that Faraday's impact was going to be significant long after the kudos Marcus would receive upon bringing him to Langley. He had just witnessed firsthand just how powerful Christian's ability could be, both in aiding, as well as against, someone personally. The phrase 'Keep your friends close and your enemies closer' definitely came to mind.

"You're probably right, Christian," West humbled himself. "You have to understand. All of us," he motioned his finger to himself, Waymon, and Heather, "have been raised and trained in a political environment full of deceit, distrust, and organizational positioning. I think we'd all construct a better world if we could, but for now we have to operate in the ugly world which currently exists."

Not me, Christian thought to himself, I'm not going to put up with this crap.

Observing the conversation while resisting the temptation to go over and make sure Tatum was all right, Heather was hoping that the conversation was swaying Christian and they could still make things work between Christian and the government, without any more dramatic chase scenes. She remained confident and committed to Christian's judgment, and would follow whatever approach Christian decided to take, wherever that might lead her.

Getting up from his seat, Agent West decided it was time to build a positive relationship with Christian. "Would you like something to eat, Christian?" turning to his daughter he added, "Tatum?"

Marcus still had a few hours before Christian was to get sucked into a vortex of politics and positioning way above his pay grade that would leave him in the dust. If he didn't get on Christian's good side now, any glory Marcus obtained from this operation would no doubt be very short-lived.

"I ordered a small feast for us, so the galley should be well stocked."

"Why don't you go ahead, honey?" Christian suggested to Tatum, "I want to follow up with the Section Chief."

Heather glanced at Christian, watching for a clue in case she needed to step in, but everything appeared normal. Tatum joined Marcus in the galley near the front of the jet. Christian knelt next to Waymon, who was beaming with pleasure from his phone call. "How did it go, Samuel?" Christian asked as Waymon hung the phone up.

"Thanks, Christian. I guess I misjudged you. I think I see your perspective and concerns now." Waymon, too, knew how important it would be to land in Washington with Christian as a strong ally.

In a very friendly manner, Christian placed his hand at the base of Samuel's neck, positioning his thumb and fingers very deliberately. "Thanks, Samuel. Between us, I'm sure we can make a difference." Waymon smiled as Christian stood up and squeezed his hand. Waymon's body instantly fell limp in his seat.

Heather looked at him quizzically, "What the—"

Christian placed his finger up to his lips, signaling her to remain silent. Marcus had been busy in the galley and couldn't see Waymon's sudden unconscious state. The plush oversized leather seats were so large he wouldn't have seen any movement from the other side even if he had been looking.

Heather played it nonchalantly, not saying anything or making any gestures that would make Marcus suspicious. Christian leaned over to her and whispered, "I always liked Star Trek as a kid. I never really believed there was any science to that Vulcan nerve pinch thing, but there really is!"

"I thought that you were beginning to accept working with the government," Heather said quietly enough to ensure Marcus couldn't hear. "What gives?"

"Immediately after Waymon hung up, the Director told the staff in his office that he would be damned if he would be extorted, then instructed them to separate Waymon from me immediately upon arrival. As we speak, he's making some calls to his old law firm to make sure things are cleaned up and any potential evidence destroyed. And you want me to trust these guys?" Christian quietly replied. "There is no way if they get me to Washington I will ever again have any say in my own life, or that of Tatum's."

Standing up, Christian walked up to the galley. "What feast do you have for us here, Agent West? I'm starving."

Tatum held up her plate, which had just come out of the microwave. "This really looks great, Daddy," as she showed Christian the omelet, sausage, and hash brown potatoes on her plate before she headed back to her seat.

"Omelet, bagel, or cereal, Mister Faraday?" Marcus asked as he poured Christian a cup of coffee.

"The omelet looks great, I'll go with that." Christian replied as he smiled and placed his hand on Marcus' shoulder.

As soon as Marcus set the coffee pot down, Christian applied the same pressure to Marcus as he had on Waymon. As Marcus became limp he began to fall, he knocked over the cup of coffee. Christian tried to keep him from hitting the ground but lost his grip, causing a loud thump as Marcus hit the floor.

The sounds carried into the cockpit where the pilot and co-pilot looked at each other with concern.

"I knew I should have arranged for an attendant," the pilot commented. "I guess I ought to go check and make sure everything is okay," he continued as he unbuckled his seat belt and began to climb out of his seat.

Working quickly, Christian signaled to Heather to get up front while he grabbed Marcus under the arms and dragged him back to the seating area.

Just as Christian sat Marcus down in Heather's seat, facing the back of the plane and out of view of the galley, the door to the cockpit opened and the pilot emerged. As he stepped into the cabin, Heather pretended to be getting off the floor, holding one of her heels in her hand as if it had just fallen off.

"I always forget that I shouldn't be wearing these on a plane before I'm fully awake!" she informed the pilot with a helpless look on her face.

"You okay, ma'am? Do you need any help?" the pilot asked as he observed Tatum eating and the men appearing to be otherwise engaged.

"Thanks, but I'm okay. Other than being a klutz of course!" she laughed as she replaced her shoe.

"How about you, gentlemen? Is there anything you need?" only being able to see Christian fully and the arms of the two agents on their armrests.

"Actually," Christian said as he stood up, "I'd love to see the cockpit of one of these things."

The pilot looked at Heather to make sure it was okay. This particular pilot had flown both Marcus and Heather often and was well aware of her authority.

Heather nodded to him as Christian approached.

"I think Agent West has a question about our ETA," Christian commented as he reached the front of the jet.

The pilot leaned into the cockpit, "Tom, why don't you give Mister Faraday a little lesson in the Gulfstream while I see what I can do for Agent West?"

"Will do, partner," Tom replied as the pilot walked back towards the agents.

Christian stepped aside for the pilot to pass then removed the cloth from his pocket, knowing there was just enough chloroform left in it. He quickly placed the cloth over the pilot's nose, supporting him firmly so there was no disturbance to make the co-pilot suspicious.

Heather stuck her head in the cockpit and closed the door just enough so the co-pilot would not see Christian dragging the pilot to a seat. "Would you like some coffee, Tom?" The co-pilot was also an acquaintance of Agent Johnson's due to many previous flight missions.

Tatum looked up at her father as he positioned the unconscious pilot in the seat Christian had just been occupying. "You know, Daddy, it's really weird eating while all these guys are passed out next to me," she whispered. Then, changing her facial expression to a more serious one, she added, "They *are* just unconscious, aren't they?"

"They're fine, sweetheart. You just eat your breakfast and we'll be back on the ground in no time."

Christian walked back to the front of the jet. While taking the co-pilot's coffee cup from Heather, he pleasantly surprised her with a gentle kiss on the cheek. Staring straight into her eyes, he whispered, "I knew I could count on you. We make a pretty good team, don't you think?"

Returning his kiss, but this time on his lips, she replied, "Better than I could have possibly imagined." Giving him a pat on his butt, she added, "Now try not to crash into the Rockies."

Christian was a little stunned, and definitely flustered. "Actually, that's not a bad idea, Heather. That's as good a place as any to disappear for a few hours."

Entering the cockpit, he handed the cup to the co-pilot. "This is really exciting, I've never been in a plane's cockpit before. Thanks for showing me around."

Expecting Christian to stand behind him, Tom began to explain the controls as he sipped his coffee. Before the co-pilot could object, Christian slid into the pilot's seat.

"You're really not supposed to be doing that, Mister Faraday," the co-pilot choked while swallowing his coffee.

Ignoring his objections, Christian pointed to a switch on the control panel, "What's this for?" knowing precisely its purpose, that of shutting down all outgoing communication.

As Christian flicked the switch, the co-pilot began to grow concerned, "Please don't touch anything, Mister Faraday!"

Christian then disengaged the transponder, making the jet both silent and invisible to stations tracking it.

"Captain!" Tom called to the back.

"I'm afraid he's taking a little nap, so I'm taking his place till we land."

As sure as he was of himself, Christian still wasn't totally comfortable having had his daughter's life in his own hands when flying the helicopter the night before; there was no way he was going to fly this bird by himself with both Tatum and Heather in it.

The co-pilot began to get up as Heather appeared at the door, holding a gun. "Work with him, Tom. If you don't, you'll have to join everyone else back here in slumberland."

Tom looked at Heather in total disbelief. Heather was one of the field agents he respected most, out of all the ones he had served.

"Don't worry, it's only a tranquilizer, but effective nonetheless. Now be a good boy and help Mister Faraday get to wherever it is he wants to take us."

As the co-pilot sat back down, in total amazement of Heather's actions against the Agency, Christian continued quite nonchalantly,

"Now, Tom, right about now Langley is noticing that we've disappeared. Since we're over the Rockies, they'll most likely be thinking that we've gone down somewhere."

The co-pilot listened, silently. He wasn't sure what to make of all this.

"In fact, right," stopping abruptly and pausing a few moments, "now, an order is being issued to scramble a few jets out of Peterson Air Force Base to search for us."

"You know, we can't go anywhere that they won't see us."

"Actually, I can," Christian replied with a smirk on his face as he began turning the plane around. "I'll navigate us around all the radars and make sure we don't cross paths with anyone, you just make sure I don't accidentally do something silly and kill us all. Okay?"

"Anything else you need from me, Christian?" Heather asked.

"As a matter of fact," Christian replied as he began writing a phone number on a piece of paper. "Give this to Tatum and have her call Parker on the secure phone. He'll be comfortable if the call comes from her. Tell her to have him meet us with the van he just bought at the abandoned Sutcliff Airfield north of town in ninety minutes. Also, discard any traceable devices your colleagues back there have."

Chapter Twenty-Three

Parker had purchased an burner mobile phone at a Seven-Eleven the night before. He was startled, yet relieved, when it finally rang. "Where the hell are you, Christian?" he answered.

"This is Tatum, Uncle Parker. Daddy is flying the jet." Tatum replied.

"Flying the jet? He doesn't know how to fly a jet. He can't even handle a hang-glider!"

"Yesterday he didn't know how to fly a helicopter either, but he got us from Reno to California in one piece."

"For Christ's sake, just don't let him near a space shuttle."

"Like I have any control over him. You know better than that."

"So, what's the latest, Tatum?"

"Daddy says to meet us at some abandoned airfield in an hour and a half."

"Sutcliff." Heather helped her.

"Who's that, Tatum? Is there more than just the two of you that I need to prepare for?"

Tatum smiled at Heather, "Jury is still out, Parker. But I suspect you'll be seeing a fair amount of her in the future."

"Has someone finally cracked into that man's heart?"

"I sure hope so, Uncle Parker," she said, giving Heather a smile and a wink.

"After the last twenty-four hours I don't think I'll be surprised by anything ever again. Anything else I need to bring?"

"Just the van, whatever that is."

"Okay, sweetheart. I'll see the three of you at Sutcliff in ninety minutes."

"Bye, Uncle Parker. Thanks."

Heather gave Tatum a gentle hug and reassured her, "Don't worry, Tatum, I'm here for as long as the two of you will have me."

≈

After a safe landing, Christian taxied the plane into an abandoned open-sided hangar and shut the engine down. "Thanks, Tom. Did pretty good, didn't I?"

Tom was still none too happy about the mutiny that took place on his aircraft. He barely spoke to Christian the entire trip, while Christian zigzagged back to the Reno area. "What now?" he asked as Christian got out of his seat.

"Would you help me with your boss back here?"

The co-pilot followed him into the cabin as Heather opened the jet door, releasing the steps to the ground.

Outside, as he drove the van up to the jet, Parker received his first glimpse of the woman that apparently had captured Christian's long neglected heart. *Oh. My. God. Lightning really does strike twice! How does that man do it?*

"I really don't want these guys to sit in this metal can in the heat," Christian said to the co-pilot. "Would you mind helping me get them into the van?"

"I can fly them out of here, you know? Won't be any problem."

"Cute, Tom," Christian smiled as he pointed to Agent West's legs, "but you're coming along."

Christian grabbed Marcus under his arms, while Tom grabbed his legs and they carried him to the door.

Parker entered the plane and greeted them, glad he didn't have to hide in the van any longer. "What have you done this time, buddy? Now you're hijacking government jets?"

"Parker, meet Agent Johnson," Christian nodded his head towards Heather as he continued carrying the CIA agent. "Heather, this is my best friend, Parker Farr."

"Miss Johnson," Parker put on all his charm for his friend's apparent love interest. He took her hand and gave it a kiss while keeping his eyes on hers, "welcome to our world."

"So, you're the famous Parker Farr," Heather replied. "You've got quite the sneaky housemaid."

"Sunye is one of a kind, for sure."

"Quit flirting and grab one of these men, will you, Parker?"

As Christian and Tom laid Marcus in the van, Christian put his hand on Tom's shoulder. "Thanks, Tom. Parker and I can get the other two." Firmly squeezing his fingers in the appropriate spots, Tom collapsed into the van.

Once Christian and Parker had the four men laid out on the floor of the van, Christian ordered everyone else inside, "Let's go guys, we don't have much time, and we have a lot to do."

Parker got in the front with Christian, the girls climbed in the back, and they drove out of the abandoned airfield.

≈

"The reports from the scout jets are negative, sir," the analyst reported to Jacob Blanton. "There's no sign of the aircraft anywhere."

"No radar sightings?"

"No, sir. Also, no sightings from any commercial or military aircraft in the area."

"Satellites have fully swept the area?"

The analyst nodded affirmatively.

"Damn it. Planes just don't disappear. I want all available search units to cover every inch of that area of the Rockies. We can't risk losing those passengers, especially Faraday."

≈

The green van pulled up to Christian's house, which was now silent and empty as all Intelligence Community resources were dedicated to the Benny Malone case or one of the many other investigations Christian's intelligence had opened up. With Christian believed to be safely on his way to Washington, his residence held little interest to the understaffed organizations that were involved up until his capture.

Parker jumped out of the van and opened the garage door so Christian could drive the van into the middle bay of the three car garage.

"Tatum, I need your laptop in my office, right away," he instructed his daughter. "Heather, could you help her pack please? Not too much stuff but assume we won't be coming back here for a very long time."

"Sure, Christian" she responded, "Need me to get anything together for you?"

What a perfect woman! "Yes, Tatum will help you. She knows what I like."

As Tatum and Heather opened a door and prepared to climb out of the van, Christian gently grabbed Heather's arm for her to stop and she turned to him, "And Heather, we're at a bit of a 'no turning back' point here. What do you want to do?"

Heather slowly approached him, her eyes locked on his. Just as her lips were about to meet his she replied softly, "I think you know," followed by a gentle, yet passionate kiss.

After he recovered from her kiss, Christian composed himself and continued, still staring into her eyes, "Okay, we can work with that, can't we, Tatum? You and Tatum are about the same size, I'm sure not everything she has is from Abercrombie or Hollister." Turning to Tatum, who had been watching the exchange with great delight, "Do you think you can attire Heather for a few days, sweetheart?"

Thrilled about the prospect of spending more time with her new friend, as well as her father's new love interest, Tatum could hardly contain her excitement. "No problem, Daddy!" Tatum grabbed Heather's hand and pulled her out of the van. "Come on, Heather. Let's go play in my closet!"

Turning to Parker, Christian got back to the logistics at hand, "Okay, Parker, can you get these guys into the house? I've got a lot of stuff to take care of before we can get out of here."

"No problem. You go on ahead, I've got these guys under control," Parker replied, as he hoisted the pilot over his shoulder.

Christian ran into the house and sat down at his desk. He turned on both his desktop and laptop computers.

"Here you are, Daddy," Tatum entered with her laptop and handed it to him. "Anything else?"

"Yes. Don't listen to a word that woman has to say about lingerie."

Tatum laughed as she turned around and ran back upstairs.

Christian began furiously working on all three computers, moving from one to another as they were busy processing, or he needed to simultaneously enter data into more than one site. As he worked, screens appeared on the monitors which included government agencies from several countries, financial institutions around the world, and other sites. On these pages he quickly entered usernames and passwords, ignoring the 'Top Secret' and 'Restricted Access' warnings which were displayed on almost every screen he accessed.

Each login was another thread severed between him and the life he'd had yesterday.

Parker poked his head in the door and informed Christian that all the men were inside. "What now, boss?"

"Tie them up, please. Securely and apart from each other. You may find cuffs on both agents. I have some rope in the garage as well if you need it. When you're done, let me know. We need to load my motorcycle into the van."

Parker gave him a puzzled look, curious what Christian was up to. As he turned to deal with the men, Christian called out to him, "The cuffs are for the men, Parker, not your toy box!"

"Come on, Christian," he called back as he retrieved a pair of cuffs from Waymon's jacket pocket. "These are the latest models."

After finishing up his business on the internet, Christian turned on the voicemail machine and pressed the 'Play' button. There were nearly a hundred voicemails on his system, and he skipped most, stopping at the ones of interest, and only slightly paying attention to those as he typed relevant information into a document in his computer.

"Mister Faraday," came one voice from the machine, "This is Sarah Williamson from the National Center for Missing and Exploited Children," the message began as Christian furiously typed names and addresses into the document. Christian spent more time doing this than he should have given the pressure he was under. However, he felt that there were at least a dozen of them he should be dealing with, including such organizations as the American Cancer Society and the Drug Enforcement Agency. He felt that he should probably wait on the call from the Vatican to make sure his response was worded properly; the last thing he needed was yet another group chasing him down.

Once finished typing on one of the laptops, he kicked off a printout. He then turned to the desktop keyboard and started an encryption-and-wipe sequence of the hard drive. He couldn't afford for a computer forensic expert to retrace what he had just done.

Joining Parker and the girls in the living room, Christian brought in the laptops and the small stack of paper. "Girls, why don't you get your bags out into the van? Parker and I will be right along."

Handing the laptops to Parker, he went around to the men one by one and gave them each another nerve pinch. "That should take care of them for a while."

"You've really got to teach me that trick, Christian."

"Now listen," Christian began as he handed him the top grouping from the stack of papers, "Get this information to the people identified on them. I made another set of notes that will help you avoid any problems with the Feds. And this," Christian began as handed over another stack of paper, "take to one of your more nefarious notaries and make sure it's dated at least six months ago."

"This is your Last Will and Testament. What is this all about?"

"You remain executor of my estate, but it keeps everything clean given what's about to happen. After I'm dead I'll get you more direction on how things need to be handled."

"After you're dead?"

"Don't worry, you'll understand soon enough. Don't accept any of the reward money from the kids' families. Any other reward money donate back to a fund for the kids who were kidnapped. Now, let's get the bike in the van and get out of here."

≈

Christian pulled the van up to Parker's garage, "Time to go girls. You get to take Parker's Porsche from here."

"My Porsche? You know I've got nothing left to drive," Parker objected as he pressed the code on the keypad for the garage door to open.

Grabbing the girls' bags and carrying them to the trunk of the Porsche, Christian reassured Parker, "Give that Gutierrez dude a few hundred more bucks and he'll have Juliette's car out here in no time. Do the same for the valet at the Mediterranean and you can have your Bentley back, too. Besides, you'll be able to pick up your Porsche and my bike once we take off."

"Take off to where?"

"Just program Sutcliff Airfield into the Porsche's navigation system for Heather, give her the mobile phone you have in case I need to reach her, and I'll explain it all to you in due time."

Turning to Heather and Tatum, he continued, "I'll meet you two at the jet in about forty-five minutes. I've got to get the Feds off our ass for good." Christian gave the girls a group hug and kissed each of them on the cheek. "We'll be okay, girls. I promise."

Going over to Parker as he programmed in the girl's destination, Christian put out his hand, "I'll be in touch real soon. Don't worry about us."

Parker reached out to his very somber looking best friend and shook his hand.

"Call the Feds in twenty minutes and tell them that I'm nuts and am heading down Phoenix Canyon Road in a green utility van in a complete rage. Make sure you tell them that I have Tatum and Heather with me as well."

"Will do, buddy. Will I be seeing you guys again?" Parker couldn't help but think that this was the last time he and his best friend would be together.

"Don't worry; you're not getting rid of me this easily."

Giving the girls one last kiss goodbye, he climbed in the van and headed out of Sierra Vista.

Chapter Twenty-Four

Parked on the shoulder, Christian awaited the arrival of the FBI helicopters that had been dispatched to pursue the green van reportedly driven by him. As the first helicopter approached close enough to get a clear look, he jumped out of the van, paced like a man unraveling, and—for theater and identification—hurled a rock skyward. He then dove back in and drove away as fast as he could down the road.

The helicopters stayed in close pursuit, informing the ground units of its location, as well as his deranged behavior. Christian began driving in what appeared to be no particular direction, waiting for the sedans and squad cars to approach. Once he knew that they were within a mile, he turned onto a road which took him up a steep canyon slope. He continued driving up the hill until he reached a small turn-off, which was partially covered by trees. He pulled over, leaving the motor running. Christian climbed into the back, grabbing the metal briefcase Alex Gutierrez had given Parker when he purchased the van. He opened the rear side door and jumped out, hidden by the trees.

As the helicopter hovered overhead, unable to see Christian as he exited the van, sirens from the ground units could be heard in the distance.

Christian crouched down in the trees and opened the case, exposing a control panel and a video display showing an image from the perspective of the driver's seat in the van. A six-inch control steering wheel with several controls popped up in the center of the case.

Christian pressed the 'Drive' button on the control panel and took hold of the steering wheel. Pressing his thumb on one of the controls on the wheel, he watched the display as the van began to rapidly accelerate. Manipulating the steering wheel, Christian guided the van back onto the road and back on course.

At this point, the ground units were rapidly closing in as the helicopter continued in close pursuit. Christian guided the van, continuing at the full speed that the three hundred fifty horsepower engine was capable of, and watched as police and FBI vehicles on the road sped past him, where he hid unseen, in the bushes.

Christian watched the display as he remotely navigated the vehicle around several curves on the mountainous road. After reaching the crest of the small mountain, the van began traveling downhill at an even greater speed. Reaching a straight stretch with a sharp left curve at the end, Christian again accelerated the van to its full speed. As the display showed the van rapidly approaching the curve, Christian kept his thumb on the speed control, not turning the van, except a nudge to the right as he reached the edge of the curve.

The helicopter pilot watched in horror as the van flew off the road and disappeared over the three-hundred-foot cliff.

Slamming on their brakes, the pursuing sedans screeched to a halt and the agents and officers rushed out of their cars.

Christian casually sat at the controls and watched as the video displayed the van heading straight for the large oil storage units at the bottom of the mountain; one of the storage tanks rapidly getting larger on the display. Christian began to stand up, shaking and stretching his legs out. As the display turned to snow, he heard an enormous explosion in the distance.

The explosion was so severe, the men at the top of the cliff stepped back and covered their eyes.

Closing the case, Christian walked to his motorcycle, which he had unloaded and hidden prior to going back down the hill to await the authorities. Putting on his helmet and strapping the briefcase on the back of the motorcycle, Christian casually mounted the bike, started it up, and slowly entered the road, driving in the opposite direction of the accident.

≈

"So, you and my dad, like… officially a thing now," Tatum commented to Heather.

"Well, he hasn't said anything to that effect, but I'm getting the feeling that's where we're headed," Heather replied. "You'll definitely have no objections from me."

The two girls had arrived at the jet fifteen minutes earlier, and were enjoying the opportunity to get to know one another better.

"I don't know what he's up to, but something tells me we won't be enjoying these beautiful mountains any longer."

"Given your dad's good taste," Heather reassured her, "I'm sure you'll be happy with wherever he has in mind."

Just then, the girls heard the motorcycle approaching. After pulling into the hangar, Christian dismounted. "How's it feel to be dead, girls?" he asked as he removed his helmet.

"Oh my God, Daddy. What have you done now?"

"Just totally incinerated the three of us in a giant fireball."

"You really don't know what you're getting yourself into, Heather," Tatum commented.

"I'll take my chances," Heather replied, winking at Christian.

Giving them each a kiss, Christian put his arms around them and guided them towards the jet. "You sure, Heather? It's barely afternoon and already I've hijacked a government jet, knocked out some senior agents, and blown up three very wonderful people."

"Can't fool me, handsome, you're nothing but a big softie," Heather replied as she put her arm around him and ticklishly pinched his side.

Christian slightly jumped and smiled, facially, and in his soul. "There are four of your respected colleagues tied up and unconscious in my house right now who I'm afraid don't share that opinion."

"They'll get over it, I'm sure. So where are we off to now?"

"Once we get airborne and I tie up a few loose ends, I'll explain it all to you," he said as they entered their new private jet.

≈

Given the day he was having, the ringing of his iPhone, even though he had just entered the ornate private bathroom, was not too much of a surprise. Not recognizing the source of the call, however, was most unusual.

"Yes?" President Beucler simply responded.

"Sorry to bother you in the restroom, Mister President, but it is urgent I speak with you privately."

"Who is this?" The President's voice revealing a slight agitation.

"Christian Faraday. I assumed you wouldn't mind having a conversation directly with me."

"Christian Faraday, eh? So just how did you survive the flaming aerobatics I just witnessed on video?"

"Listen, sorry to bother you at such a private moment and I know your top intelligence advisors are awaiting your return to the Oval Office. There are a few things I needed to immediately speak with you about personally."

"And just how do I know this is actually Christian Faraday?"

"You just put your suit jacket on the valet stand in the wash room. In the left inside pocket is a brief memo about me that your secretary just moments ago handed you. And this morning you had a very encouraging discussion with your daughter about a project she's working on in school."

"I'm listening."

"First, I don't want to startle you as nothing is imminent. However, there is a plan in the works to kidnap your sister, Renee, from her Arizona horse ranch. Just the latest terrorist approach to making your life difficult."

"Thank you, Mister Faraday," his tone now more conciliatory. "I'll notify her Secret Service detail immediately."

"Their action is planned to take place within days. They're currently holed up in a sleazy place called 'Sedona Sky Motel', not too far from her ranch. There are only three of them there now, with two more joining them tomorrow. Lots of weaponry there, too."

"I can't say how much I appreciate the heads up, but that certainly isn't all you called about."

"Too much to cover just now but suffice it to say we are going to have to have a very close, and very secret, relationship from here on out. You've been fully briefed on me, and I can assure you that my ability is real and quite powerful."

"It's been quite impressive thus far, Mister Faraday."

"Just the tip of the iceberg, Sir. I want you to understand that my goal over the last twenty-four hours was not to make the government's life miserable, but you know as well as I how the political machine in government agencies works. The motivations of the CIA and FBI alone that I uncovered were not only deeply disturbing but would have severely limited the positive impact I could have on society on an international basis.”

“Trust me, I understand completely. I appreciate your own motives, and you have my promise that I will isolate you from that with all the ability of this office.”

“Believe me, Mister President, if I didn’t have complete faith in you, we wouldn’t be talking right now.”

“So, what can I do right now, Mister Faraday?”

“Within a few days, you’ll be receiving a call from my attorney, Parker Farr, with detailed instructions for a private meeting between the two of you. He’ll lay everything out so that we can get some real work done absent destructive politics.”

“I’ll have my secretary look for his call and give it top priority.”

“He’ll be calling you directly, Mister President. This needs the highest level of discretion. Apart from a few others I’ll be involving, no one other than yourself can be aware that these discussions are even taking place, or that I’m even alive. You’ll just have to take all the credit for the results yourself.”

“Fair enough. We’ll give this a go. Anything else?”

“Yes. Encourage all agencies to stand down on issues relating to me, including Parker Farr and anyone else I involved in this. I’m a little tired of throwing them off, and it’s a waste of your Administration’s resources.”

“Will do, Mister Faraday.”

“Oh, and one other thing. Take it easy on the four guys currently tied up in my house back in Reno. Someone might want to find them soon, by the way.”

“You left someone tied up in your house?”

"FBI, CIA, and a couple of pilots, I'm afraid. Really, agents Waymon and West did everything humanly possible to keep up with me and bring me in. I'm afraid no one could have prepared for the curve balls I threw them. I'm surprised myself. They both deserve commendations and promotions. They are exceptional agents. Please hold Director Allen to the promotion he just promised Agent Waymon."

"I think I can make all that happen, Mister Faraday."

"You should be getting back to your meetings, sir. Sorry to have disturbed you in the washroom."

"The best thing that's happened to me all day, Mister Faraday. Thanks for opening up the dialogue."

"From now on, it's Christian, if you don't mind."

"And thanks again for the heads up on Renee."

"My pleasure, Mister President."

Christian put down the phone as the plane leveled out at twenty-five thousand feet. Heather came up from the back and sat in the co-pilot's seat. "So, what's the plan, Christian? Do you think you can keep them off our trail?"

"It will take them years before they even have a clue."

"I'm sure that someone is going to notice an unauthorized jet with no transponders flying around their airspace. We're going to need to get fuel before too long."

"Actually, you're right. That's why I've re-enabled the transponder and we'll be landing in Montreal in about four hours to refuel as well. You might want to get some rest until then."

"Aren't they going to know it's the missing CIA jet and stop us?"

Christian laughed, "Actually, no. I've modified the transponder identifiers in the CIA and FAA databases. This particular jet is now believed by all computer systems to be a top-secret State Department jet under special status that allows it to proceed at will within all U.S. territories and many of our allied countries. It's been cleared in the FAA and international systems to our destination in a way that will raise no eyebrows. I've also assigned, through the CIA internal system, a co-pilot to help with the rest of the flight. Fuel will automatically be billed to your Agency. You don't mind, do you?"

"And just where are we going?"

"Well, I just this afternoon purchased a beautiful, secluded estate on the island of Majorca," he informed her as he smiled. "Compliments of the budget for some illegal covert activities of your colleagues. At enough of a premium to make it immediately ready for occupancy."

"Aren't they going to be able to trace all this?"

"I put the fund transfers through a maze of transactions that would take the best forensic accounting minds years to even begin to grasp and are simply impossible to fully track. Each of us, you included, now have a Swiss account that will take care of our needs until we figure out how we are going to manage this situation."

"You stole money?"

"Actually, I just reallocated it from some very bad people and organizations, including our friend Benny Malone. It's amazing what you can do with internet access, knowing where to go, and what the access codes are. There are literally no sites that I cannot get into and move around in at will. CIA, White House, NASA, FAA, Bank of America. You name it, I can do just about anything," Christian informed her. "There are some very, very bad, I mean really bad, criminals that are going to wake up to empty bank accounts tomorrow morning. There will also be some very needy organizations waking up to find their budget problems solved."

"And by the way," Christian added, "do you have any idea how many slush funds there are in the CIA alone? You cannot imagine the scam that is your budget."

"Wow. What else were your dancing fingers doing on those keyboards?"

"Well, the staff of the estate will be greeting us once we land. They are currently preparing the house for our arrival. They think you are some super important business executive; I'm just your kept man, I guess. A complete wardrobe will be delivered to the estate over the next few days, including some of your favorite lingerie pieces," he turned to her with a grin. "I'll be anonymously supplying information to organizations that I can help, but mostly we'll be getting plenty of rest."

Heather smiled and stood up to go back and spend time with her other new friend, "I better go check on Tatum." Leaning down to give him a gentle kiss near his ear. "But I wouldn't plan on getting too much rest if I were you."

Epilogue

"Glad I could help, Mister President," Christian begins wrapping up his call as he admires his lovely bride directing her windsurf board along the white beach. It's been two years, and he still refers to Heather as his 'bride.' Although their social life is almost non-existent as he has become the most reclusive, and speculated about, man on the island, he really didn't care. His days with Heather were as precious as life gets.

The two were hardly ever apart, and they savored every moment of it. Besides, with their own private Gulfstream G600 and essentially un-limited financial support from a special fund quietly administered through the United Nations, Christian, Heather, and Tatum are able to enjoy an extremely fulfilling life.

"I look forward to our next conversation. Parker, try not to corrupt any more Congressmen and Senators while you're in town."

Christian places the phone on a nearby table and watches as Heather runs towards him from the water. The sight of her shimmering bronze body and beautiful smile never wears on him; he is in constant awe of the special treasure he has found in her.

Christian refuses to speak with anyone in the U.S. Government other than the President and a special bipartisan group of Senators and Representatives that Christian personally selected. When setting up this group, Christian wanted to ensure that any information he provides the government is unfiltered at the highest levels and not used politically. He has this same arrangement with the United Nations, as well as several countries, and they all know Christian is providing the others any information he feels necessary to keep them all honest and at peace.

A secure satellite network was built around him; all contact was routed through Parker. No agency could find him. Officially, he did not exist. No person or Agency had any way of tracking him down. In fact, all aspects of his life are completely untraceable. His very existence is a secret from anyone outside the group he speaks with personally.

Early on, there were rumors that he didn't perish in the fiery blaze, and it was always suspicious that the missing Gulfstream was never recovered, and Christian ensured any serious digital trail vanished as quickly as it appeared.

Everyone that he invited into the exclusive group of 'The Knowing' knew the consequences of divulging any information about him. Parker had a personal discussion with each of them, accompanied by a phone call from Christian, who brought up just enough of their personal information that they thoroughly understood.

Even the President's Chief of Staff had no idea what this secret Congressional panel which his boss participated in was about.

Christian liked it this way and his approach to diplomacy ensured that the international community is generally at peace, as they are no longer able to deceive one another.

Heather leaned over and gave Christian a kiss then sat next to him at the edge of his lounge chair while drying her hair with a towel.

"How was your talk with Tatum on the phone this morning?"

"I'm worried about her. She was complaining about some of the other girls in school. What's your take on her emotional well-being?"

"I swear Christian, sometimes you are so adorably daft. She is so playing you," Heather replied as she moves to a position facing him, gently grabbing and wrapping his legs around her waist. "She's about to graduate with honors from the most respected and challenging private school in Monte Carlo, has earned her own way into Harvard, she's off every weekend with her friends skiing in the Alps or snorkeling in Greece, and she's got the most wonderful dad in the world just a quick private jet ride away on his own private estate on a gorgeous Mediterranean island. On top of all that, in four months she'll have that baby brother that she's always wanted."

"I guess you're right. It could be worse for her. But wait till she finds out he's got my knowing gene in his DNA."

"That's going to be quite the challenge for all of us! Can you imagine what the terrible twos are going to be like?" she laughs as she places the towel on the sand. "But for now, you just lean back," Heather commanded as she seductively crawled on top of him, her lips hovering over his ear, "and let me give you something more important to focus on."

<u>ABOUT THE AUTHOR</u>

Robert Lange grew up on a farm outside of Charlottesville, Virginia and currently resides in Western North Carolina.

Robert graduated from Virginia Tech, has two children, two rascally grandsons, and wishes he could find worthy backgammon opponents a little more often.

Robert's word processor has already begun work on the sequel to *The Knowing Gene*. Hopefully, *From Under His Radar* will find itself on the bookshelves sometime in the next decade.

www.ingramcontent.com/pod-product-compliance
Lightning Source LLC
Chambersburg PA
CBHW032026310726
48972CB00002B/549